THE SONG OF THE SIREN

The singing echoed and rang, and Wirrun shuddered with longing. He saw the Yung-gamurra at last and knew her from her singing, and the knowing held him while he looked.

She was silver and lovely. Her hair flowed over slender shoulders, and she combed it back with delicate fingers. She smiled with the sweetness of honey. She was dark and silver like moonlit water, lovely and remote like a dream. She longed for him, the singer in the dark.

His longing flowed back and he began to slide over the ledge into the water.

"THIS IS STRONG AND ORIGINAL FANTASY BY A RE-MARKABLE STORYTELLER. MS. WRIGHTSON'S WRIT-ING HAS THE EVOCATIVE POWER OF THE FIRST THINGS AND THE GREAT ONES OF THE LAND; AND HER VIVID SENSE OF HER CHARACTERS MAKES THEIR ADVENTURES BOTH GRIPPING AND POIGNANT."

—Stephen R. Donaldson
Author of *The Chronicles
of Thomas Covenant*

Also by Patricia Wrightson
Published by Ballantine Books:

THE ICE IS COMING

THE DARK BRIGHT WATER

✦✦✦✦✦✦✦✦✦✦✦✦✦✦✦✦✦✦✦✦✦✦✦✦✦✦✦✦✦✦✦✦✦✦

Patricia Wrightson

A Del Rey Book

BALLANTINE BOOKS ● NEW YORK

A Del Rey Book
Published by Ballantine Books

Copyright © 1978 by Patricia Wrightson

Library of Congress Catalog Card Number: 78-8793

ISBN 0-345-29486-6

This edition published by arrangement with Atheneum Publishers

Manufactured in the United States of America

First Ballantine Books Edition: December 1981

Cover art by Michael Whelan

Contents

Author's Note

Twice lately I have explained that, in stories of my own making, fairy and monster characters were drawn from the folklore of the Australian Aborigines. I have to refer to it again this time in order to make a confession.

All the spirits of this story come from the same source—except for one species that I have invented. These are the nameless, shapeless shadows I have placed in the deepest underground. It seemed right that at those depths and in that dark something should move that was quite unknown to man.

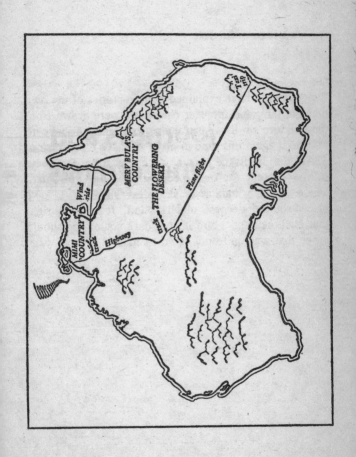

1

Journeys and Homecomings

One

The old south land lay across the world like an open hand, with the weight of summer heavy in its palm. The wind washed over it, polishing its gibber-plains; the sea leapt and worried at its endless coast; but the land lay flat and still, full of summer and secrets. And in one far corner, north and west across mirage-shrouded lakes and polished plains and beyond the haze-hung monoliths of the Centre, the first cyclone of the year was building.

It began as a tropical wind over the ocean, building grey-green hillocks of water that hurried before it until they were rolled and broken into foam. As the wind neared the land it found an area of low pressure and soared upward into it, curling its tail. Now it was trapped, and it screamed in mounting fury—a wind-dragon howling after its own tail as it still swept on towards land. Clouds were caught in its whirling; it darkened the sky and hurled rain senselessly. Small and big ships fled from it where it lashed at the funnelled, flying sea. It let them go and howled on towards land, breaking over the coast at its north-west corner.

To the old south land lying broad and still under the weight of summer this fury of wind was no more than a swarm of bees; but to all who lived in that one country under the cyclone it was more. There were no towns there; only a few grim-faced Inlanders, a handful or so of the dark People, and the unknown earth-spirits of the land itself. To them the cyclone was a fury.

It hurled the sea high over rocks and inland over beaches. It pummelled the country with fists of rain and wind, tore down buildings, tossed cars and boats about, uprooted trees or stripped them of leaves. It gathered up rivers, flung them down again, rained new rivers into them and split them over the country. And all the time, while men cowered, the cyclone shrieked and howled and the earth-spirits howled back. Some of them fought it, some hid from it, some mounted it and rode the circling wind.

The water-spirits rode the floods, out of the fierce river-currents into quieter water. All but the Yunggamurra. They could be as wild as any wind. Their fierce eyes flashed, they dug their long sharp nails into root and bank and fought the current with joy. They joined hands, a chain of sisters reaching from bank to bank of their flooded river, their grey-slimed bodies knifing through the water. Their dark hair netted flood-wash and bound it to rocks, and they sang a wild-dog chorus to the storm. One of them stopped to listen and laugh, loosening her hold for a moment—and in that moment she was torn from her sisters and blown and tumbled away down the river. That startled her, for she had never been alone before, and while she howled for help she was rolled and tumbled out to sea.

She hardly knew when she had reached it, all the land was so wild and wet and the muddy floodwaters reached so far into the grey sea. She went on calling for her sisters into the noise of the storm until the storm itself paused to listen. The wind quietened. There was only the roar and crash of water, and the Yunggamurra quivered with fear. She knew the storm had not passed but was looking down at her through its great central eye, and it was terrible to be alone. She knew the wind would start again, and there were no banks to dig into and no chain of clinging hands. From land to sky, only the waves drove and smashed; they seized her and dragged her out, out, and their salt burnt her body. In terror the Yunggamurra dived and flicked away with the speed of a spirit. It was some time before she was calmer and began to look for the shore. By then she had left the storm behind.

She could see no shore. She had come a long way in her panic and thought of going back through the sea; but by now her soft slimy body was badly burnt from the salt. She needed a river—a flood—a storm—even dry land. Here there was only a wide and shallow sea, quite calm, but grey under cloud that the cyclone had pushed ahead of it. She saw a rain-squall coming, and lay on the water and waited for it until the rain gave her some relief from the burning. Then she dived again in search of an upward-sloping sea-floor. Her dark eyes were hard again; there was no panic in them.

She met fish and shark, strangers to her. They gaped and slid quickly away and she barely noticed. The sea-floor was rising to the south and she knew she was coming near land. The sea tugged at her in pulls and currents, but she slid through those as easily as the fish did. Then, like a feather spiralling up from below, she felt the lightest touch of another current. Fresh water! She hung where she was, sensing and testing. The swell lifted her dark hair like weed, and that feather-touch of fresh water rose through the swell. There must be some current or pressure to make it flow upward like that.

She followed it down to the ooze, and the flow strengthened a little as she went. She dug down with her sharp nails, working in a swirl of grey-brown ooze that hung in the sea as she stirred it up. She found a basin of sandstone filled with sand and ooze, and cleared it until she had found a fist-sized hole. The water gushed through more strongly. Being a water-spirit, and slimy, she was able to slide into the hole.

After the strong salt sea, this water was as gentle as a summer evening; but the sandstone was rough and scraped the soft slime from her body. The hole widened as she went, working her way in darkness on and up, sure that she was leaving the sea for land, waiting for the moment when her tunnel would lead into some sunny pool. When she had found it, and rested and recovered, she would find the river-roads back to her sisters. Until then she would not think of them, for she needed them too badly. She would think only of the water.

Yet she would rather not think too much about the water for it had begun to worry her. It was a strange sort of water, with no smell or taste or feel of river or pool.

'It is old water,' said the Yunggamurra, and turned her thoughts away from it. Whatever it was, it was life to her for she could not stand the sea. Pressed in the narrow darkness and longing for space she fought her way on, driving her own sore body with the ferocity of her kind. The tunnel went on and up, on and up. 'It will surface somewhere,' hissed the Yunggamurra.

Suddenly she slid forward into freedom and wider water.

She could feel it all around, and above and below. She took two quick turns for the joy of free movement, then lay for a long time and rested. She had reached the pool. She felt like a man who has run a long way through fire.

After some time she raised herself unwillingly, for she had to take notice of something. It was the darkness: it was still there. Not as close, but just as thick and solid. With an eel's wriggle she rose through the water feeling for the surface. There was no surface, only more rock, above as below and on all sides. The water, the old water, was imprisoned in rock. Yet she could feel its sly and secret flowing.

She knew then what the water was and where it had led her: into deep and hidden secrets of the land. These were the waters the thirsty land had locked away in store, drop by drop and age by age, far down under rock and desert. They were rains and floods and melted ice that had seen younger suns, when men were small and hairy and beasts were giants. They were the old land's private thoughts, its youth remembered. The Yunggamurra shuddered and clenched her sharp nails into her palms. She felt the might of the land locking her in. She must go back through the tunnel and back through the sea.

But she could not go back. Could a man run a second time through fire? She thrashed to and fro in the pool, and its waters stirred as they had not for an age. It frightened her; she cowered at the bottom. There was a gentle touch of slime on the rock: that was comforting, for it was life, even here. She scraped some off with her nails and ate it. After that she was able to still her terror, and even her longing for light and company. She could wait, and listen for the old slow thought of the land. And as the water stilled and settled she heard it.

It was in that sly and secret flowing, the tendril of movement that curled through the quiet water.

'It flows in as well as out,' whispered the Yunggamurra. 'It will surface somewhere.'

She crept along the thread of current till the stirring of water hid it. Then she waited, ate more slime, allowed her body to heal and rebuild its own soft cover. In this way, little by little, she tracked the water to its entrance and found a second, larger, tunnel. She went into it and on into the depths of the land.

Darkness, even First Darkness, is not the same to an earth-thing as to a man; an earth-thing has more seeing. Loneness is not so heavy, nor silence so deep; there are rhythms and pulses to feel. Harmonies and discords that vibrate from other spirits; the strong, deep singing of stone and the soft consent of water. And there is life making its tiny response in the growth of a fungus, the groping of a cricket, the scurry of a spider. All this is intelligence to the old things.

But this was an old thing of running waters and open sky, not of waters quiet under the weight of a land. She had lost her own country, which is darkness and loss to her kind as it is to the People. She was used to wild laughter and singing, savage play and the joining of hands—all her life, wherever she looked, she had seen herself everywhere in her sisters. Alone she had no self. Most bitterly she missed her sisters.

But she went on, from tunnel to pool and from passage to cave, not knowing night from day and choosing only one direction: up. Even that was not always possible. Often the water was hot, and she fled in fear. The current led nowhere and often disappeared: there was no pattern in it. Yet in time she did reach levels so high that the dark and bitter water lay only in the floor of cave or passage, and others where she felt it only in the shale under her feet. She was glad to be free of it at first, for it was a powerful and stinging water, but soon she was forced to seek it again. By degrees she grew used to it and it ceased to sting.

She grew used to many strange things. Sometimes there were heavy, choking airs that she had to escape by diving under water. The first time she knocked a stone into a cave-pool she thought she was hunted by spirits, and ran and hid—for the water sang a clear note like a magpie's, and the rocks picked it up and sent it back and forth till caves and passages rang with magpie-calls. Afterwards she knew the voices of water and rock calling each other, and sometimes roused them for company. Her eyes grew wide and sharp; she saw a grinning shape and ran in terror before she felt what it was—the skull of some ancient monster, dead an age ago. Later she saw stone with the sparkle of rain and shaped like the flowing or dripping of water; but it was stone, hard and still and brittle.

Once she heard a sound that was the strangest thing of all in this deep place: the distant shrieking and howling of wind. The air in her cave sucked out and breathed a cold breath in, yet she knew it was too deep for wind or cold. She stood listening, quivering, all her wildness frozen still. This was no wind for a Yunggamurra to howl at. It was a spirit-wind. She slipped into a pool and lay still.

It was some time after this that she strayed into a cave of ice. She had never seen ice and thought at first that it was hot and burnt her. But she found it was a burning cold and remembered, from the talk of earth-things she had met in past times, that this was ice.

She longed for other spirits but dared not meet them, for here she was a stranger and an intruder. Sometimes there was a brooding heaviness that hung in niches or blocked a passage, and she knew that some spirit of the place was near and she hid in water. Once or twice she saw a moving glow and crept after it, not daring to come near, until she lost it. Then she sat in a pool and wept angry, lonely tears, since she must not howl.

There came a time when she followed such a glow and found it growing stronger as it went. She grew afraid and turned away into a passage that ran beside the cave where the light travelled. But the passage turned back suddenly into the cave, and the light was there before her eyes, and she saw earth-things. It was so long since she had seen any of her own kind that she could not slip away. She stayed and watched.

She was lucky. It was a gathering of earth-things of several kinds, aware of each other's strange vibrations and so not aware of hers. She was able to climb high up in the darkness of rocks and look down at them. Their faint glow seemed a strong light after her long time in the dark, but soon there was added another stronger light: the leaping red and yellow of fire. That worried her, for she hated fire, but now it was too dangerous to climb down again. And she wanted to stay, to watch.

It excited her to see these other spirits; she shook with the wild Yunggamurra laughter that she had to hold back. There were shapes like men and women of the People, except that they were tailed like dogs. There were more fearful shadows, shapeless at the edge of the light, flowing a little forward and a little back as the firelight wavered. There were women without heads, groping in spite of the firelight—the Yunggamurra held her laughter all the tighter. Most of the spirits were a starry-eyed Little People with voices that rumbled together like stones. They were as small as young children, but the Yunggamurra looked at them with respect. She knew that the races of Little People have a wonderful strength.

They seemed to be waiting as if there were more to come, and she wondered if this were some corroboree. The smoke of the fire rose straight up in the stillness of the cave and drove her back. What had they found to burn? She took another look: dried grass and sticks brought, surely, from far away; handfuls of rubbish that might have been scraped from the sides of pools; ancient bones such as she had seen here sometimes. And—strange!—laid out beside the fire there was food. Not food for all of them, but a meal for one: a limp sooty bat, a pale lizard, three or four strange grubs. It was not a corroboree, then. They were waiting for some important being. The Yunggamurra waited too, and looked where they looked.

She felt them stir. Another spirit had come out of the shadows into the cave. This one was tall and stick-thin, with dark round eyes and a wisp of hair that floated as she walked spring-kneed. She drooped a little as she walked, a shy and timid creature; but when she saw the fire and the waiting crowd she straightened and lifted her head. She looked proud then, but the Yunggamurra failed to see it.

The Yunggamurra had crushed her hands to her mouth and bitten them to hold back a wild, fierce cry, for this spirit was a kind she knew. It was a Mimi, a rock-spirit from a country near her own—a frail and gentle type, in constant fear of the wind and of breaking; and a stranger here, as the Yunggamurra was. Of all the earth-things she might have chosen to help her home, none could have been better than this.

'She shall help me,' whispered the Yunggamurra savagely into her fingers, 'or I will break her into tiny straws. Let her only see me and she will know and tremble.'

Two

The Yunggamurra was so filled with wicked triumph that she quivered like a string. The creatures below must have felt her presence if they had not been welcoming another stranger. A rock-spirit! What else could travel so surely through these roads of rock? And where should she travel but to her own country, so near the Yunggamurra's? The river-spirit crouched in the darkness above, ready to spring. A Mimi—what was a Mimi to a Yunggamurra?

But she did not spring; just in time she remembered the others below. The bright-eyed Little People were many and strong; the tailed creatures had a free, fierce manner that matched her own. For the headless women she felt only scorn, but she dreaded the shapeless shadows. They most of all seemed to belong to the dark, imprisoning heart of the land. They would not tolerate an intruder here.

It was clear that they had expected the Mimi and welcomed her. She had paused, lank and frail, at the edge of the shadows while her large round eyes took in the scene. Now she turned away with shy ceremony, folded her wispy length down, and sat on the rock with her back to the fire. At once the others surged forward with a murmur and rumble of voices, inviting her, bowing their heads and speaking with respect. The dark formless shapes flowed towards her. The Yunggamurra watched sharply, frowning. She had never seen so much respect shown to a stranger and a Mimi.

'We have fire, we have food,' the Little People coaxed.

'We have heard the word,' said those with tails, 'and we have heard the wind and felt the ice. Our roads are open to the Fighter of Ice.'

At these words the Yunggamurra quivered again, with curiosity and angry disbelief. She and her sisters had heard no word of ice, but she had seen it here in a cave. No Mimi had fought it; she could not believe in a Mimi fighting anything at all. She watched while the Mimi rose and turned, standing very straight with her dark eyes glowing green, yet looking more defiant than proud as she walked to the fire.

'See her!' The Yunggamurra whispered, scratching her own arms with her nails as she hugged herself in scorn. 'Too timid even for a proper pride! Wau! When I have her alone! I will make the fighter wilt like a broken fern!' But she listened sharply, and grinned when the Mimi's first words confirmed her disbelief.

'You shame me, for I am no fighter. My part was only to help the fighter on his way. The word that came to you was his word, for he is both good and brave.'

'Who are we to know these things?' said one of the tailed women. 'We know only that the Ninya came this way with their cold wind, building ice, and now they have gone back. You have the knowledge, Great One. Inform our ears.'

The Little People had been busy laying bat and lizard and grubs in the ashes of the fire. Now they looked up with their star-like eyes fixed on the Mimi. 'You tell,' they begged in a soft rumble, and made room beside the fire.

The Mimi folded herself down again like one who has travelled a long and weary way. Smoke rose in the heavy stillness, the smoke of burning bones and rubbish, of singed fur and scales. The Yunggamurra cowered between her rocks, but the Mimi sniffed gratefully and gazed at the fire as if she saw her story in it.

'The Men of Ice,' she murmured, and all the earth-creatures were still and listened. She knew they had heard the story for all the roads were buzzing with it, but they needed to hear it again from her. And had they not met to bring her fire and food?

'They came from their home under the red sand,' she said, 'for they planned to lock the land in ice as in the old days when they were strong. But first they would find the Eldest Nargun, the one with the power of fire, lest it should defeat them with fire before they were strong again. And so they came, through your country and many more, east to the sea and down to the far end of the land in search of the Eldest. And we followed, to warn the Nargun and rouse it.'

Still the listeners were silent, for to the name of the Ninya was added the name of the Nargun, and that name was known in the deep rocks. The Mimi gazed at the fire seeing what she had seen; and at last another of the tailed creatures spoke.

'It was a terrible ice. It cracked rocks. You have seen them? Great rocks that never saw the light, a dreaming of mountains whose time is not yet come. And the ice, swelling like a frog, has burst them apart.' He spoke solemnly, but a quick red spark in his black eyes made the Yunggamurra grin.

The Mimi saw it too. 'The land will shape the unborn mountains, child of Kooleen,' she said sternly, and the spirit shifted its eyes. 'The ice was our affair.'

'You tell,' urged the Little People, bringing singed food set out on stones.

'We tracked it to the beach where the Eldest lay, but the Eldest was beyond its time. We fought the ice with the fires of Men. There never were such fires. They too cracked rocks, child of Kooleen.'

'The fires of Men . . .' A crowd of eyes, bright and dark, stared at her. Even the Yunggamurra was caught up in the tale.

'Men and spirits fought together under one leader.' The Mimi's twiglike fingers grasped the bat by the leg but she had forgotten it. 'That was a fight. The Ninya crawled back into their holes, and the People of their country came to sing them home.'

'And the leader? Who was that?'

'A man. Wirrun of the People.'

Voices rumbled, half believing. 'A man of the People!' 'Are the old times come again?' 'Was this an Old One beyond his time?'

'A young man of this time, one who lives in the towns of the white men. But he hears the voice of the land and carries an old power. Wirrun of the People, the Fighter of Ice . . .' Her head drooped and she stared unseeing at the singed and broken bat. 'I grieve to lose him,' whispered the Mimi, who had nagged and scolded Wirrun down half the length of the land. The headless, groping women swayed towards her, the Yunggamurra sniggered, the Little People were respectfully silent, the shadow-shapes fluttered and were still, and one of the tailed women gave her tail an insolent flick.

'And what was your part, Great One? How came a Mimi from the far north to cross the land and fight the ice with this great leader?'

The Mimi lifted her head in sudden pride that made the Yunggamurra frown. 'I rode the winds, wife of Kooleen, as the Mimi cannot do. I was carried off from my home and rode the winds from sea to sea and was not broken. This was my part: to help the Fighter ride the winds. And to use my eyes and ears for him, and acquaint him with strange spirits.' Her eyes fell to the fire again, brooding. 'The land ordered it; but I am weary for my country. Weary with wanting.'

'Soon now,' the Little People comforted her. 'You eat. You rest.' They offered her the grubs, which were their own secret kind and a great restorer of strength.

The Mimi ate politely but absently, drooping beside the fire. She had played her part as an honoured guest; she had sat by their fire, eaten their food, spoken what they needed to hear. She hoped there would be no corroboree. The journey home, through so many countries and with so much honour, was wearier than ever the journey with Wirrun had been, and the nearer she came to her own country the sharper was the pain of her need.

The Yunggamurra watched narrow-eyed from above, avoiding the smoke as well as she could. She had never before had to endure smoke—at home she and her sisters would have dived deep into the sweet water—and it filled her with a shuddering unease. She dreaded that the smoke would bring her drifting down like a withered leaf on the crowd below. Besides, she needed clear eyes and ears to see, to hear, and to think.

She had heard the Mimi's story with some awe, for even a lost Yunggamurra knows how the land must be served. But this serving was over, and the ice had never reached her country. She had seen only the remains of it in a cave. Her own need for her country was as sharp a pain as any, and she knew fiercely that this Mimi must take her home.

But while the Mimi rested there beside the fire in the care of so many, there was nothing to be done but to wait and think.

It would not be as easy as the Yunggamurra had hoped. The Mimi was no fighter, that was confirmed, but her story showed that she had courage and pride. And if she should refuse to help—what use was a broken Mimi to the Yunggamurra? Yet she thought that the Mimi would not refuse, for there had been that moment when they two might have been sisters: when the Mimi had spoken of the weariness of waiting, and the river-spirit had felt the weight of loneliness and despair.

'Let me only come to her alone,' whispered the Yunggamurra, clenching her nails into her palms. Yet even that would not be easy, for all the spirits of the land had a duty to watch for and welcome and help this Mimi.

On the rocks below the fire was dying. The tailed creatures and the headless ones stood apart in groups. The Mimi, watched over by shadow-shapes and Little People, lay sleeping by the fire—or was she sleeping? The Yunggamurra, peering, thought she caught a green glint of eyes and drew quickly back. She waited and listened. It seemed a long time before she heard a stirring and crept forward again.

The Mimi had roused and the tailed figures were scattering the fire. There was only the dim glow of the spirits themselves as they prepared to set the Mimi on her way. No light came from those shapeless shadows, the most dreaded. They were only a movement of dark at the edge of the glow, and the Yunggamurra bit her lip. She must go carefully. She watched the group trail away into a passage at the far end of the cave and their glow fade. She waited for a moment longer, then, swift and silent, climbed down and followed.

The next cave held a pool of the secret water. She had to wait behind a rock while the Mimi stooped and drank; all the others drank with her. When the water's clear call had been answered by the rocks and was silent, the Yunggamurra slipped without a splash into the pool. She was glad of it, for it restored her slimy skin and rid her of smoke.

She knew the water-ways better than those of rock and for some time could follow the travellers by those ways, winding through tunnels and cutting back through flooded caves that they must go round or under or over. The sense of their nearness guided her, and the murmur and rumble of voices; echoes in a cavern; sometimes a reflected glow. It was good travelling, swift and safe.

But a moment came when the dark threads and pools of water would not lead her to the voices she could hear. The Yunggamurra, refreshed again, had to leave the water and climb over rock. She crawled into a cleft and saw the spirit-light at its other end. She went through quickly, pausing in the dark mouth of the cleft to look into the cave beyond.

It was one of those caves where sparkling stone had grown into the flowing and dripping shapes of water. At first she thought it was ice, but it glittered with colours and had no burning cold. Lit by the spirit-light it shone against the darker rock behind, a dreaming of water in stone. At the centre of the cave a pool caught this sparkle and colour, so that all the cave shone doubled in the water. The Yunggamurra caught her breath and came forward almost into the light. She had not known that any stone could live like this in light. It was another of the land's private thoughts, kept in darkness.

Just in time she clutched at rock to hold herself back from the earth-things in the cave. They were clustered beyond the pool, far too close for safety, but by good fortune turned away from the pool and towards the Mimi. She faced them alone, speaking her farewells. The Yunggamurra, looking out across the pool from her dark cleft, saw this with a curling back of lips from sharp white teeth, a dog's snarl. The moment was near; she stood ready.

'You have brought me far on my way,' the Mimi was saying. 'I thank you for your kindness and will trouble you no more. From here my own road is fastest.'

A spirit's speed is fast indeed, and the Yunggamurra tensed. She must not lose the Mimi in the moment of parting, while she waited for the others to go. She leaned forward, poised.

'We come, we watch,' the Little People were begging. 'We go your road.'

The Mimi stood tall and frail, looking not at the Little People but over their heads.

'I would take you if I could,' she said, 'but the road is dangerous to strangers, and there are evil spirits as well as good. And I must go by my own road, fast and straight and alone, for my country is near and I hunger. You know that hunger.'

She lifted a hand in farewell, and turned to the dark rock and blew on it. A great blackness opened for a moment in the rock, and the Mimi stepped into it and was gone. The rock closed again.

The Yunggamurra slumped back into her crevice. She did not know how long ago the Mimi had seen her and read her purpose. She did not care that the Mimi had kept her secret and saved her from the earth-things of this place. She felt only bitter fury that she had forgotten what she should have known of the ways of the Mimi and their camps and roads within rock.

She lay in her fury until long after the Little People and the tailed people, the headless women and the hovering shadows, had gone. She was alone in the dark, and blind again after the light. She stumbled into the cave that was a wonder of beauty if only it could have been seen, and found her way into the water. There she lay, feeling the emptiness of the cave, the closeness of the dark, and the hugeness of the land that had caught her in its secret heart. After a time she forgot danger in the pain of her loneliness and longing, and she lifted her head from the water and howled.

That wild-dog howl went crying and wailing down caverns and tunnels in the dark, and was caught and answered and built into a pack of howling as though all the Yunggamurra howled with this one. The spirits of the place heard it and cowered; they thought the land itself was howling in its heart. And when the sound had come and gone and died away, when the dark places were silent, the Yunggamurra crawled on her weary way into the depths of the land.

. Three

Of the men who live in the old south land the brown-skinned People are the eldest race. The two white races, Happy Folk and Inlanders, are two branches from the stem of the first white settlers, and very recent comers. They are so new to the land that the Inlanders still struggle to manage it while they slowly adapt to it; and the Happy Folk, engrossed in the serious business of happiness, do their best to forget the land altogether. The coming of the People was long before, and by now the land has made them its own and flows in their veins. Yet there is an older race still: the old things that the land itself has bred, of whom only the People are aware. The earth-creatures, of spirit kind.

They are scarcely seen even by the People, but they are many, for their time is not yet past. As the land bred them so they live by it: by rock, sand, forest, river, and the quiet breadth of night. Any tree, any whirlwind may harbour its spirit; the surface caves and deep caverns are full of them. They are fearful or charming, cruel or kind, by no law but their own or the will of the land. Yet though they are many and everywhere, few of the spirits themselves know the camps and roads of the Mimi. These lie within solid rock, in the First Dark. The Yunggamurra would have remembered this if it had not seemed to her, a spirit of the open rivers, that she herself was enclosed in solid rock.

When the rock closed round the Mimi in answer to her blowing, its dark stillness wrapped her in peace and the certainty of home. She was sorry for the river-spirit trapped in so strange a country, but she had told that spirit the truth: she could not travel by slow water-paths, or with so wild and fierce a companion. She remembered the day when she herself had been taken by the wind up into the dizzy sky; how she had dreaded that she would never see her home again! How helpless she had been, and how afraid. She had not known herself then. A hundred ages had not taught her what she had learnt in the last few weeks. So she set off fast and true on her own road home, knowing what she would meet when she reached it and how she must face it. And on a day when the Wet was beginning—when the swamps lay open to the clouds that came down, and only within rock was there peace and a fire—she came back to her kind.

'Wa!' they said. 'You are here.' They said no more just then, for they knew no more and needed time to adjust. No word from the south had reached them, and in their warm wet country they knew nothing of the ice. On the day the wind had carried one of them off they had found her bark dish and her digging stick where she had dropped them, and had guessed what had happened and hidden it decently.

The Mimi are too light to resist the wind, and so frail that it breaks them easily. For this reason they gather their food only in still weather and every Mimi obeys the tabu of the wind. So to be caught by the wind has become improper, and if possible some other reason must be found to explain such accidents. They had preferred to believe that this Mimi had been carried off by a more evil spirit; they had mourned her suitably, revenged her by magic, and given her up. Now here she stood and the truth would have to come out.

All this the Mimi knew. 'The wind took me,' she confessed with drooping head, 'and the land saved me. It had work for a Mimi.' And she told them the story as briefly as possible with no pride. Pride was her secret from now on, for she knew what was right in her country. She would be no Great One here; it was only right.

Her kind listened, tall and wispy and embarrassed, avoiding each other's eyes. They still had no knowledge of the ice, for words are only words, but they did not know how to punish or reject one who had been called to do the work of the land. Yet it was wrong that one Mimi should come down safe from the wind and perhaps lead into it many others who would not be saved to do the land's work. They needed more time to see what grew out of this. Silently they went away.

The Mimi made her fire where she was and sat by it alone. She was not depressed by the coldness of the others for she had known how it must be. She was back in her dear north country with the swamps filling outside, and her stick-like body was silently singing for joy. She wanted to dance with the slender flying grace of the Mimi, but she must not for her people's sake. She stayed demure, downcast, and alone.

In the next few days she spent much time alone, hearing the voices of her kind and hiding a smile of content. She followed out all her adventure, needing this time to make it a secret part of her. She felt again her parting from Wirrun, and opened her wispy fingers and let it go. She thought of the wild water-woman trapped inside the land, and pitied her but not too much: if she did not find her home again, at any rate she would find herself. She sat alone and thought of these things while the others watched her secretly for any sign of a swollen head. They watched her gathering wood and food in the shelter of rocks, making a digging stick or spinning string, eating alone by her fire, always decently timid and drooping.

They began to come in twos and threes, late when the fires were low, to whisper to her. It was always the same question, morbidly eager: 'Is it terrible on the wind?'

She answered soberly with a shiver: 'It is terrible . . . It is rising and falling and twisting, with the limbs cracking . . . The land and the sky change places and roll about. The stars are sharp, and the wind-spirits cry . . . You are nothing. There is no fire and no home.'

The inquisitive ones would creep away in silence, burdened. By day they turned to look at her and whisper, and she knew they spoke of it. In a little while they spoke of it aloud, pointing her out with pity and at last with kindly scorn. 'See, here is the one that the wind caught. It took her ears away, but she thinks with a better ear now.'

Then the Mimi knew she had won back a place among her people; a lowly place, but it would do. She never told them anything but the terror of the wind. She never spoke of battle or the young man of the People, but she thought of him often and wondered if he too had come home.

* * *

And Wirrun of the People was as near home as he could be. He was in that eastern country by the sea that was his own country, even weighed down as it was by concrete and bitumen. He was in the town from which he had set out, and in which not long ago he had gone to school with the children of the Happy Folk. He had not yet found a job, for the world of spirits and moonlit seas still hung about him and he could not cast it off; but he had borrowed money from his friend Ularra to pay his rent and restock the noisy old refrigerator in his room. He told himself restlessly that he would find a job next week. Next week would be better and more real, or he tried to think so.

He was sitting now in a dimly lit milkbar, sprawling in a high-backed bench with Ularra sprawling in another across the narrow table. These two had each another name among the Happy Folk, but when they were together they used the names known to the People. Wirrun's eyes were shadowed, for he had been telling the story that Ularra had a right to hear. Ularra was grinning with delight and disbelief, and sometimes laughing loudly and throwing his long arms and legs about as he went back over the impossible story.

'And that old bunyip, eh?' he said again, boisterously because he was not much older than Wirrun. 'I bet *he's* scared a lot of little kids.' Wirrun stirred restlessly, and Ularra saw and looked subdued. He was concerned for his friend without knowing how to say so or what to do. The adventure sounded like a crazy game to him, and young Wirrun had won it and done all right for himself. He ought to be wagging his tail a bit. But there was something different about him, and Ularra couldn't pick it.

The broad east-country face, so different from Ularra's longer northern one, was the same yet not the same. That hair, always tangled into curls like a kid's, that was Wirrun all right. The quietness, with the wide white grin coming through . . . it still came through, but it wasn't the same grin. He'd always been quiet, but not . . . stern. Stern? Ularra heaved around on his bench, knocking over a cup. Not stern . . . tired, maybe. It had been a rough time. What was it? About two weeks? Not enough, you'd think, to turn a boy into a man. In the old days it took longer.

'It was good seeing the mob from Conner,' he said; for the men from Mount Conner who had brought Wirrun home belonged to the country near Ularra's own, and his eyes had lit up and his laugh had been loud while he talked to them. 'They think a lot of you.'

'They're good men,' said Wirrun, smiling; but then he sighed.

Ularra tried again. 'I heard the pub down the street's looking for a yard man. Not bad, a job in a pub—I wouldn't mind it. But look, you don't want to worry about it. I got cash, and if I run short there's others. It's only right.'

Wirrun knew it was only right, for the Ninya—the Ice-Men—had been the People's concern and not just his; but he also knew he must get a job as soon as he could. It was the only way to live in the Happy Folk's town—and the only way to get out into the country as he needed to do, and walk on the land and feel it flowing into him through his feet.

'I'll see them Monday,' he said, and hesitated. 'Only there's something I gotta do first. If you can spare the cash.'

Ularra's hand was in his pocket. 'How much?'

'Five should do. Gotta go north to that mountain and put the power back where I found it.'

Ularra pushed a note across the table, waited till Wirrun had pocketed it, and said, "You're crazy. You'd do better to stay home and get some sleep—looks as if you need it. What's the point? It's yours, that stone. Who else is around to look after it? Keep it, man.'

'Can't,' said Wirrun, not trying to explain because Ularra knew the reasons. He knew the age and power of the great quartz crystal in its wrapping of possum-fur string; that it was a power for a man and Wirrun had never been made a man; that he had been led to it only by the old spirit of the mountain—by Ko-in, who was Hero, and whose stern, strong voice Wirrun heard so often in his mind . . . *I will speak to no more men till the ice comes again.*

'Crazy,' said Ularra uneasily, because he could see that for some reason Wirrun had to go back to the mountain.

So Wirrun bought a train ticket that same night, and made the short journey north and slept by a stream. And the next morning, with his travel-stained pack on his back, he walked to the mountain.

Four

This mountain that Wirrun sought was the one on which his adventure with the ice had properly begun. He walked to it with his long, loose stride away from the highway, along dusty roads that he remembered; and the power, the magic stone hidden so deep in its fur-string wrapping, hung in its bag from his belt. He knew that Ularra was partly right: he need not have made this short journey so soon just to put the power back in its place. They had done the land's work together, and he was used now to having it in trust; he and the power did each other no harm. He could have waited until he had a job and money of his own for the trip, without borrowing Ularra's. And he did need rest. That was partly what he came for; that, and to be alone.

They'd always said he was a loner, and he knew they were right—but in his wanderings round the country he had always liked to meet and talk to the People. He had felt at home with them. He'd been glad of the People's help in fighting the ice. Good men, all of them. So why had he needed to get away from them to be alone? He had spent weeks talking only to spirits, and it had felt easy and right; he had travelled a long way with a Mimi and parted from her sadly. He missed her more than the People and it worried him. He was real, and life in the town was real, and he couldn't get it started. He was tired and empty and spirit-haunted and he couldn't believe in a job on Monday. He needed . . . rest . . .

But how could he come from that shadowy company and rest with a motorbike revving outside a broken window? How could he come from a moonlit, calling sea to Ularra's laughter in a murky milkbar? He knew he was

21

running away to the mountain, to something that was unreal and yet more than real. He needed to be alone.

He saw the heads of mountains looking at him over a wooded ridge, and sat down for a while and looked back. And he knew he was partly fooling himself: he didn't come here only to be alone, but to be alone with his mountain. That mountain had shown him old terrors and old evils as well as old powers; he had walked on it at night and heard its voice. He wanted to walk on it again with everything put right, and perhaps the mountain would know. Perhaps it would feel like home again.

I will speak to no more men until the ice comes again. But that had been Ko-in, not the mountain.

At midday he came to a village on a ridge with the scrub-draped, forest-hung mountains standing over it. He did not go to the village shop to buy supplies; he had carried a heavier pack all this way in order to avoid it. It was only a couple of weeks since the Inlanders of this place had watched him with hard suspicion, and he had known they thought of bushfires and careless shots meant for rabbits and the noisy nuisance of a silly young drunk, and other realities of their lives. He did not want to be seen again so soon. He skirted the village and took his old path to the one mountain, the nearest one.

He knew the way up through the lower forest, between the boulders of the steepening slope, to the sheer heights of rock and scrub. He went straight to the sheltering ledge where he had camped before, and began to build his fire in the old place where the shoulder of the mountain hid it from the village. Often he paused to stare at a hollow tree or an outline of rock, remembering. It seemed so long ago . . .'

He did not light the fire but sat beside it in the shade of the ledge and ate a cold lunch, looking from the mountain across the ridge to blue-hazed valleys in the summer heat, and farther mountains, and the dark tree-lined course of a river, to a distant misty blue that might be the sea. It felt like home, but the mountain did not speak.

After a time he took his canvas water-bag and climbed around to the steep rocky gully where the stream trickled, and down into the gully. It was deeply shadowed, for the sun was already behind the high wall of rock that closed the head of the gully. Wirrun sat for some time by a little pool between rocks. The moss was still black from that impossible summer frost, but new curled fronds were showing among the blackened ferns. He touched one gently, saying that everything was all right again. His fingers strayed from the fern to the net bag hanging at his belt.

Now he was here, in the very place. In three minutes he could return the power to that dark hole where a dying man had hidden it long ago. He might as well climb up there now, to the hole in the cliff at the head of the gully; but he only sank his canvas bag into the pool, wetting and filling it, holding it carefully to draw in clean water. He would sleep another night here on the mountain with the power. Tomorrow was time enough.

He climbed back to his camp as the day's heat was ebbing, hung the water-bag in its place on a root that curled over the ledge, and lit his fire. Then he sat feeding it, waiting for the good red coals that would grill his steak, watching the sunset reflected in the eastern sky from behind the mountain. He saw the gold drain away, and pinpoint stars shine in the clear green of evening; sitting with his hand on the power, feeling the soft ball of cord and the hardness of the stone within, and the roundness that swelled to the roundness of the world inside his hand. He felt again the lift and swell of the mountain under him, but it did not speak.

When the coals were right he cooked his steak, then built the fire into a blaze and ate by its light. The dark breathed in and out as the flames rose and fell, but there was no thickening of fearful shapes in it. He could just see, farther along the ledge, the tree that he knew had a hole in the trunk from which Ko-in had dragged forth the Mimi. How spindly and cantankerous and staunch she had been, and how much he missed her. What a lot of sadness there was mixed up in the joy of restoration . . . and as he thought this the hard sadness softened and began to flow.

He put his head down to rub the wetness off his chocolate-brown cheek on to his knee; and when he lifted it again he saw that a shape did stand at the edge of the firelight, watching him. The red-yellow light washed over it: a man of the People, tall and strong, painted with white markings and carrying a firestick.

'Welcome to my country, Hero,' said Ko-in.

Wirrun goggled at him as he came forward into the fire-light. 'I never hoped—' he stammered. 'You said no more—I brought the power back.'

'The power is yours and in your keeping. Hero must honour hero, and you were in need.'

'I was that,' Wirrun confessed. 'I'm in a lot better shape for seeing you. You know it's turned out all right?'

'I know and I honour you.'

'It was others, mainly—the Mimi most of all. Did she get home safe? Do you know that?'

'All is well,' said Ko-in on a note of exasperation. 'I never met a man so hard to honour. Again: I salute you, Hero.'

'You needn't. I'm no hero. You know well enough what I am.'

Ko-in bowed his head in agreement. 'Better than you know. And there are words to be spoken.' He crossed the firelight and sat himself formally, cross-legged, by Wir-run's side. 'We will speak at your fire, for the time is past when I might carry you through the wind to mine.'

'I know that,' said Wirrun a bit roughly. He was no little kid looking for favours. The time had passed with the need.

'Hear me,' said Ko-in, 'for you know only what you will not know, and what you will know is all greenness. You have come to this country as a tired man comes home, and I welcome you. But you must know the truth. This country is my home. Yours is wider.'

Wirrun gazed at him under lowered brows, and the fire-light hid his eyes in shadow.

'Hold back your anger and hear me. You came here first as a boy with down on your chin, knowing nothing, only listening to the land. I gave you knowledge and power, and sent you forth with help beside you. I could do no less, for the land called you and the men are gone and there was no help at hand but mine.'

'And I'm thankful,' muttered Wirrun angrily. He burst out, 'I remember every word you said, always! You said your love would follow me, and I rested on that. Is it any wonder if this place feels like home? Was it wrong to come back and say what's done?'

'It is no wonder and it was right. Have I not welcomed you? But tonight I have stood by your fire and watched, and I see more than a young hero returned. I see a man, a man whose country has found him. I came to salute you and welcome you to my country. I stay to show you yours.'

To be called hero was a thing that washed over Wirrun like firelight, but to be called a man touched him like a finger. He smiled wryly, rubbing his chin. 'Still a bit fuzzy,' he said. 'Can't change much in a couple of weeks.'

'No?' Ko-in smiled gravely. 'The men would have taken a little longer, but you have been made a man by other means. You have not learnt the lore of this country, but there are lores for all countries. Which of the youths of your People has journeyed to manhood in the arms of Tu-ru-dun? Has made his man's journey with a Mimi for companion? Has been taught spirits by the spirits themselves? Has fought beside and against them, and led them to victory? I could say more.'

'Don't bother. I don't feel no different, any rate.'

'Only because you will not know. By shoulders, mouth and eyes a man reveals himself and not by the hair on his chin. Such a man-making cannot be denied; you must accept it. Come, Hero. I will show you your country.'

Wirrun rose with him unwillingly and followed beyond the firelight to the dark edge of the mountain. Grey starlight lay over ridge and forest, outlining the lift of hills and the long arms of spurs. The old south land, released from the day's heat, stretched and expanded in the breadth of night. Wirrun laid his hand on the power and found it was throbbing. The land reached for him, night-murmuring and hung with stars. Ko-in spoke beside him.

'From sea to sea, there lies your country.'

'It's a lonely country,' said Wirrun, 'too big for me. I'd sooner have just this bit.'

'You cannot take back your name from the places where it is known. There are makings that cannot be denied, Hero, and names that must be accepted. You have said that you remember the words of Ko-in: remember these, for in time you must believe them.'

'Eh?' said Wirrun. 'Of course I—you know I—' He saw Ko-in's grave smile and pulled himself together. 'It's all a bit big for me, that's all, like the country. All I know is, you're chucking me out of the place I thought I had . . .'

'If the name is too big you must grow. And do not envy me my country, for it too is yours. When your fire burns where it burns tonight I will come to you. Now rest well,' said Ko-in as he had said once before, 'and wake well, and journey well out of my country.' And he sprang up into the wind and rose between the trees and was gone.

Wirrun went back to his fire confused, like a man between sleeping and waking. He could not seize on and remember the words of Ko-in; they slid away as he reached for them, and would not hold together. He gave up trying at last, and sat and stared at the fire while it died; and then one sentence did come back clearly in the strong voice of Ko-in.

When your fire burns where it burns tonight I will come to you: he could never have hoped for such comfort as that. He climbed into his sleeping-bag, taking the power with him as he always had, and fell deeply asleep.

If the scrub stood closer about his ledge while he slept, he did not know it. If the darkness gathered in fantastic shapes and whispered, 'Hero, the ice is gone,' he heard nothing. He had been given rest. Tiredness and haunting drained away; partings were made and finished; all the realities merged into one and grew whole. Even the words of Ko-in sank through his sleep into deep places in his mind, to be remembered in time. Only when grey starlight thinned to the first grey of dawn did his sleep thin a little, and then he was hushed by the sound of water. There was a rushing of water rising and falling through his sleep, sometimes with words singing in it. It held him and charmed him till the sun probed under his ledge and he woke. He turned his head to look for the water, saw where he was, and forgot it.

He felt good. Even the spiderweb tangled on his dark face and hair felt good. Beyond the shelter of his ledge there was dew that the sunlight struck into sparks. He looked at it for a while, then sat up and looked farther: out from the mountain and down to the ridge where the village lay under a thin streak of mist . . . He had been given a land for a country. To a man of the People it was a stern gift, as Ko-in had known. But he had been given manhood to accept it, and the mountain was part of it too. He got up and went to the water-bag to splash his face with cold water.

He ate breakfast, tidied the camp, buried the fire, and left his pack rolled under the ledge. Then, with the power hanging at his belt for the last time, he set off for the gully. *The power is yours and in your keeping*: well, he was putting it back in its place. His time with the earth-spirits had finished while he slept—a man had to go back to town and find a job.

The gully was full of morning sunlight as he climbed down into it and up its narrow bed to the cliff. The rock had warmed already. The frost-blackened mosses would not be green again before autumn, he thought. He climbed a little way up the cliff by a narrow ledge, towards that hole in the rock where a man of the old People had hidden the power. Balanced and leaning against the rock, he unfastened his belt and slipped off the net bag. But he held the bag for a little while, and put one hand into it to hold the soft roundness of fur. He had held it like that often . . . but only once, at Ko-in's bidding, had he unwound the fur cord and looked at the pointed, hexagonal crystal of quartz, glinting and veined with pink. He held it—and felt it throb—and suddenly there was the sound of water, and a daylight dreaming.

He thought a waterfall poured over the cliff above him and into the gully. He saw the swirl of water and the whiteness of foam and heard its roar. It wavered, the water dwindled to a silver curtain, and the song of water softened; and again it broke forth, and leapt and tumbled and foamed. It wavered, and rushed and roared again, and he heard words singing in the sound of the water.

> *Are you not coming?*
> *sings the bright water,*
> *are you not coming?*

Wirrun snatched his hand away from the power, holding only the net bag. The waterfall vanished: but still the sound of it was in his ears, and the words singing from low to high and drifting down again like a wind-dropped leaf.

He thrust the power into its hole and pushed it back into darkness as far as he could reach.

He had just woken to the ordinary things that a man had to live with. He would not be caught again by a dreaming.

2

The Name of Hero

One

On Monday Wirrun went to the pub down the street and got the job as a yardman and cleaner. It was not as good a job as his last one at the service station, but he could have all his meals in the hotel kitchen and that would make the money go further; and there was a clean, dull room across the yard near the garages, where he could live and save the rent of his old flat.

'You'll clean it yourself,' said the stout white woman who ran the hotel, 'and get a change of linen from the housekeeper once a week. You'll stay out of the house unless you're sent for. The room's your own but there'll be no rowdyism. That clear?'

Wirrun nodded. His thick-lipped, broad-nosed People's face was heavily serious. The woman noticed it.

'We've got no prejudices here,' she said roundly as if he had accused her. 'The same rules for everyone.'

Wirrun nodded again. He was not resentful; the Happy Folk had rested in his hands along with the beetle and the starfish and would never again be large enough for anger. He was simply holding on to the ordinary things that a man had to live with.

Ularra approved of the job, partly because of the free meals and cheap beer that went with it but chiefly because it seemed to have ended Wirrun's restless unhappiness. On Monday night, when he helped Wirrun to move his belongings from the flat to the room behind the hotel, he was noisy with pleasure. Standing tall and loose-limbed under the light, he looked at Wirrun's new home and nodded.

'More room and cheap beer. You'll be all right here, man.'

'No rowdyism, mind,' said Wirrun with the wide grin that lightened all his face. He had taken a bottle from the small refrigerator and was pouring beer. Ularra took his chipped glass with noises of approval, and his eyes gleamed against the darkness of his skin.

'That's the stuff,' he said, and dropped untidily into the one armchair with his feet on Wirrun's bed. 'What's it like any rate?'

Wirrun had taken his own glass over to the old wardrobe; it had a deep bottom drawer in which he was storing the things he wouldn't be needing for a while. His sleeping-bag and camping gear; his collection of maps; clippings from newspapers, pasted on to sheets of paper. He glanced at those as he laid them away: SUMMER FREEZE ON TABLELANDS. But suddenly it was the rushing music of water that filled his mind, and a haunting drift of song . . . *are you not coming?* He shut his mind to it quickly.

'I said, what's it like?' shouted Ularra.

'Eh? Oh . . . all right. Good tucker. Funny eating in the kitchen with them watching, but I'll get used to it.'

'You can bring home some of that take-away stuff for a change. What about time off?'

'About usual. Finish at four-thirty. Couple of weeks' leave a year, maybe—I'm not sure. Makes no difference.'

'Go on—that's not you. You'll be off somewhere for a few days sooner than that.'

Wirrun shut the drawer with a bang and began to unpack clothes into smaller drawers. 'No money,' he said firmly. 'Got to keep my head down till I pay what I owe.'

Ularra sat up and reached for the beer. 'You know better than that, man.' He sounded hurt. 'Never's soon enough—you paid it back before I lent it.' The beer had already made him earnest. 'I got rights too, you know. Maybe I missed out on these Ninya and Mimi and those, but any rate I can put a bit of cash in. They're nearer my business than yours.'

'I know that,' said Wirrun quickly, for Ularra's home was near Mount Conner and the country of the Ninya. Into the silence came the distant roar of the hotel's bar, where the Happy Folk were avoiding rowdyism in their own way under the eye of the stout lady. 'If that's how you want it. Only I still gotta keep my head down. Time I settled down a bit. A man's not a kid all his life.'

Ularra threw himself back in the chair, hurled his legs

on to Wirrun's bed, spilt a little beer, and laughed for some time. 'Listen to him! Couple of weeks and he's got grey hairs coming? Man, you'll have that gear out and be off for a weekend before you're a month older.'

> *Are you not coming?*
> *sings the bright water*

'Not me,' said Wirrun. 'It's a year till I get any leave. Then we'll see.'

'I've got a fiver says it'll be in a month,' declared Ularra.

He would have lost his money. Wirrun settled into his room and his job, worked silently by day and read the newspaper at night. He grew used to the roar of the bar, began to exchange grave smiles with the staff and to like some of them. He often spent an evening with Ularra, in a milkbar or in his own room; and Ularra's easy chatter began to dry up, and he sometimes looked at Wirrun with puzzled respect.

Wirrun looked at concrete and smog and painted metal; he watched the Happy Folk eagerly chasing happiness or sternly marketing it; sometimes he saw the People lost and searching. He would not look at far-off moonlit seas. He closed his mind to the haunting sound of water. That water-dream still haunted him, but he held on to the ordinary things that a man had to live with and grew older and sterner; and more than one month went by.

One evening Ularra brought two strangers to the milkbar: men of the People, visitors from an inland country. They were shabbily dressed, with stubble on their chins, and they sat silently at the table gazing at Wirrun. He asked them about their country and they answered with short, blunt shyness. He could see that someone had told them stories about him and he looked reproachfully at Ularra. But Ularra only stared intently at the waitress, for this was his latest game. He called it 'eyeing off a chick'. Wirrun was glad when the evening was over and the strangers went away, still silent and respectful.

'You got no right cheating men like that,' he said roundly to Ularra, and got only a look of puzzled surprise.

A few weeks later, on an evening when Wirrun was at home reading the newspaper, Ularra brought another stranger of the People. This one too was shy and silent and only looked with shadowed eyes at Wirrun while Ularra, a little nervous and therefore showing off, shouted for beer.

Wirrun produced it. He had noticed lately that an evening at home with Ularra used up more bottles than it would have used once. Ularra talked a lot, Wirrun a little, and the stranger not at all until the third bottle was empty. Then he leaned forward suddenly and laid a hand on Wirrun's sleeve.

'Had to see the hero,' he said very earnestly. 'Couldn't—go home and not—tell 'em.' He lifted his glass unsteadily. 'All the men—thanks.'

'You want to forget that,' said Wirrun shortly.

It was a terrible evening. Even Ularra seemed to realise it, and rose and stretched and took the visitor away. When they had gone and Wirrun had closed the yard gate behind them he went quickly into his room and opened a fourth bottle of beer.

He reproached Ularra when he came alone the next evening. Ularra looked dogged.

'What's the harm, letting 'em come and look? It means a lot to them and it don't cost you a cent. How can you turn 'em down, man? What else can I do?'

'You can stop filling 'em up with yarns, and then it won't happen,' said Wirrun.

Ularra stood under the light and gazed down at him. 'You been telling me lies, then?' Wirrun frowned with anger. 'If it happened,' said Ularra, 'it happened. No good pretending it didn't.'

'What's done's over and best forgotten,' snapped Wirrun. 'I'm just a bloke like them—I got nothing to give 'em but a bit of free beer. You ought to grow up, man, it's time.'

Ularra lowered his brows. 'You could do a bit of that yourself, for a man that grew up quick. I tell 'em nothing they don't ask. They come looking—what do you expect? There's been near a dozen, I reckon, but you never saw 'em. Only the few that need it.'

'Need it!' Wirrun was shaken, even shocked. He had seen the People as lost and searching; he would not have them cheated with false hopes. For a little time he had been an instrument used by the land and guided by its spirits, nothing more. 'They need to get out and stand on their own feet, that's what they need. And you and me too.'

Ularra dropped into the armchair and grinned. They had been close to a quarrel, but he would not quarrel with Wirrun. '*You* need it. Me, I'm getting out soon as my leave's due, only you won't come. Where's this beer? And won't that heater do any better? I can't wait to get out of this and away to the sun. You oughta come, man. You need a break.'

'My turn'll come,' said Wirrun, kicking the heater closer. He knew he would not dare to leave the town while the water-music haunted him; and lately it seemed to be growing worse. He listened while Ularra talked of his own leave, due in only a month, and of the trip he would make to his People in the centre of the land. The thought of it shone in Ularra's eyes and boomed in his voice. It led him into fantasies about a dark-eyed girl of the People, one he remembered from his last visit; maybe he might bring her back as a wife.

'You couldn't do better,' said Wirrun firmly, and he meant it.

It was a long journey that Ularra planned for his leave: more than a thousand miles across the old south land. It never occurred to him to travel as Wirrun had once or twice, by the speedy and expensive routes of the Happy Folk. There would need to be a strong reason for such extravagance. Ularra would go by the slower routes of the People, from country to country, seeing as many friends as he could on the way and spending only a few days with his own People. The journey had to be thought out, planned and discussed; a month was only time enough. For a month Wirrun listened and nodded and approved, and forced himself to speak warmly while the grooves on his face deepened. He could scarcely sleep for the haunting of water-music. He was glad when at last the evening came to see Ularra off on the first stage of his journey by train.

'Have a good time, man. I'll miss you.'

'Serves you right, too. You oughta be coming.'

. . . sings the bright water . . .

Wirrun went home with relief. It was true that he would miss Ularra, yet a strain had crept into their friendship. He told himself that he needed time alone—that he had to sort himself out. He went home to quietness.

For a few days the quietness helped. He worked hard all day and retreated to his room after work. The noise of the streets sounded far away, shut off by the brick wall of the hotel yard. He was used to the background roar of the bar and occasional footsteps stumbling across the yard. There was nothing that needed to be heard, nothing to distract him from his newspaper . . . or his thoughts . . . or the water-haunting . . .

Try as he would he could not shake it off, and neither could he understand it. In his mind he went over all his adventure with the ice and remembered no singing of bright water. If it had been wind, now: one who had ridden the wind might well be haunted by a song of wind. But this haunting came from nothing but a dream that had soothed him on the mountain, and then had leapt at him out of the power he had carried for weeks—or out of the rocks of the mountain itself. And the mountain had only a trickling stream that would dry up in a hard summer. There was no waterfall rushing and fading, no bright stream . . . *alight with the glancing of glimmer-bright eyes* . . . Wirrun twisted and groaned. He had never even heard that phrase before, not even in a dream on the mountain. Where had it come from, into his mind in a voice like wild honey, its notes drifting down a scale like falling leaves? He wondered if he was going mad, and was glad when Ularra came home.

Ularra brought no dark-eyed bride but came back enlarged by his journey. He talked of sun-gold days and frosty nights round fires, and gave news of the People whom Wirrun had once visited. The journey lasted weeks in the telling, and for a time Ularra drank less beer than usual; but now and then his flow of talk would falter, and he would look doubtfully at Wirrun from under his brows as if there was something more to say for which he could not find the words.

At last, one night, he found them and they startled Wirrun. 'There's bores stopped flowing,' said Ularra. 'They want you to go and see.'

'Eh?' said Wirrun. 'What bores?'

'Bores, man, you know the bores they get water from. There's some stopped flowing.'

'Bad luck for the Inlanders,' said Wirrun lightly. 'Didn't know they had bores in your country.'

'Not bores, they don't,' said Ularra. He was clearly finding it hard to explain. 'They got a spring—same thing. They got word about the bores. They're worried. Want you to go and see.'

'But a lot of those bores don't flow no more without they pump 'em.'

'They know that, man. These do. And there's the spring. It's drying up.'

'You said it was a bad year, no rain. Bound to dry up.'

Ularra had stopped looking embarrassed and began to look irritated. 'There's been other bad years. You think they don't know that spring? Never dried up before. You've got leave. You could go.'

'What for? I don't know bores.'

'You think they're stupid?' shouted Ularra. 'There'll be more, won't there? I don't know what—they're not saying. Only they want you to go. They think a lot of you, like you used to think a lot of them.' He flung himself into the armchair. 'Never thought I'd see you hiding in a pub yard turning your back on your own People.'

'What are you talking about?' roared Wirrun in rage. 'I'd sooner turn my back on 'em than cheat 'em any rate.'

For a long, angry minute they stared at each other in silence. Then Ularra got up and went away.

Are you not coming? No, said Wirrun angrily getting into bed; he was not. If the People wanted to make some sort of hero of him, maybe he couldn't help that. But he wasn't going half across the land on a white man's business like bores.

For weeks after that he did not see Ularra at all. The winter grew restless and blew cold and warm; spring was on the way. Paper bags and drink cartons scuttled furtively along pavements and lay still when Wirrun looked at them; then, as he passed, they rustled again and were flung into spirit-dances. Bits of paper that had been trees, thought Wirrun. Square-cut stones that had been rocks on a hillside. Bricks and concrete and bitumen out of the dark earth. All of them crumbling and wearing away; creeping secretly back into the earth, too slow for a man to see. Sometimes he was frightened and did not know why.

The winds died and the days brightened. It was still strongly daylight when Wirrun sat in his room after work. The doorway darkened, and when he looked up Ularra was standing there. Wirrun hoped this was good.

'There you are, then,' he said in greeting.

Ularra smiled widely and nodded. 'I brought someone,' he said. Wirrun had turned like a good host to the refrigerator, but he turned back at that. 'This is Tommy. Tommy Hunter. From out west, near my country. He's come a long way to see you.'

'Glad to see him,' said Wirrun cautiously.

Tommy smiled and put out a hand. Wirrun took it and felt healed. Tommy Hunter was an older man, straight-looking and firm, a man who lived outside the tightening circles of the Happy Folk and their cities. He wore frayed corduroy trousers, a checked shirt and an old waistcoat, and he waited with dignity to be shown where to sit. Wirrun turned the armchair towards him and Ularra sat on the bed. Tommy said nothing at all until the business of pouring drinks was over and Wirrun sat by him at the table. Then he took a slow sip, put his glass down and wiped his lips with his hand.

'I come to fetch you,' he said.

Two

Wirrun lowered his brows and gazed steadily at old Tom Hunter: not a curious traveller come to look at a young man of whom he had heard strange tales, but a steady and mature man who had journeyed more than a thousand miles with a purpose. Here it was, then: the battle he had to fight with his own People for the sake of the truth as he saw it. He was glad it should be fought with a man like Tom Hunter, one who would understand what the battle was about and that Wirrun fought for his People and not against them. He thought maybe Tom understood already, for his gaze was as steady as Wirrun's. And though he must have journeyed to see a man, he would know that manhood itself is a long journey and that Wirrun had only begun it. He would understand that the wise men of the People should not depend on one as young as Wirrun, or put the name of hero on him because for a little while he had been guided by spirits. The name was too big.

And at that, though he gazed at Tommy Hunter, the figure of Ko-in filled his eyes. *You cannot take back your name from the places where it is known . . . If the name is too big you must grow.* And maybe I will, thought Wirrun; if they give me time.

'You're needed in my country,' said Tommy Hunter, watching him. 'They sent me to fetch you.'

'I'm no good to 'em,' said Wirrun. 'Any man there knows more than what I do.'

Tommy smiled gently, an old man's smile to a young one. But he went on relentlessly. 'We heard there's bores stopped flowing, and we got this spring drying up.'

'Ularra told me,' said Wirrun. 'I don't know bores.'

Ularra poured himself another drink and said nothing. He sat back on the bed and watched both men as closely as they watched each other.

'No harm looking,' said Tom. His voice was deep, rumbling on its low notes. 'A young feller that's been where you been, seen what you seen, he might see something we missed.'

'I've never been down where the bores go. I can't see deep under, more than you can. You know your own spring better.' Wirrun spoke firmly, and hardly knew that part of his mind was asking questions. Why?—why send for him to look at bores and a spring? What other mystery was there that the men were not telling?

Tom chuckled deeply. 'Know Ninya better too, but we never saw what you saw. Lucky you came that time, eh? You're one that's got the eyes for it, a man born Clever.'

'I'm a man,' said Wirrun wearily, 'and I don't know what else. I did what I was sent for. I had help. I can't go under where the bores go.'

'These Ninya can,' said Tommy. 'What about that, eh? You think maybe they're up to something with this spring?'

Could that be it—the reason why they had sent for him? Because they suspected the Ninya again? Wirrun thought for a moment. 'I've been told that all's well,' he said, 'and you don't tell me nothing else.' And he said it as a challenge.

Tommy was silent for a while, staring into his beer. He might have been listening for some word. At last he looked up again and spoke.

'There's this ridge,' he said, 'and under it this stretch where the white gums grow. Like it was a river, only there's no river, wet or dry. But this bit's greener. There's a river down underneath, see. Deep down, and the trees know it. Always been there. My old grandfather told me about that river deep under. He reckoned it came from under the ridge.' Wirrun listened and waited. 'No rain for a long time now,' the older man went on. 'Trees dropping their leaves in the river-beds, everything drying up, just red sand all round . . . but that green stretch, she's greener. She's flowering.' He held Wirrun's eyes and saw in them shadows of doubt and wonder. 'That old river's flooding down under there, coming higher, making it greener. But there's been no rain. And the spring's drying that never dried up before.'

The glimmer-bright water alight with the glancing . . . No, said Wirrun to his water-haunted mind; that'd be dark water down there.

'Better you come and look,' said old Tom. They drank in silence. Ularra sat on the bed watching their faces.

Tom glanced up almost shyly and spoke again. 'There's these old Pungalunga, or there was. Like men only big, tall as a hill. Did a lot of damage in the old times, ate a lot of People. You can see their bones lying around still, only they're rocks now. A long time back, it was. None of them been about since white men came. Only now there's new tracks. One of 'em's left his prints on the ridges.'

Wirrun heard Ularra's sharply drawn breath; evidently the Pungalunga were new to him too. 'Tracks?' asked Wirrun with a keenness he could not hide. 'Where from? Where to?'

'Can't tell,' said Tom. 'Too big.' In reply to Wirrun's

incredulous stare he tried to explain. 'Those sand-ridges, they're bare on top. A man walks up one, he sees a, like a big dish, pressed in the sand. Sixty feet long, might be, and no reason for it. He's got to see it three or four times before he sees the shape right. A month or so, maybe another man goes up another ridge, finds another one. It takes time.'

'Must do,' said Wirrun. 'I don't know how you'd be sure.'

'We know,' said the old man. 'Five or six ridges now, all with a dent on top. A Pungalunga's walked over there, one ridge to the next.'

Wirrun sounded doubtful. 'Maybe. What's it mean any rate? A Pungalunga's a long way from a dried-up spring, isn't it?'

'Can't be sure. We think it's all of a piece. Better you come and see.'

Ularra leaned forward, grasped the bottle, and spoke for the first time. 'You got time off coming, man. Might as well go somewhere.'

Wirrun swung towards him. 'How many times—' he began, and stopped.

'That's right,' said old Tom. 'You come. We'll look after you all right. If you don't see nothing—you can't help it, that's all. No harm trying.'

Wirrun sat gazing at Ularra, who was filling his glass again. Ularra felt the gaze, looked up, shifted a little, and leaned back trying to get out of range. Wirrun's frowning gaze followed him.

'Easy for you to talk,' he said at last. 'Maybe you think a man just walks out and calls up a few spirits when he wants 'em. I dunno what you do think and that's a fact. Well, last time I gave up my job; this time you can give up yours. Maybe I will go and have a look, only if I do you're coming too.'

Ularra splashed beer over the edge of the bed and brushed it off with his hand, staring at Wirrun. 'Me? What good'll I be? I'm not Clever.'

'It's your country. Well? Are we going?'

On Ularra's long dark face a wondering grin was dawning. 'If that's all you want. Sure we're going.' He sat rocking to and fro on the bed and grinning.

Wirrun ran his hands through his hair, startling it into curls. Why had he said that, when he had never meant to go? A glimpse of Ularra caught in the circles of the Happy Folk, sitting on a bed with his third glass of beer and believing too easily in Wirrun's powers. A story of the desert flowering in the dry, a tale of the Pungalunga stepping from ridge to ridge. Was that all it took to make a man give in when he knew he was right? He couldn't get out of it now, any rate; not with Ularra grinning in pure delight and old Tom nodding with some inner certainty of his own.

'It'll do no good,' he warned them—and felt his conviction loosening its grip as he spoke. When old Tom answered it was as if his words came from somewhere deep in Wirrun's mind.

'Maybe. Can't say. A man can't turn his back on his own country.'

From sea to sea, there lies your country. Ko-in had said it, but the men of the Centre could not know that.

'I'll give a week's notice tomorrow,' said Ularra, still grinning.

They began to talk about the journey. Tommy had taken two weeks to come by the devious routes of the People, sent forward by one group to the next: from the huge quiet Centre northward to the coast, east across the cape, and southward stage by stage as the People of each country arranged; in little boats and in trucks, on foot and on horseback, even once or twice by taxi. He expected to take Wirrun and Ularra back by the same routes, and to Ularra it seemed a reasonable plan. But Wirrun, after thinking in silence, shook his head.

'Best if we fly and save time.'

Ularra stared at him. 'Three of us? Man—that'll take a lot of money!'

'Trains cost near as much and take longer. Use up all my leave to get there. Best if we can keep one job between us—that's more money than flying.'

Ularra threw himself back on the bed and laughed with excitement, for he had never flown and had envied Wirrun his one trip. 'Me up there in a little tin plane? I'll be broke twice over—going up and falling down!'

Wirrun grinned broadly. It was good to be at one with Ularra again, good to see his eagerness and his willing sacrifice of job and money. He found himself wishing that one day before he died Ularra might ride the wind and find a real adventure.

As for Tommy Hunter, at this talk of planes he sat very straight and unmoved, staring ahead. He had never travelled the wind's way or wished to do so, but he had been sent with a call for help to the new young hero and he must travel as the hero did. It was his fate.

He slept in Wirrun's bed that night, accepting it with dignity and no argument as an older man and a guest, while Wirrun unrolled his sleeping-bag on the floor. Wirrun lay awake for a long time, listening to old Tom's grunting snores and wondering how much more of the story Tom knew and had not told. He knew the ways of his People when they were troubled and unsure. First the message about bores and a spring, then the tale of the flowering desert and the Pungalunga's tracks; Tom had told him just enough to bring him and only what could be shown. As Ularra had said months ago, there would be more: something that they wanted him to see or feel for himself. It saddened him to know that they had put too big a name on him and there was little chance that he could help. But at least he was taking that chance and not turning his back.

He remembered his last visit and the wonder it had wakened. The tired red country and its delicate hazes; the early morning when the Ninya had walked and the country hung upside down. His cramped spirit uncurled and expanded— maybe it wasn't right to go, but it was good. He fell asleep to the rushing of water and the singing of words: *Are you not coming? . . . coming? . . . coming?*

It took the whole week of Ularra's notice to arrange the journey. Wirrun had to ask for his leave, to which the stout lady agreed after a little fuss. A leathery old man called Charlie, who was to do Wirrun's work while he was away, came once or twice to chew his moustache and watch what had to be done. There were two or three visits to the airlines office, where Wirrun or Ularra asked shy, curt questions and took the answers home to be discussed. It was as well that Wirrun had been saving up for a year and that Ularra had severance pay to collect: the fares for three travellers, one way only, cost a frightening sum. When Ularra finally bought the tickets he handed the three bright folders to Wirrun with awe.

'That pretty little book, that cost all I've got. We'll have to get a job in Alice when we need more.'

'I got a bit more,' Wirrun reminded him, but Tom Hunter looked at them proudly.

'You won't need no more,' he said.

They knew what he meant: they were travelling on the People's business and of course the People would take care of them. But it would be a long way home, and travel cost money, and few of the People had much of that to spare.

Meanwhile the weekend had arrived and Wirrun had something to do alone. He took his camping gear, caught the train again, and spent another night on Ko-in's mountain. To have even a slender chance of seeing whatever it was the People wanted him to see he must take the power with him.

He did not light his fire in the old place but made a new camp farther along the ledge. He did not want to summon Ko-in—partly for fear that the summons might fail and prove that all he remembered was a dream; partly because, in answering the People's call, he was groping towards some knowledge of himself and he could not yet face the largeness and certainty of Ko-in; and partly because he was still too young and shy to call up the ancient hero except at need.

Haunted as he had been all these months since he laid the power away within the rock, he dreaded the moment of drawing it out again. He went as soon as he had made camp. It was late afternoon, the sun behind the mountain and the gully already filled with shadow. Though the days were lengthening these walls of rock held a chill, but Wirrun saw that the moss was green again. He climbed to the ledge he knew, thrust his arm into the rock-hole and closed his hand on the power, his fingers remembering its roundness and the harshness of twine and the softness of fur . . .

The rush and roar of water was all around him, with the high, bird-sweet voices singing through it. It dwindled, died, and broke forth again, and the song soared high and drifted down. Then all the singing voices were silent except one, and that one soft as moonlight and sharply sweet as wild honey, singing the words he had heard or had not heard but remembered. He was frightened and enchanted, gripping the power and sternly drawing it forth. He climbed down from the ledge not knowing the moment when the music stopped and the singing was only in his mind; but when the power hung in its place on his belt and he climbed up from the gully into the gold and perfume of wattles the dreaming had gone.

It did not come again, though he sat late by his fire gazing at the village under the stars and holding the power with fear and longing. The power was still, and the song only haunted his mind as it had done for months.

'It's in the mountain, then,' muttered Wirrun, daring at last to climb into his sleeping-bag with the power. The song must be in the rocks and not in the power; he would be journeying away from it and not towards it. He was deeply relieved and shaken with loss. Yet he slept as he always did on the mountain, deeply and in peace.

In the morning he left as early as he could, and was back in his room before sunset. Ularra's eyes and old Tom's passed over the bark-fibre bag at his belt but neither of them spoke of it.

And now, with only two more days to wait, Wirrun was as eager as Ularra for the journey to begin. All the decisions that could be taken were taken; there were only questions left, and the answers lay far away. He felt the long miles of the old south land stretching westward. They plucked at him. The city, feverish with Happy Folk, tightened round him and he fretted to break free. He felt like a schoolboy waiting for the holidays, and told himself that this *was* his holiday and he needed the break. And at last the morning came when, long before daylight, he closed the door of his room behind himself and old Tom.

The streets were very quiet. The lights stretched away one behind the other into loneliness. Wirrun, passing under them beside Tom, looked as he had a year ago when he followed the ice: wearing old shorts and strong boots for walking, with a sweater for the dark cool of morning; his camping gear on his shoulders hiding their extra width, the net bag at his belt. The lights threw shadows on his strong dark face. It could have been a boy's.

The city was a dark bulk behind the lights, holding the Happy Folk caged and contained. Ularra was waiting at the corner, a tall shape bulging at the shoulders with a

pack like Wirrun's but newer. The dark city strung with
lights and the sense of the journey to come had quietened
him; he only said, 'Here we are, then,' and fell into step
beside the other two. They walked on in search of a taxi.

Three

At the airport Tom and Ularra fell in behind Wirrun
and followed him doggedly through the confusion of glass
doors, flashing signs and giant voices, a tunnel that suddenly entered a plane, a girl dressed up like a doll who
smiled as she robbed them of their packs. Wirrun, remembering, had curtly asked for three window seats and was
given them: one behind the other, with Tom in the middle
and Wirrun behind. The plane shook with a fearful power
restrained—Ularra's eyes were fixed and Tom's were
closed. The city and the sea fell away; hills flattened,
crouching like cats; roads revealed themselves. The journey
became theirs and they the travellers.

The land lay under them, grey-brown and immense,
draped with the purple shadows of clouds. With majestic
authority it set forth its cratered hills and looping rivers, its
endless plains relentlessly fenced into squares, the patched
fur of its forests. The dark eyes watching from little round
windows darkened again with awe. Each man travelled
alone.

A children's game of trays and tea brought them together for a moment. They twisted around in their seats to
exchange embarrassed looks, but they were glad of the tea.
When the trays were emptied they were alone again, each
to himself.

The grey-brown land became red misted over with slate
and stranded into channels. The dunes lay folded, the hills
bared fangs of rock, a purple haze dissolved land into sky.
The land opened its fearful and beautiful heart; they saw it

as the wind sees it and felt it as only the earth-things or the
People can.

Old Tom leaned hard against the glass of his window,
looking down. He turned to Wirrun and made signs, jab-
bing at the glass with his thumb, then leaned against it to
look again. Wirrun leaned against his own window, peering
down at the dunes to see what Tom had seen.

'Tracks,' said Tom's voice in his ear over the back of the
seat. 'Them Pungalunga prints.'

Wirrun searched. Just as the dunes were falling away he
saw them: a line of craters, shallow and elongated, one
depression in the red and sandy top of each dune as though
something big had gone leaping from ridge to ridge.

The plane swam down like a shark towards jagged hills.
Tom was looking a question: had Wirrun seen the prints?
He nodded and pointed to the sign about fastening seat-
belts. The men had been right. From the ground those craters would be too large, too far apart, for easy reading; only
from the air would they show as a line of prints. What had
startled Wirrun was the singing of his own blood in his ears
when he saw them.

He had spent a year in banishing the earth's old spirits to
the darkness where they belonged, in holding on to the ordinary things that were real. Now his blood sang in his ears
that the old things were real and the city a dream, and
perhaps he had chosen wrongly and lost the spirits. From
the air anyone could see the Pungalunga's tracks. Wirrun
longed with a fierce terror to see the Pungalunga.

When Wirrun had seen the Centre before it had been in
a spring that promised a hard summer. Now he saw it in a
year when the rains had not come. In the blue-china bowl
of the sky the air shimmered with heat; mulga, ironwood
and ghost gums folded their leaves and endured it; the red
earth, sparsely covered here and there, received it and sub-
mitted. Only the jagged, tip-tilted ranges proudly breasted
the heat. Only in the town had gardeners with hoses kept
the green alive.

In the streets he saw only Inlanders and People. There
were no Happy Folk hung with cameras; they had taken
offence at the season and withdrawn to places where happiness was better understood. Wirrun and Ularra visited
stores and bought supplies while old Tom hovered uneasily.

'You don't want no more now,' he objected. 'There's time.'

'What about water?' said Wirrun.

'Time for that too.'

Since it was now too hot to find a camp outside the town, they bought cold cans of beer and settled in the shade in a park to wait for evening. Passing Inlanders glanced at them and looked away frowning. Tom politely emptied one can and rose to leave. 'Back later,' he said, and slouched off down the street.

'Gone to spread the word,' said Ularra.

Wirrun nodded, watching the old man with affection. 'He's grown since we got off the plane.'

Ularra smiled, then frowned. 'It's no good, man. I see what you meant.'

Wirrun turned away on his elbow. 'What did I mean?'

Ularra growled a little and pulled up a grass-stem. Wirrun stared through leaves at the sky and waited. Ularra jerked his legs and spoke.

'Well—now we're *here*, man. We spent all that money and lost my job, and what can you do?'

'I dunno what,' said Wirrun, gazing at leaves. 'It was worth it, just coming.'

'You never wanted to come. And now they're expecting something. And here we are like a couple of ants on a billiard table, don't even know what we're looking for. It's no good.'

'You won't make a hero that way,' said Wirrun. 'We've come, that's all. We don't know what we're looking for, but maybe . . . if it's here, if it wants us, it'll find us don't you worry.'

Ularra glanced at him sideways and glanced away again.

'Can't stop 'em expecting,' Wirrun told him. 'Can't live their lives for 'em. All we can do is watch and listen, and do what comes up if it wants doing.'

They lay in silence under the heat for a long five minutes. Then Wirrun spoke to the leaves, telling Ularra about the Pungalunga's footprints on the ridges. 'It was—like there was more to it. I dunno what but I'm waiting.'

After more moments of quiet Ularra said, 'You gotta see it from a plane before you know. I never thought of it like that, all spread out.'

Then, because of the heat and the beer and because it had already been a long day, they slept on the grass.

They woke to find that the park, which had been sunlit splotched with shadows, was now shadow lit with sun. They could feel the heat rising into the sky like a monster leaving its nest. Tommy Hunter stood there with a man more grizzled than himself, both of them holding white-wrapped parcels. Tommy had grown again and was looking at them with a smile pink and white in his dark face.

'Don't you want no tucker? Me and Jump-up thought you might.'

Jump-up greeted Ularra with goodwill and Wirrun with a respect that made that young man sigh. They took up their packs and went through the streets, out of the town; and dark eyes watched under heavy brows as they went. In twos and threes, from benches and bars and side streets, little knots of men and women and children collected and trailed after them towards the river. The People were gathering.

Tom and Jump-up took Wirrun and Ularra over sunburnt flats and the dry sandy bed of the river towards the rock wall of the range. 'Good cool camp over here,' said Tom. 'You'll want water.' He bent and lifted an iron lid that lay on the sandy river-bed. Under the lid was a hole roughly lined and half full of water. 'Good water,' said Tom.

Wirrun and Ularra knelt and filled their waterbags with the sweet, secret water that flowed under the dry sand. *The glimmer-bright water* . . . secretly guarded in the land's indomitable heart.

Near a gap in the range by which road and river passed through, they reached a clump of ironwood trees that clung near the base of the rocks. Behind the trees was a shaded cranny where the older men waited with expectant grins.

'Couldn't be better,' said Wirrun, admiring the camp they had found for him. 'Cool all day and handy to water. You ever had a better camp, Ularra?'

'Put your fire safe under the rocks,' said Jump-up, chuckling. 'Quiet here, no one round.'

'Just what we want, man,' said Ularra.

Gratefully the travellers dropped their packs on the

rocks and hung waterbags and some of their supplies safely from branches. They all went back across the river, where the People had gathered on the bank and were collecting wood and making a few small fires.

The sun had gone leaving only a red-gold shining in the west. The land expanded and breathed in the cool of evening. Food was spread on paper wrappings on the grass; children played, young people laughed, women called to each other from fire to fire, older men sat watching and smoking. The good smell of singed fat was already beginning. Tom and Jump-up handed their parcels to the women and took Wirrun from fire to fire.

It became clear that Tom really had grown larger in the eyes of his People: not only had he travelled far and brought the hero back, but he had brought him back by plane. He had seen the land as the wind sees it. He told them in short phrases and wide movements about the plane and the tea-trays and his terror, and they roared with laughter. He told them in words and in silence about the breadth and wonder of the land, and they too were silent. There was no need for Wirrun to talk, nothing that he needed to explain.

Ularra had found friends among the young People and sat with them on the grass near one of the fires. The dusk came down and the air chilled. Trees stood dark against the luminous sky; behind them the town hung out its lights, and in front the range rose dark against the stars. And Wirrun noticed that the People, the noisy laughing groups, stayed closer and closer by the fires. He saw that they looked often over their shoulders, and that if a child wandered to the outskirts of a group its mother sharply called it back. He saw that the People were afraid. He watched and listened.

When the meal was over the talking grew quieter and fell away. The firelight showed faces turning often to Wirrun. They were waiting for him to speak.

'You been having trouble,' said Wirrun.

Silence and a turning to the fires. Older men coughed. Tommy Hunter began to speak, telling again about the spring that had never dried before and the flowering desert. 'Better you look,' he said. 'We take you tomorrow.'

'Dunno what I can do,' said Wirrun. 'I wouldn't want to fool you. Last time I was helped. All I know is to look and listen—maybe something'll come, I dunno.'

Voices murmured to each other round the fires. They weren't fooled, they said; look and listen and wait; couldn't do more.

'You know more than what I do,' said Wirrun. 'It's your country and your trouble.'

But this they would not have. The murmurs round the fires dissented. Jump-up coughed and spoke.

'It's bigger. There's men here from three—four countries, come on purpose. Plenty fights sometimes, but not now. None of us knows the whole of it, had to get you here. It's bigger.'

That was something to know; and perhaps it explained why they would not talk but insisted that he should look for himself. Wirrun began to fish a little.

'I seen those prints on the ridges. From the plane you can see them clear.'

The silence thickened. There were movements towards the fires and a flaring of fresh fuel. They would not speak of the Pungalunga while the dark moved round the fires; or of any spirit, Wirrun guessed. Behind him Tommy Hunter said, 'Tomorrow. We fetch you in the car before light.' He saw that this meeting had not been held to inform him but to welcome him and show the People he was here.

'We best get to bed, then,' he answered. 'A long day today and another one tomorrow. Right, Ularra?'

Ularra's long form rose from one of the fires. Jump-up and Tom moved too, but Wirrun, remembering the spirits, waved them back. 'No sense walking two ways for nothing. We know the way.' He and Ularra shouted goodnights. The People called back and sat close to the fires and watched them go.

'Must be a terrible feller, this Pungalunga,' muttered Wirrun as he and Ularra crossed the dry river by starlight.

'They're worried all right,' said Ularra, sounding puzzled. 'Too worried. It's not enough, this Pungalunga's not.'

'Big as a hill? Eats People? Gone a long time and coming back?'

'Yeah, but they *know* it, man. They'd stay by the fires

but they wouldn't be scared to talk. That's something they don't know, something else.'

Wirrun agreed. 'Something we gotta see for ourselves.'

At the camp by the Gap they unrolled their sleeping-bags, finding what flatness they could between the rocks. They were so tired that Wirrun said the men would have to stone him awake in the morning. He was asleep almost before he had finished saying it.

He woke some time later to a prickling awareness—of what? Beyond the shade of the ironwoods moonlight flooded the flats and the dark winding snake of the highway, turning the tawny-gold rocks of the range to dull brown. He lay still and alert, searching the shadows near at hand. There was a throbbing at his shoulder: it was the power. Under his eyelids he searched the camp.

Ularra stirred in his sleeping-bag and settled again. On a moonlit rock above his head Wirrun saw the intruders. Two of them, perching together and watching Ularra with evil little faces. They looked like wicked little men of the People, perhaps three or four feet tall, hairy all over and with long dark beards. One of the pair was stick-thin, the other stout and round-bellied. There they crouched, side by side, watching Ularra.

Wirrun sat up suddenly, holding the power and speaking sternly. 'Clear off, you. Get back where you belong.'

Their heads swung round at him, startled, but they sneered and answered mockingly. 'Too far,' they said, pulling faces and jerking their hands insultingly. 'Too far for you, earless.' They slid off the rock and vanished into shadows.

Cheeky rubbish, thought Wirrun. What did they mean, too far? But he was warm with strength and pleasure. He hadn't lost them, any rate. He had seen and dealt with these earth-things as easily as if the Mimi had been with him, and they too had known the power as Ko-in had once promised. He chuckled at the thought that Ularra might have wakened to see them perched above his head, and fell asleep wondering if Ularra could have seen them at all.

It seemed still to be night when he woke again; but the air had the chill of morning, the moonlight had paled a little, a small fire crackled under the rocks, and Ularra stood over him with a little icy water in a can. He stepped back grinning when Wirrun rolled over and yawned. Wirrun heaved himself up, fastening the power to his belt.

'What woke you, then? You were sound asleep when those two old hairy things were looking at you in the night.'

Ularra scoffed. 'What are you talking about, man?'

'I'm telling you. Two of 'em, sitting on that rock. Keeping an eye on you, they were, only they cleared off when I showed 'em the power.'

'Pull the other leg,' said Ularra uneasily.

'Nasty-looking little pair, one of 'em half-starved and the other fat as a pig. You ought to know 'em.'

'Never heard of anything like that in these parts,' said Ularra firmly. 'You were dreaming.'

'No fear. The power woke me and I sent 'em off.'

'Next time you wake me up first, man. I want to see 'em myself.'

'Next time I will,' said Wirrun, rolling his sleeping-bag. 'You ever see an earth-thing? Any time?'

Ularra was silent, thinking back. 'I might've,' he said shortly, and left it at that.

They ate breakfast quickly and stowed things away among rocks. In the chill quiet morning they heard the chatter and grumble of a motor long before it was near and saw headlights, one bright and one dull, coming from the town. When the car drew up with a rattle Wirrun and Ularra were waiting by the road.

The driver was a young man named Harry. Ularra squeezed in beside him and a middle-aged man named Duke. Wirrun sat in the back seat with Tom Hunter and Jump-up. The car headed north.

Harry drove fast along the highway, between rough hills and across high plains curving with the curve of the earth. Watery moonlight turned to watery dawn. The sky was a pale and polished blue flushed with gold when they turned off the highway to the east. For a while the track was good and Harry still drove fast in a race with the sun. Later they bounced and rattled over salt-crusted clay and red sand, between spinifex and mulga, with a dust-cloud rolling behind them and blue-hazed hills in the distance to left and right. The sun climbed higher, the heat closed down, and for hours they rattled on. The men spoke little and drank often from bottles of water.

The land called up its heat-magic, it shimmered and wavered. Mulga branches writhed and twisted, mocking and beckoning. Remembered lakes and seas spread over the sands, magical water that lay invitingly ahead: *Are you not coming?* I've come, thought Wirrun, I'm here; show me.

When the heat pressed down like a great flat hand Harry turned the car towards mulga on the shady side of a scooped-out ridge of rock. Tom went ahead on foot into the mulga, to look for broken-off stumps that might spike a tyre. The car followed and drew up in shade flickered with sunlight. The men climbed out and stretched. Harry loosened the radiator-cap, flicking his fingers, and steam rose from the radiator. Duke brought a battered old cooler from the boot of the car. The men sat or lay in the shade to rest, eat, and wait out the heat. They were silent, not looking at each other. Wirrun noticed it.

Ularra too was looking puzzled. 'Man, I'm too soft for it . . . Is this the best shade you got? What's wrong with the ridge?' The shade of the ridge was deeper and he knew its rocks would be cooler.

Something like an electric shock passed through the men. No one spoke; no one moved. Wirrun looked at them and frowned.

'Come on, Ularra,' he said. He waited while Ularra slowly stood up, and they two walked back towards the ridge. The men did not speak or watch them go.

Broken and stony ground led them upward to a patch of boulders. They went with care, Ularra looking sharply among the boulders and now and then glancing at Wirrun's face. Wirrun's eyes went from the boulders at his feet to the shaded cliffs ahead. There was a deep cleft in the rocks, black with shadow, a place where the cool of night might linger. He aimed for that, dropping his hand to the power and feeling its throb.

They climbed upward, sweat drying on their faces. A little below the cleft they stopped and looked, trying to penetrate the darkness in it. It gathered and moved. Wirrun stepped forward. The darkness snarled, savage and menacing, with a glint of red eyes.

'*Man!*' breathed Ularra in horror.

Four

The darkness was a dog, huge and red-eyed. It stood hunched to spring and its snarl rattled between the rocks. Wirrun fumbled the power out of its bag and held it like a shield. He stepped forward, and the snarl rattled viciously. He took another step. The angry dark slunk back and hung for a moment. At his next step it drew off into the cleft.

'Man,' whispered Ularra again.

Wirrun kept the power in his hand as he turned away, stumbling a little. 'I told you, didn't I? I said if there was something it'd find us.'

They went back down the rocks, stopping now and then to remind themselves where they were.

'They knew,' said Ularra angrily. 'They never said a word, just let us go.'

'They had to let us see for ourselves,' Wirrun reminded him. 'It's no use bellyaching, that's the way it is. There might be more yet.' His face softened into half a grin. 'One thing any rate—we know you've got eyes for the old things. You saw that one all right.' Ularra muttered darkly. 'Well, you said you wanted to see.'

They returned to the men who sat or lay where they were and did not speak.

'Not so cool back there,' said Wirrun. 'I reckon you blokes knew better. What do you call that brute any rate?'

At last the men looked at each other. 'Don't call him nothing,' said Jump-up strongly. 'None of us knows him. He don't come from no country round here.'

Wirrun frowned heavily. 'Must belong somewhere near.'

They all stared obstinately at the ground or the sky. After a moment Tom Hunter spoke. 'Old Ngunta, he's a very old man, he says they got these dogs on the Darling somewhere. Jugi, they call 'em there.'

'The *Darling*? Why'd he come here, then?' Silence. 'How long ago?' They all looked at Duke.

'Near three months ago I seen him,' mumbled Duke. 'Only they never believed me.'

That was it, then. What they knew and could show they had told him. What was foreign and wrong, what rested on the evidence of one man, to that they would not commit themselves. He must see and judge for himself.

'Mm,' said Wirrun. 'So you don't know the songs to send him off.'

'Don't know nothing,' said Jump-up firmly.

The sun had moved a little. Old Tom dragged himself into deeper shade. 'That rock where he is, that belongs underground. Land used to be all up there till the wind took it. That rock goes deep under.'

It was another thing that they knew and Tom must have thought it had meaning. 'This Pungalunga,' said Wirrun. 'Where does he come from?'

They knew the Pungalunga and could talk of them by daylight without fear of strange and ancient ears that listened in the dark.

'Used to be in the ranges,' said Tom. 'There's bones out there near the Olgas, I seen 'em, only they're stone now. It was that long ago.'

'I seen 'em too,' said Harry.

'One killed hisself,' added Tom, 'stepping across a gorge on a cloudy day. Missed his step in the clouds, crashed down and got smashed. Bones everywhere. That was old times. Dunno where they been hiding since.'

'Underground,' said Jump-up. 'Only place.' He spoke with a certainty that Wirrun did not like to question; for now that the men had begun to talk he did not want to dam the flow by reminding them that he was a stranger. Ularra, watching his face, rolled over to argue.

'I dunno—some of these ranges are pretty wild. A lot of room for a Pungalunga. More than underground.'

Jump-up scoffed at the idea. 'All these cattle and mines, Inlanders everywhere and now these airy-planes. Someone'd see a monstrous great thing like that. Like a hill walking. They're all gone or they're underground—and this one ain't gone if it's walking. Eh?'

'Underground's a big place,' said Tom severely. 'You know that.'

Still watching Wirrun's face, Ularra gave in.

'He's a bit upset,' said Wirrun, excusing him. 'Couple of old things sitting over his head last night, and he slept like a baby and never saw 'em. Nasty-looking pair, kid-sized, all hairy with long beards. One fat and one skinny. What do you call those?'

The men were troubled; they refused to look at each other or at him. 'Don't call 'em nothing', grunted Jump-up. 'Never heard of 'em.' And the others agreed, when Wirrun pressed them, that no such old creatures as those belonged in any of their countries.

It was a strange picture that had emerged while the men talked. Wirrun brooded over it with tingling nerves. 'Any more like that?' he asked at last. 'Any more stories of old things out of their places?'

The older men stared at ground or sky and said nothing, but Harry stirred.

'Danny,' he said.

The others frowned and looked away, but Harry went doggedly on.

'Camped two—three miles out and let the fire go down. Woke up with hands pulling at him, some woman dragging him off. He said she had no head.'

Ularra's eyes flared. 'No *head*?'

'Moonlight night,' said Harry. 'He says he saw her clear. Came driving back like she was still after him and wouldn't go outside for three days.'

'And none of the men know about this woman?'

None of them did. None of these would speak again about spirits strange or familiar. Harry, out of his impetuous youth, had broken the agreed pattern of telling only what they knew and leaving the hero to see the rest for himself. They waited for the sun to pass over, repacked the car and topped up the water in its radiator, and at four o'clock drove on to show him the spring that was drying up.

To Wirrun the heat seemed unbearably worse than ever and the baking country seemed to reject all life. He hung grimly to a door-handle to steady himself in the bouncing car and thought about what he had heard. The sun beat through the rear window on to the back of his neck; the distant hills were a tingling, living blue. By the time they reached the ancient spring even Wirrun could feel that the heat was not so fierce.

The spring lay on another of those low rocky hills that the wind had quarried out of the land. They had to scramble up to it on foot and found a wide pool deeply cupped in the hill's flat top. Through ages of evaporation it had built itself a rim of sediment overlaid with red sand, wind-plastered. The water lay eight feet below the rim, walled by dried mud that was cracked and scabby. Jump-up pointed to a rock, black with old slime, that lay only two or three feet under the rim.

'Oughta be under water,' he told Wirrun. 'Always under water, that old rock. Always.'

To Wirrun the spring was not a sight worth travelling over a thousand miles to see. It told him nothing, but the men brooded over it, measuring its fall with their eyes. 'Any more drying up like this?' he asked.

'No more,' said Jump-up. 'There's more down south, don't know if they're drying. We only got the one. That's the old water, that is. From underground.' He looked sideways at Wirrun.

'It's her own water, that is,' added Tom, 'that she keeps deep down. All these things wanting water—sun, people, trees, snakes—she's gotta keep some hid away for herself. Eh?'

. . . sings the dark water . . .

Bright, thought Wirrun correcting his wayward mind. It's bright water. That's different.

. . . of dark-floating hair, sang his mind. More words that he had never heard.

They went down the hill again, and back to the car. As they bounced and rattled eastward the mountains to the south curved to meet them. At sunset the range shone ahead, red and gold, with one dark ridge lying nearer than the others. Along the base of this ridge lay the flowering desert.

There was no depression where water might flow in the wet, yet the large old gums with their ghostly white trunks showed that water lay below. Wirrun knew that there were such places, yet now when even the river-beds were baked it was a strange sight. There was green grass under the trees, and the gold of flowering acacia and the pink-white of hakea. Wirrun and Ularra walked through it with Tom and Jump-up while Harry and Duke made camp for the night, unloading supplies from the car.

'And it's not always like this?' said Wirrun.

Tom shook his head. 'Not in the dry. Just the trees. You can dig down and you won't find water; she don't lay near, she just soaks up. From deep down. Only now she's soaking more . . . Where's she getting it from?'

'From the spring,' Wirrun suggested. 'The old water finding a new way.'

'And what's it want to do that for? What's going on down there?'

'Them Ninya, might be,' said Jump-up, and they both looked at Wirrun. He shook his head, frowning.

'Don't see how they'd do nothing with the water. Except freeze it, and they're not doing that. Any rate there's all these old things, strangers coming in that don't belong. All the ones that I met, they didn't like the ice. I reckon they'd keep away if it was Ninya.'

Tom glanced quickly over his shoulder in the fading light.

They went back to the camp before dusk and found that Duke and Harry had lit three fires. It was too many, but Wirrun understood when he saw how the men kept between the fires. They ate stew and drank strong black tea and watched the stars looming close from the clear chill sky. Leaping flames lit up small green stars on the ground: the eyes of the big huntsman spiders crouching by their burrows. When the men had eaten they went early to bed, for the homeward race against the sun would begin before daylight. They kept the fires burning.

Wirrun lay for a while and felt the land wide around him, felt it stirring with silent life under the burning stars. Tell me, he begged it; show me. But only the old haunting sang in his mind: *the dark-flowing water like washes and ripples* . . . He thought of the old water, her own that she kept deep down, and of the Inlanders' bores that drilled into it and stole it. Well, he and his People could not deal with that; they must wait for the land to deal with it in her own inescapable time . . . Duke got up softly to feed the fires, and Wirrun slept.

He woke to a sky that glowed like a black pearl and to a chorus of singing. They were women's voices, free and wild, unlike the sweetness of his haunting. He felt the throbbing of the power, and the stiffness of the men lying awake and listening with him. The singing came near and swept by, shadowy women dancing by in the moonlight and singing as they went. He saw shields and spear-throwers lifted, and a flowing of limbs and breasts and hair, then the shapes and the singing were gone. The men lay unspeaking until Tom got up and fed the fires. One by one they stirred.

'Were those some of yours?' asked Wirrun at breakfast. 'Or were they out of their place?'

'Eh?' said Tom. 'Them. That's them Unthippa, them women.' He went back to his breakfast. 'A long time,' he said at last. 'A long time since we seen them around. We got unused to 'em.'

'Restless,' said Jump-up, frowning. 'All restless, them old things. There's something's up.'

'Better move before the sun,' said Tom. 'Got to get back. Tomorrow you'll see them prints.'

'No need,' Wirrun told him. 'I seen 'em. Tomorrow I want to go north. If I can. There's someone might help.'

'Where north?'

'Right north. Mimi country—it's a Mimi.'

All the People had heard that story. The men considered.

'Harry'll take you,' said Jump-up.

3

A Trouble in the East

One

By evening of that day the old car came back along the highway to the town. Wirrun knew the People would expect him to spend another evening by the fires on the riverbank, but this he could not do for he needed a lonelier fire and the night at his shoulder. He sent messages instead.

'Tell 'em we've seen and heard and now we gotta find our road. Maybe Harry'll bring word down from the north if we find it. And we'll see 'em again later when things are back in their places.'

The men accepted this soberly and drove off, Harry promising to come again before daylight; and Wirrun and Ularra spent another night in their camp by the Gap.

'We need to chew things over,' said Wirrun; and Ularra looked pleased, for he had thought his part was to fetch and carry and maybe to stand with the hero if he was needed. But at first there was no chewing over. Wirrun only sat on a rock with his arms draped over his knees, weary and silent, frowning at nothing.

Ularra checked the water supply, unrolled sleeping-bags on rocks, laid the small fierce fire of the dry country, and looked over cans of food consideringly.

'These women, these Unthippa,' said Wirrun at last. 'They big business?'

Ularra paused. 'N-no. They got mixed up in it a bit, got 'emselves in a dance or two. But they're not real big, just weird.'

'They're that. Where do they live?'

'Underground. In these caves where it's always sunny with rivers running. We got a lot live there.'

'Underground again,' muttered Wirrun.

Ularra chose a can of stew and ventured to ask a question. 'This Mimi friend of yours. Can you find her? There's a lot of rock up there.'

'If I'm lucky I reckon she might find me.'

'She's a long way off. Will she know what's going on here?'

'She knows most things—and why not, the way things are shifting round out of their places?' Wirrun kicked suddenly at a rock. 'That's got me, that's what I can't understand. All these things out of their places—why? What are they after? What's bringing 'em?'

Ularra restored the tin opener to his pack. 'Some of 'em aren't,' he pointed out. 'The Pungalunga and these Unthippa. And they're restless too.'

'They would be, wouldn't they, with all these strangers coming in. No wonder they're restless. I want to know what brought the strangers.'

Ularra placed a couple of flat stones near the fire and set the stew in place. He said carefully, 'Last time you said you were told; the land told you. Maybe she will again.'

Wirrun swore. After a moment he confessed, speaking harshly and in jerks. 'There's just this haunting. Months now—ever since I got home. Waterfalls and singing. I can't hear nothing else.' He pressed his hands against his eyes. 'I can't get rid of it . . . And if I did,' he muttered, 'maybe that'd drive me mad too.'

Silently Ularra stirred the stew. A haunting; months of it; all that silent time in town. There was more than you'd think in being a hero.

While they were eating he pointed with his fork at the power hanging in its bag. 'Reckon this haunting might come from that thing?'

Wirrun shook his head. 'It came out of the mountain; out of the rocks. But maybe the stone might've brought it.'

'Well . . . can't be helped, you gotta trust the stone. And you've gotta get some rest. Between haunting and bouncing round in the heat all day, you look about done in, and we're off again before daylight. Get yourself off while I clean up.'

'Cleaning up's my turn. You did the cooking.'

Ularra tossed his limbs about. 'Listen to him, he's crazy. What else am I for? Have *I* got a power? Or a Mimi friend? Nothing talks to me, man, you're the one we count on. Turn in and get some rest.' He had Wirrun in his sleeping-bag a little after dark and himself half an hour after that.

They were so tired that they slept without stirring while the night moved and whispered around them. They woke in time for a quick breakfast and a hasty packing up and were waiting with their packs by the road when Harry's lopsided lights came creeping from town.

'We'll get on a bit in the cool,' said Harry, 'and doss down somewhere till night. Travel better at night.'

Wirrun agreed, remembering the last time he had travelled by night: on foot, with the Mimi holding to the cord of the power lest some wandering wind should catch her. That was when the land had spoken to him, through his feet or through its old spirits as he met them. Perhaps if he walked again . . . But he couldn't walk in this country, two hundred miles from one water to the next and a thousand miles in a few precious days.

Even in the car it took a morning and two nights, though Harry drove fast up the long highway north. The car probed ahead with its lopsided lights like an old camel with one good eye. Harry, removed from the stern gaze of the older men, sometimes talked of restless spirits and sometimes drove in silence for long hours. Twice he stopped to fill the tank from drums of petrol that he carried in the boot; twice he filled it from lonely outpost pumps and wordlessly failed to see the money that Wirrun offered. When it was time to sleep he turned the car aside into some waiting and expected shade.

The first morning they crossed mulga flats between low hills and slept out the day at the edge of a worn, stony tableland, heading north again in the sunset. All night they saw only the yellow-lit road, and sometimes a shine of green eyes beside it; but they felt the ridges that the car nosed through and dark bluffs that cut off the stars. Towards morning the moon rose and they saw plains stretching ahead, and broken hills on either side misted by moonlight. They saw the sunrise drape these hills in silken hazes of lavender and apricot; and in a little while they camped in a tumbledown shed on a marshy sand-plain.

On the second night's driving the road seemed to go on forever with nothing to mark it but a hotel or two for tourists; but just as the moon had risen the highway began to swing farther west. They had been climbing imperceptibly; the moonlight showed rolling grasslands and the silvered trunks of gums. Harry found a track that Wirrun might not have seen and turned east off the highway, driving more slowly as the track grew rougher. A darkness of trees received them; Harry stopped the car.

'Need daylight for the next bit. Sleep a couple of hours and start early.'

They climbed out gratefully to stretch and stamp about. Wirrun felt the watching of owls and possums and other soft small things. Beyond the trees lay a stretch of grassland and a city of low, rough towers dark in the moonlight: termite mounds, some as tall as Ularra, pointing their jagged fingers at the stars. The men gathered sticks to light a small fire and ate, sitting with their backs warmly to the fire and resting their tired eyes on the moonlight beyond. The pointing fingers of the termite mounds uttered some silent message that they could not read. Ularra stopped chewing for a moment, leaning forward to look.

'What's moving?'

'Where?' said Wirrun, trying to follow his gaze into the moonlight.

'By that mound, the near one . . . It's gone—no, to the right—there's something—' He stopped with a strangled grunt.

Shadows moved between the mounds, shadows that swayed and beckoned in the silver light. They heard soft laughter and the voices of young girls calling. They were like girls of the People; their slender forms drew near and drew away.

'Get in the car,' said Harry wrenching the door open.

'But—hang on, man—' Ularra was staring. 'I know that one, she's from up near Darwin!'

'What's she doing here, then?' said Wirrun sternly. 'Get back, man.'

Ularra gave a short, excited laugh and stepped forward instead. Wirrun grabbed his arm and pushed in front, holding the throbbing power. The girl-shapes laughed uneasily and began to drift away, swinging their hips in the moonlight. He followed a little way; in the moment before they disappeared, each one into a termite mound, he saw the nearest closely. He had seen a girl like these before, but not from a termite mound.

He went back to the car where Harry was thrusting an angry Ularra into a seat. 'They won't give no more trouble,' he assured him.

'Get in,' said Harry. 'We're shifting all the same.' Wirrun climbed in beside Ularra and Harry started the motor. 'Out of their place,' he muttered. 'Can't trust the country any more.'

'What are they?' Wirrun asked.

'Mungga-mungga,' said Harry shortly.

Ularra stirred and laughed his short laugh. 'Them. Always reckoned I wouldn't mind meeting one. Only for you two I'd give it a go.'

'You'd change your mind when you saw their big sharp claws,' Wirrun retorted. 'Only then it'd be too late.'

Ularra laughed again.

Harry drove carefully for a mile or so along the rough track and over the feet of ridges. He stopped again on level ground clear of termite mounds. They rested in the car, eyes closed but not sleeping. When the moonlight began to pale they did sleep a little.

Wirrun and Ularra were wakened by the movement of the car to find the sun well up and Harry driving carefully over the bumps. When he saw that they were awake he said, 'Not far now. Sleep a bit more when we get there—safer by daylight.'

By now there was hardly a track to be seen. They travelled along the spines of ridges above gullies that Harry said would be rivers in a week or so if the wet was on time. The old car bucked over rocks hidden in the grass and kept gallantly on. Wirrun had begun to watch for the faces of sandstone that he glimpsed from time to time; that seemed to hang in the sky beyond the reach of any car. They crawled steeply up another long ridge—and suddenly the cliffs were in front to the north: red-gold, sheer and shadowed, pencilled with the darker lines of clefts and gorges, and reaching away to east and west. The blood sang in Wirrun's ears at the sight of them.

Harry drove into the shade of trees and stopped the car. 'Close as I can come,' he said pointing to the cliffs. 'You'll have to walk the rest. After a bit of tucker and a doss down.'

Ularra climbed out and stretched with his eyes on those brooding faces of stone, immense and endless. 'Mimi country, eh?' he said and stole a doubtful look at Wirrun. It seemed impossible to find one Mimi in that.

Harry confirmed his doubts. 'If this ain't right we'll have to try again.'

Wirrun was not troubled; as far as he had thought at all he was counting on his Mimi to find him. He sat on a log, eating whatever Harry or Ularra passed to him, and looked at the cliffs reaching away against the sky. He could climb to them in half an hour, once he had slept. He let his mind go to them now, not exploring but only feeling the age of the stone and the depth of its shadows. He was not aware of the heat or the sting of an ant; but he heard the grass whisper and the birds call, and under those the surging of the land. When Harry passed him a blanket he spread it in the shade and lay watching the cliffs till he slept.

He woke in the late afternoon. Harry and Ularra were still asleep and he was alone. He got up and began to walk. His feet found their own way—stepping around the lizard and over the log, waiting before the rocks for the snake to pass—and his mind lay ahead of him brooding in the shadow of the cliffs. They drew him.

He reached them when the sun slanted low along their faces; he wandered along beneath them, clambering over the lower crags, laying a hand on the rock and feeling it like a note of deep music. He looked out as the rocks did, over folded grass and forest, down where the waters ran in the wet; and he smiled a little and waited for the Mimi.

She did not come; and yet he was sure she was near and knew he was there.

He found a shadowed gorge and wandered in seeking her. It was only a shallow cleft between soaring walls of rock; he laid a hand on them, calling her out, but she did not come. He left that cleft and found a deeper one and sat down there. He was so still that a spider scuttled over his leg.

After a time he went on, entering clefts or climbing outcrops, certain and waiting. He opened his mouth to call her

and instead began to sing; the song soared high and
dropped in falling phrases.

> *Are you not coming?*
> *sings the bright water;*
> *are you not coming?*
>
> *The glimmer-bright water*
> *alight with the glancing*
> *of glimmer-bright eyes.*

Nothing answered. The silence deepened suddenly, but
he did not hear it.

> *Are you not coming?*
> *sings the dark water;*
> *are you not coming?*
>
> *The dark-flowing water*
> *Like washes and ripples*
> *of dark-floating hair.*

She was there. She stood by him in the shadows of a
cleft. She was outraged, rigid and quivering, her stick-like
body towering over him, her large dark eyes glinting green.
When she could, she hissed at him furiously.

'Sst, Man! Be silent!' hissed the Mimi.

Two

Wirrun was so full of joy at seeing the Mimi that at
first he saw only herself and his face broadened in content-
ment.

'I knew you'd find me,' he said. 'I need you bad.'

The Mimi gave her snort that was like the sneezing of a

cat, and suddenly folded herself down on a rock as if her spindly legs had given way.

'What's up?' said Wirrun. 'Shouldn't I come? But there's trouble.' She was still rigid and silent, so he tried coaxing. 'I'm no good on my own, you know that.'

'You do me great wrong,' hissed the Mimi, and now he saw how angry she was. He had never seen her so angry, even when he dropped her roughly off the wind and endangered her fragile body. He stood up, hurt and disappointed.

'I never meant any wrong. I came looking for a friend.'

'Is it friendly, then,' hissed the Mimi, 'to shame me among my kind? To sing me for all to hear with an evil love-singing?'

He could only stare.

'Is a man's friendship in itself no shame to a Mimi? Yet friendship is sacred, and for yours I have earned the sneers of my kind. I have been called earless, the wind's plaything, and this I have endured and remembered you with friendship by my fire. Earless indeed! For now you seek me with a love-singing as if the Mimi could be trapped like an earless girl of the People!'

'A love-singing!' He stammered, walked away, came back; then Wirrun too sank down on a rock.

The Mimi's dark eyes followed smouldering; but when she spoke again there was a note of resignation in her anger. 'You did not know. I had forgotten how little a man knows. Yet I see you have still your power: you will give me the cord as before, and we will go farther off where the rocks do not listen.' Then, as Wirrun still sat and gazed dumbly, 'Stiffen your spine, Man. The cord.'

He unwound a length and passed it to her through the mesh of the bag. Protected so from the winds she walked with him, spring-kneed like a mantis, away from the cliffs and down the ridge. They sat on a log.

'You have spoken truly,' said the Mimi, 'for I think you do need help. Where did you find that singing?' She watched him sternly.

He was still too bewildered to answer clearly. 'Ko-in's mountain . . . out of the rocks . . .'

She looked away. 'So far east? And from rock?'

'I . . . can't get rid of it. It haunts me.'

She hissed. 'And will. It was made for that.'

'Just now . . . it came of itself. I never knew—I never even heard it all before.' He saw that she was frowning. 'Oh, Mimi! Would I come this far and call you up on a trouble of my own? I came for something bigger!'

She was still frowning and he could not read her dark possum-eyes, but when she spoke he knew he was forgiven. 'What is bigger than the friendship of heroes?' said the Mimi grandly. He could have smiled except that her anger and distress still troubled him and her greeting rang in his ears.

'Why do you have to be ashamed here? Don't they know you're an Ice Fighter, a Great One?'

'In my country Great Ones are not taken by the wind.'

'That's rubbish,' he said hotly. 'I better go up there and tell 'em the story. Put 'em right.'

She cat-sneezed at him. 'Have I worked and waited for a place among my kind and the right to live in my own dear country, and will you take it from me out of friendship? Tell me your trouble. And speak softly. And sit low in the grass like a lizard and be still.'

Wirrun looked obstinate; but he slid from the log down among the tall browned grass and endured the ants. 'I came on a trouble of the land and I reckon you know what it is. You must do.' And he told her, speaking softly, how a restlessness had seized the earth's old creatures; how some of them were driven out of their places to countries far apart; how the spring fell and the desert flowered as if the old water had found a new way; how it seemed that the trouble might come from under the ground.

'You'd know about that, wouldn't you, living inside the rocks like you do? Ever hear the Ninya's wind in there these days? Ever feel a chill?'

'The Ninya are quiet in their own ice-caves and few in number. There is no trouble under the ground in my country, Man.' Yet she was frowning again. 'There is ill humour,' she admitted, 'and wandering, and spirits out of their places. Not many but a few, from east and west and south. This is your trouble, Man, and not the Ninya who keep at home; it is this that makes us restless and ill-humoured. For when strangers come in, may we not need to fight for our places? And how can the countries feed many where there should be few?'

Wirrun broke off a grass-stem. 'I know. But why are they coming in? What brings 'em?'

'They come because strangers have driven them forth in their turn, and so the evil spreads. When a stone falls into a pool, does not the troubled water widen around it? You may see the trouble spread.'

'Where does it spread from? Where did the stone fall?'

'There are strangers from east and from west but more from the east.' She gazed down where the tree-tops spread below. 'Some quarrel, perhaps . . . some war . . . it may be even that the Ninya in their travels have left some footprint of trouble . . .'

'Mimi . . . When they called me Hero I thought it was like Fighter of Ice: something over and done. But they've put the name on me for good and called me to stop this trouble, and I can't go down under there the way you can. The land doesn't speak to me and I need help. Come with me again.'

For a moment the Mimi looked fierce and eager, but then she shook her head. 'Can I leave my kind when strangers wander near? You are the hero, it is you who are called; if the land does not speak to you yet it will hold and support you. I am an earth-thing, I have only one place. I must stay with my kind.'

His face was heavy with disappointment but he knew she must be right. She always had been. The Mimi looked at him kindly.

'Yet I would come if I could, and not only to ride the wind again. I would come to help you in your own trouble, this love-singing of which you do not speak.'

Wirrun's hand moved among the grass-stems. He was used to bearing his own trouble but not yet used to the new name she had given it. 'Forget it,' he muttered.

'You cannot. You have said so and I know. Yet how can I speak? For it may be that the land has need of your trouble and how can I know what your own need may be? I cannot think for a man or a hero. Only remember. . . .' she hesitated. 'Remember the kunai grass.'

He was puzzled. 'The kunai grass?'

'It grows in the west: tall, as tall as a young tree, and slender-leaved. When it burns its smoke has a power. If a day comes when you need to fight your trouble, fight it with the smoke of a tall grass.' She rose, stooping to keep hold of the cord from the power. 'Come, Man. I must return to my one place.'

He stood up and walked with her back to where the crannied cliffs brooded over the land. 'I'm glad I've seen your place. I'm glad I've seen you. I've missed you, Mimi, worse than wind-riding.'

She let go the cord and stepped close to the rock. 'And I you, Man. But the friendship of heroes will not break for a little parting.' She blew on the rock and stepped into its darkness quickly lest a wind should come.

Wirrun too walked away quickly and softly in case the rock should watch as well as listen. The thought of the Mimi went with him down the ridge; and first he thought of her returned from her great adventure, enduring shame and sneers as proudly and staunchly as ever to win back a lowly place among her kind. It seemed a bitter wrong to him, and yet it was somehow right for the Mimi. Then he thought of her sending him off to walk alone as a hero; and after that of journeying east in search of a place where trouble had dropped like a stone among the spirits; and so at last he approached his own trouble that gnawed and worried at his mind.

How it had angered her: a love-singing, and evil. Why should it leap at him out of a mountain and never let him go? Why should it come from his lips when he opened them to call the Mimi—come whole, as he had never yet heard it? And now, whole, it went over and over in his mind until he clenched his teeth and thought of the smoke of a tall grass. Maybe a man could fight a love-singing if he knew the singer—but how could he fight the love-singing of a mountain?

'Oh, Mimi!' whispered Wirrun striding fast down the ridge in the sunset. But there was only Ularra to travel with him: Ularra now just ahead by Harry's car, cooking something over a couple of burning sticks as he watched Wirrun coming down the ridge.

And Ularra too watched him with the eyes of a friend. 'Just in time, man!' shouted Ularra pouring baked beans on to a plate. 'Half an hour and we'd have gone off and left you. Come and get outside this—Harry wants to shift.'

Harry stared doggedly at the baked beans. He was not at all sure that he did want to drive over an invisible track through rough country after dark; he merely hoped that it might be safer than camping at night a stranger among restless and unreliable spirits. Wirrun knew his problem and hurried on to the fire. Ularra passed him a plate and asked anxiously, 'Didn't find her, did you?' At Wirrun's nod he gave a whistle of delighted surprise.

'Wish I knew this country like you do,' said Wirrun to Harry by way of thanks, and Harry looked even more dogged with satisfaction.

They ate quickly, bundled things back into the car, and true to Ularra's threat were retreating down the ridge within half an hour. Harry drove as fast as he could to make the most of the evening light, Wirrun and Ularra hung on and no one had time or breath for talking. Only Wirrun kept twisting his head to catch glimpses of the haze-hung cliffs of the Mimi's country.

It grew dusk, and then dark; Harry picked his way with care, but he kept on till they reached their last camp which now had the safety of a familiar place. Here, at last, he stopped the car with some relief. 'We want the moon,' he said, putting his head out of the window to stare at the sky.

'Not due for hours yet,' Ularra pointed out rubbing an elbow that had caught a door-handle at the last bump; but Harry was not looking for the moon. He had caught the sound of wind in the trees.

'Westerly,' he grunted. 'No cloud. Wouldn't want to be caught too far out in rain. Got to watch it from now on.'

They got out of the car to feel the wind; it swept down on them in gusts and lifted eastward over ridges. Harry built a bark shelter for a small fire, for safety and companionship rather than for warmth, and he and Ularra sat by it to wait for sleep or hunger or a moon. Wirrun was too restless; he wandered close to the fire and away again, stared at the stars, leaned against the car feeling the wind. Ularra watched him.

'Where to after this, man?'

Wirrun tangled his hair with a hand. 'What's the best way east?'

'East?' said Harry. 'There's bad country that way. How far east?'

'Right across, say.'

'Couldn't do it in the car—too far for me. Take you north to the coast, that's not far, and pick up a boat or a truck. One to another the men'll get you across.'

'Mm,' said Wirrun swaying to a gust of wind. 'That'll take time.'

Ularra tugged at the lobe of one ear. 'Back where we came from? Is that what your friend said?'

'She didn't know too much,' said Wirrun. He added gruffly, 'She couldn't come . . . I just gotta try my own way . . .' and gazed up at the stars. They hung low, beckoning. The wind's tide swept over him again and poured away through the treetops. Harry placed another sheet of bark to shelter the fire.

'Hum,' said Ularra. 'Better start thinking, then. You got any money left?'

Wirrun shook his head, one hand going from habit to his pocket and finding the power instead. It was thrumming; the wind pounced and tugged, lifting him a little. Wirrun gave a shout.

'Ularra, get your pack on—' he wrenched open the car door and reached inside—'here, quick! Harry—' he paused, struggling into his own pack, for how could he leave Harry alone with the spirits? Yet was he not Hero, and travelling on the land's business? 'Harry, I hate leaving you like this after all you've done but it's a right wind. There'll be power enough left after we're gone to keep you safe till morning. Ularra, hang on to this cord and don't drop it—*don't let go*—and run when I run. Thanks, Harry! *Now,* Ularra—run!'

Stumbling on stones in the dark, they ran together into the wind and were lifted and tumbled in its tide. There was a glimpse of Harry's firelit face, eyes staring up and mouth gaping. Wirrun, gripping the power and breasting the wind like a surfer, felt its wild tumbling ease and knew that now it carried them with it. He shouted at Ularra to stop threshing about and wind that cord round his hand.

A ridge fell away below as the dark and windy sky gathered them up. Wirrun remembered a night that seemed long ago, when he had wished that Ularra too might ride the wind before he died.

Three

When the wind at last gave its message to Wirrun it gave him too some of its own rushing freedom. He had been called hero by Ko-in and the Mimi, but the laws of their kind were strange to him: he had been called on as a hero by the People and had groped his way with worry and doubt. But when the wind itself had called on him to mount and ride then Wirrun of the People knew himself. It was all the knowledge he had but it was enough, for now he could travel wherever he was led and do whatever he must. He was released.

And at first he needed all his power to cope with Ularra, for Ularra gaped and gasped and threshed and struggled. He tugged on the cord of the power like a drowning man, he tangled Wirrun in it as he sank low and shot high with a flailing of arms and legs. He even grabbed desperately at Wirrun's head for support. It reminded Wirrun of his own struggles when Ko-in had carried him over the treetops. He managed at last to seize Ularra's free hand in his and place it firmly on his own shoulder, which steadied Ularra and allowed Wirrun to shout reassurances into his ear.

'Don't fight it, man! Let go and ride it like a wave. Here—wind that thing round your wrist before you lose it!'

'Man!' gasped Ularra at last on a windy breath. 'You shoulda warned me!'

'I know that. Sorry, mate. Only you gotta grab the right wind when it comes. Right now?'

Ularra looked down into depths of darkness that were gullies and on to forested ridges touched with starlight. He looked up into depths of sky at the coldly burning stars. He gave a sudden shout of joy and laughed like a giant.

'Riding the wind, eh?' he said. 'Poor old Harry!'

'He'll have a story to tell when he gets back home any rate, and that should suit him.' Harry would shut himself into the car until morning; he and Ularra were flying to meet it. He could see a far-off lightening in the sky where a pale slice of moon was now hanging.

Ularra was trying to settle the pack he had shouldered so quickly. Suddenly he gaped in fresh dismay. 'Hey, man— I hope you know what you're doing! Wherever we're going we've left most of the tucker behind!'

For a moment Wirrun gaped too. Except for a few things tucked into pockets of their packs their supplies and water-bags had been left behind in the car; and he did not know where the wind might set them down or how long the journey might take. Then he laughed in his new freedom as Ularra had.

'She's putting us on our way, man. She won't let us starve!'

'Hum,' said Ularra. 'She mighta thought we'd take all our stuff.'

The wind had been drawing them higher: up into dawn while the land was still shadowed below. Hanging between the shadows and the pearly sky Ularra's worry could not last. His face shone.

'I'm dreaming, man, only I never did it so good before. It's like . . . what? Lying on a big pillow that keeps pushing at you . . . only that's too soft. You gotta keep your balance or you lose it.'

'It's like nothing,' said Wirrun, 'only riding the wind. There's nothing the same.' Ularra's delight doubled his own.

They blew on into morning: one moment banners of colour and light in the sky and the next a dazzle of sun in their eyes. They were crossing a broken, sandy coast still grey in the dawn; they watched sunlight come sweeping towards it over the sea. To their left the broken coastline swept north and vanished. To their right it turned south-east with a sweep of sandhills; for a while they travelled along it over the islanded sea.

'Is it the Gulf?'

'I reckon—what else?'

'Harry was right, then. It wasn't far.'

'A bit longer going up and down ridges,' Wirrun pointed out.

Gulls swung and wheeled below. The shallow sea lay broad and quiet, shaded blue and green in the contours that lay beneath. The coast turned more southerly and threaded away into haze. There was only sea under them, and Ularra looked sideways at Wirrun.

'You reckon you can find land?'

Wirrun grinned. 'No, mate. It'll have to find me. But we gotta hit the Cape sooner or later unless the wind changes.'

'Man, that's a long way,' said Ularra, but he said no more.

Hours went by with only sea below and deep blue sky above. Wirrun, his left hand aching on the power, managed to use the pocket of his shorts as a sling. Ularra had tied the possum-fur cord round his hand for safety. Between them, bobbing and tumbling out of control for some moments, they succeeded in drawing from a pocket in Wirrun's pack a cake of chocolate and a carton of orange-juice. The sea was painted with lines of movement that never seemed to move. The push of wind at their backs became something solid and permanent. They were caught in a great stillness, it seemed, under a dome of glass.

Into this stillness Wirrun began to speak. About the sad staunch pride of the Mimi keeping her lowly place among her kind, hugging the secret of her fame among spirits. About the trouble that had fallen like a stone, perhaps in the east and perhaps made by the Ninya on their travels. And at last, haltingly, about his own deep trouble: how the mountain had caught him with a love-singing, and if it should be fought it must be with the smoke of a tall grass.

Ularra knew the kunai grass. In the glassy stillness of sky he listened and frowned and asked a question or two.

'Ever seem to you that this mountain's . . . got you?'

'Not that way,' said Wirrun. 'It makes no sense. The mountain's sort of a home. It's the singing's got me.'

'Been hearing it up here?'

Wirrun turned and looked at him. 'No. I've thought about it but that's me worrying at it. Not it worrying at me.'

'Hum,' said Ularra. 'Well, you're *coming* any rate, straight as you can. Can't do more, only wait and remember the smoke. I'll be there keeping an eye—just as well you told me.'

And Wirrun knew that Ularra was in his own way as staunch a companion as even the gallant Mimi.

The afternoon found them weary and silent, still blowing eastward before the wind with the shallow sea below; but now Wirrun watched a mistiness ahead and thought it might be land. He saw that Ularra watched it too, but before either of them could be sure enough to mention it the wind dropped them into its pocket, caught them out again at a lower level, buffeted and tossed them and tore their breath away, and swung them farther south.

'Man!' gasped Ularra when he could speak. 'You never told me about that. Where to now?'

'Dunno, but I hope we get there soon. I reckon this wind's getting ready to drop, and I'm not keen on coming down blind into strange country at night.'

'Me either, man.'

The sun was now low in the west. They watched a mistiness grow into a coastline, and a little after sunset saw it clearly. 'I never saw anything like that!' cried Wirrun. 'Bush coming out to meet us! Mangroves, they must be.'

The sea washed in gently between spreading trees; they passed over a forest that stood in the water.

Ularra had crossed the Gulf by boat and knew and welcomed the mangroves but they did not tell him, as Wirrun hoped, what part of the coast they were crossing. 'The Gulf—you know that, man. There's mangrove forests walking out to sea all along here.'

Behind the mangroves the sunset shone on low, rolling sandhills that held between them the wet glint of marshes. It looked a desolate country, with low flat-topped hills to trap flyers in the dark. As dusk rose towards him like the filling of a well Wirrun peered anxiously down.

'Had it yet, mate?' he asked Ularra.

'A bit of chocolate and a drink of orange don't keep up a man's strength too good,' Ularra confessed. 'But I reckon I can keep going while you can. I don't like the look of that down there much, do you?'

'Not much—but now you can see it any rate. It'll be

dark in a minute or so. Still . . . I reckon we'll trust it a bit longer if it'll take us . . .'

They kept on south while the stars brightened over them. Below there were no lights: no string of bright beads to show a township, not even the lonely yellow light of an Inlander's home. But Wirrun had forgotten the starlight which his eyes were learning to use again. He could see at least the flat-topped hills that grew more frequent as they went; he would feel them looming as one feels a presence in the dark, and by looking could pick out their shapes.

When he caught Ularra yawning once he thought of coming down on one of these hills. He even loosened his stiff fingers on the power and experimented, bringing them down a few feet. But to sleep dry and hungry on a bare hill and wake lost among marshes was not what he wanted. The right wind might not come again, and the Ninya's known route was still far to the south and east. Hilly country with streams, if he could find it, would lead them across.

By the time he had found it it was all he could do to keep his hand closed on the power and his eyes open. Beside him Ularra would doze, droop, begin to fall; wake with a start and peer ahead and down for a while; doze and droop again. Like a sleepy driver who suddenly sees another car, Wirrun was roused into panic: he had felt two changes in one moment. One was a looming of strength and power in the darkness—the land rising to meet him. The other was a change in the wind—it fumbled, dropped him six feet, roused itself and swept him higher. Wirrun grabbed Ularra's shoulder and shook it roughly.

'Wake up, man, wake up! There's hills ahead and we're going into 'em! Watch out—try not to break a leg!' His eyes found the shape of the ridge, grey-edged with starlight, reaching away left and right.

'Eh?' muttered Ularra, and woke up. 'Glory be,' he said and peered helplessly down at the dark.

Wirrun, loosening and tightening his fingers on the power to bring them down by degrees, had no choices. They were falling off the wind; they might overshoot into some deep gorge or smash into rocks. He must take the first slope as he met it. He felt it near.

Leaves struck at them, sweet and keen with the smell of

eucalyptus. A tree—he caught at it and with one foot shoved Ularra hard into its branches. Clinging with one hand he forced the other, stiff and numb, to release the power at last.

'Eh?' said Ularra scrambling among leaves. He was suddenly too heavy to support himself and slid and crashed to the ground with Wirrun on top of him.

It was darker under the tree. Wirrun rolled aside and they sat peering at each other, both unhurt. The possum-fur cord that linked them was still unbroken. Ularra untied it from his hand.

'Man, I'm starving,' he mumbled, and fell back on his pack and slept. Wirrun dragged off his own pack, pushed it under his head on the stony ground, and slept too. The dark crept around them and murmured with wonder. It had been a great riding of the wind.

They woke in the shade of stringybarks with strong sunlight beyond, on a slope looking westward over the marshes and broken hills they had crossed. They wasted no time in admiring this view but tore at their packs to see what food they had.

'Chicken and mushroom!' breathed Wirrun producing a can.

'Meatballs here—and I got the tin opener—wow!'

They ripped the cans open and ate with their knives, wriggling their backs uncomfortably from time to time because they felt bare without the push of the wind. Ularra licked the blade of his knife with care.

'That's breakfast any rate. I'm not too sure about lunch.'

'Rabbit,' Wirrun suggested without much confidence. 'Or maybe wallaby.'

'Lizards,' said Ularra. 'Witchetty grubs—they don't run fast. With all that hunting we won't get too far in a day.'

'Water first,' said Wirrun, draining the gravy from his can. 'And when we find it we'll light up and brew—I got the tea here.'

'Brew, what in?'

Wirrun thought quickly. 'In these two cans . . . Lucky we both got knives.'

They flattened the hacked edges of the empty cans by hammering them with stones, rolled back the partly removed lids to make handles, and stowed them carefully in their packs. Then they climbed the steep ridge in search of a gully and water.

The flat-topped ridge showed them a wide wild country stretching east and south into sharp blue sunlit hazes and purple shadow. A sandstone country, not high at its edges but deeply chasmed and ravined, a country to know and revere. The gorges, filled with purple, were cut sharp and narrow at the top but widened under overhanging walls as they plunged down. Wirrun gazed at it in sober silence and Ularra whistled.

'Thanks, man.'

'What for?' said Wirrun, gazing. There'd be water down there all right if they could reach it; and the ridges melted away so far to the east that they must lead him to the Divide and so to the coast.

'Thanks for not dropping me in one of those in the dark.'

Wirrun's face grooved into a grin but he was still thinking. 'I bet there was ice in here somewhere. The first we knew was at Toowoomba, but that's only the one the papers told about. If we're tracking the Ninya we could start here, only we don't know where to look . . . Well, better try for some easier water.'

They turned west along the ridge looking for some younger gully opening to the plains. They found one cutting deep into the sandstone and followed its course down the ridge to a point where they could climb in. Its floor was only damp; they turned upward looking for hollowed pools where water might lie. The rock walls of the gully rose higher as they went, and closed in towards each other overhanging at the top. Above them the scrub rose higher still, deepening the coolness and shade.

They found small potholes with a little water and a great activity of wrigglers. They were thirsty enough to drink this water if it had not promised better near at hand. Higher up, among umbrella fern and forest mint and spreading crowsnests cool under overhanging rock, they found their pool and drank. A magpie's call rang as cool and clear as the water.

'Man!' sighed Ularra, and lay back in a hollow of rock to let the water settle inside him. 'I could drink her dry only she mightn't fill up again. You reckon it's a shame to make this stuff into tea?' Wirrun didn't answer; he too sat in a hollow of rock, but his face was deeply grooved and strained. Ularra glanced at him and repeated the question.

'Eh?' said Wirrun, his face relaxing. 'I reckon I'll have tea next, and after that more water.'

'That's sense. Better wash those tins out while I see if there's any dry wood in here.'

The wood was mostly damp and rotting, but he found a half dead branch fallen in from above and laid a fire on flat rock.

Wirrun had washed the two cans and filled them. Ularra set them in place and lit his fire. Smoke billowed up from the green and rotten fuel.

'Bit of a change from our last camp—now there's a country where you can light a fire. This one'll want watching.' He glanced at Wirrun. 'Wish we had something to cook on it.' Wirrun was silent and strained again, with a look of tight-lipped eagerness. Ularra looked at him closely. 'I said, what are we going to cook on this fire besides tea?'

Wirrun jumped almost guiltily and smoothed the strain out of his face. 'Don't get in a twist, man. Fetch a rabbit.'

'It's that singing again, eh? Worrying at you.' Wirrun looked away, moody and resentful. Ularra broke a branch with great energy. 'Shoulda had more sense, making a fire in all these rocks. You just watch this water boil and keep your mind on rabbits.'

High overhead there was a rustle of leaves. Something whooshed through the air and thudded down two yards from the fire. It was a rabbit, freshly killed. It lay on the rock and stared up from one glazed eye.

Four

Wirrun and Ularra sprang to their feet; they stared at the rabbit, and at each other, and then upward. A face hung over the edge of the gully, a dark face slashed by a white grin and topped by an old felt hat. An arm in a rolled-up shirt-sleeve waved over the head.

Ularra shouted between anger and delight and jabbed one hand at the rabbit. The dark man above grinned again and held up a hessian bag: he had many rabbits. As he lowered the bag the felt hat toppled from his head and floated down into the gully. It landed almost on the fire and Wirrun pounced on it.

The man above stopped grinning and held out an arm. 'Throw her up,' he called; but Wirrun held on to the hat.

'She won't travel—too light. You come down.'

'I'll take her up,' Ularra offered. 'We owe him for a rabbit.'

'Let him come. We need him more than his rabbit. This country's not for strangers.'

The man had disappeared. They could hear him grumbling, and the clumping of his boots along the gully. He did not go far before the boots rang on rock: he was taking some track of his own down the steep walls that Wirrun and Ularra would not have dared. In a few minutes he came up the gully into view.

'Saw your smoke,' he greeted them, and his eyes went deliberately over their packs and the two small cans of water on the fire. The look was the kind by which the People said much, a silent criticism easy to read: 'Strangers with empty packs and empty bellies and no sense; maybe they'll know what to do with a rabbit.'

Ularra was driven to defence. 'Man, we're glad of that rabbit if you can spare it. Left in a hurry yesterday, and our tucker's back in Alice.'

The man gave him another measuring look and answered with only one word. 'Yesterday.' Ularra was flustered.

Wirrun held out the old hat. The measuring eyes ran over him too—and went back to the bag on his belt. 'Yesterday,' said the man, and took back his hat with a slight bend of the head. 'Merv Bula. Glad you've come. You're needed.'

'You're needed too,' Wirrun told him. 'You heard we were coming?'

Merv Bula dumped his hessian bag at his feet and took out a billy; used his hat to lift the cans from the fire and empty them into the billy; set it carefully to boil; took a knife from a sheath on his belt and began to skin and gut the rabbit. Ularra moved to take this job from him, was ignored, and retreated to make the tea.

'Hoped you might,' Merv grunted, answering Wirrun as he worked. 'Saw Tom Hunter going through back east . . . Yesterday, eh?'

It would be known in any case since Harry had seen it. Wirrun said, 'We came on the wind, Ularra and me. It was sudden.'

'Ah,' said Merv, tugging at the rabbit skin.

'We needed water first, and this was nearest—and then we couldn't leave it right away. But we wanted someone like you that knows the country. You and your rabbit turned up like a storm in a bad year.'

'Or a man for an Ice-Fighter, maybe,' said Merv. He rolled the rabbit skin neatly, thrust it into his bag, drew out a pannikin and began to cut up the rabbit.

'You got trouble here too, then?'

'Trouble all over. You can't move of a night.'

'Strangers out of their places?'

'Never been anything like it.' Merv took out an ancient enamel mug and placed it by the two cans for Ularra to fill with tea. Ularra had also searched the packs and found salt and an onion, and now offered these small finds to Merv. 'Ah,' said Merv. 'That's handy.'

'From the look of it,' said Wirrun, 'I'd say you might've had trouble last time too. High rocks on the road east: a likely place for ice. The papers never said, but they wouldn't.'

'Ah,' said Merv pausing in his work to sip tea. 'They wouldn't know. No one to see it but me, and all I told was the right men.'

'There was ice, then? How near?'

'Can't see from here.' Merv sat back on his heels to finish his tea. When the mug was empty he rinsed it out, measured water into the pannikin and set it on the fire that Ularra had been nursing. He picked leaves from a small creeping plant and tossed them in with the rabbit. 'Give her a while to boil down a bit,' he advised. Ularra looked resentful, being familiar with the cooking of rabbit stew. Merv stood up and heaved his bag to his shoulder. 'I'll put

my rabbit skins to dry and be back. Show you that place.'
He pushed the old hat hard on to his head and strode off
down the gully. They heard the scrape of his boots climbing rock and saw him peer down again from above with a
grin of farewell. They waited and listened for a little longer
feeling that the ears of Merv Bula could hear farther than
other men's ears. Then Ularra huffed a little and moved
the pannikin two inches.

'I been cooking rabbit stew since I was *that* high. What
were those leaves he put in?'

'There you are, then,' said Wirrun with a grin. 'You
know rabbit stew but you don't know the leaves of the
country. That's a sizeable man. We've been lucky. Helped,
more like.'

Ularra had to agree. 'The only one seeing that ice, too.
You reckon it'll do any good going to look? What are you
looking for?'

'Told you before—I'm not looking, just waiting. If it's
there it'll find us.'

They rested in silence till the fire needed more wood
and Ularra went off up the gully to find it. When he came
back he saw that Wirrun's face had darkened again into a
hungry listening. Ularra dropped his wood noisily and began to feed the fire, calling on Wirrun to smell that stew,
rubbing his own stomach and sniffing loudly. Wirrun
roused himself to agree that he could handle the lot without
Ularra's help, and lapsed back into his own darkness.
Ularra squatted by the fire and watched him with helpless
anxiety.

'Wish I could take it from you, man.'

Wirrun only hunched a little. When he spoke it was only
to himself and like a fretful child. 'Will I ever get free?'

Ularra broke a branch savagely. 'When I find this tall
grass I'm gonna smoke you black.' He was startled to see a
flash of anger in the hero's frowning eyes. If it was like
that it was going to be tough; could you cure a man of a
love-singing if he was so bad that he didn't want to be
cured?

After midday when the sun filtered green light into the
gully they used knives and fingers to eat stewed rabbit and
drank the gravy from their useful cans. The darkness had
drained out of Wirrun leaving him only tired, and they

were both so hungry that the meal was a feast. Afterwards they made more tea, cleaned up the camp and let the fire go out.

'Been trying to long enough—it won't need no help,' declared Ularra, but he emptied the billy over it for safety.

They were bored with resting and anxiously watching the angle of the sunlight when the boots of Merv Bula rang on the rocks and he came clumping up the gully. Though he had dealt with his morning's catch he still carried his bag, rolled and roped and slung from his shoulder. He glanced at the dead fire and the packs strapped ready and nodded.

'Best stew I ever ate,' Wirrun told him gratefully as he and Ularra shouldered their packs.

Merv smiled widely. 'Hungriest you ever were,' he suggested.

His way out of the gully proved to be an easy climb, under an overhang of rock weathered into holds that could only be seen from below. After the coolness of the gully the ridge seemed heavy with heat even in the scrub.

'Watch out for warrens,' said Merv. 'I got traps.' He pointed now and then to a rabbit warren as he took them east along the ridge.

'Wouldn't like to step in one of those traps,' Ularra agreed keeping clear. But Merv had not been considering Ularra's feet.

'Do you no harm only maybe waste a rabbit. I got me own make of traps. A rabbit's got rights like anyone else.'

They nodded, for they both remembered with what agony the shriek of a rabbit in an Inlander's trap came whistling through the night.

They came out of the scrub on the edge of a gorge cutting sharp-edged across the ridge. The frowning cliffs of its opposite shore led their eyes down, past hanging rock and clinging scrub, down through blue distance to a far-away canopy of forest. The blue filled it like some magically translucent sea into which they might dive or over which they might sail.

'Take an hour to get down,' said Merv with a glance at the sky. 'We'll be there for the night.'

'An hour?' Ularra gripped his pack-straps. 'Couple of steps and I'd be down a lot faster.'

Merv grinned widely and turned along the gorge, following its course until the ridge began to dip. 'Lucky it's dry—we'll go in the way the water goes.' He led them into the dip.

It was hardly a watercourse but it had nibbled a little at the sheer cliffs of the gorge. They could see how it would run in the wet, channelling a way down the cliffs; Wirrun pictured a long fluttering plume of water free-falling past the undercut lower walls into the hazy depth. He wished for a wind but none came. He and Ularra, avoiding each other's eyes, had no choice but to follow Merv Bula over the edge of that terrifying gap.

They never really knew how they made the climb. They used no rope though Merv had one. They simply followed Merv through the tunnellings of weather, over pavements quarried by roots, behind the balusters of stunted trees. They were slow and cautious even where the path was wide, for that blue distance sang always into one ear. They watched where Merv placed a foot, where he sat and slid, where he hung on and dropped. Wind-holes led them from one hanging cave into a lower one; narrow water-courses threaded behind domes. The only moment that stayed clear in Wirrun's mind was that of leaving the cliffs for the deeper-cut shale below; and though he knew the descent had been made by way of a cave and a tree he remembered only the thought that if they fell now any rate they could roll.

It took more than an hour to reach the bottom, and there they sat resting and looking; for the far-bottomed blue of the gorge had become a wide place of grass and scrub with a creek winding through it and a complex geography of hillsides and ridges, and high above, blue and distant, a soaring of impregnable cliffs.

'Coulda gone round,' said Merv, 'if we'd had three days.'
'I wish you'd said,' retorted Ularra, and Wirrun grinned.
'What about this ice place?' he asked.
'Up the creek,' said Merv. 'When you're ready.'
The creek was no more than a trickle between small pools until they reached its head, in a gully cut deep into hills of shale. Here under hanging sandstone cliffs lay a wide deep pool with river oaks standing over it and an outflow into the creek. It reminded Ularra of mysterious wa-

ters in his own red country, and it pulled at Wirrun like a magnet. He could only stand and stare.

'How long since we had a bath?' he asked with his eyes on the water. 'Nothing but little dishes for a week.'

'You don't want a bath now, man. Sun's gone and it's getting cool. Merv's showing you where the ice was.'

'Here,' said Merv.

Wirrun dragged his eyes from the pool. 'You mean up there on the cliff?'

'Down here,' said Merv. 'Water iced over.'

Wirrun was puzzled. 'You'd have thought up there, with all that high rock to look out of.'

'Down here,' said Merv stolidly. He added, 'They mighta come down through the cave.'

'Cave?'

Merv took them through the river oaks to the farther end of the pool and they saw that the gully's head cut deep under the sandstone, making a cave with a wide, low entrance that ran back into darkness under the mass of the cliffs.

'Might have a look in there,' said Wirrun.

'You do. I'll set a few traps for morning.' Merv unhitched his swaglike roll and began to untie it. Ularra followed Wirrun into the cave.

Though the sky was still sunlit the cliffs shouldered the sunlight aside and a long evening had begun in the gorge. Four yards in from the entrance of the cave the light was failing; but they could see that the cave narrowed sharply and went steeply up in height. There was a fine soft dust under their feet, and a sense of soft, continuing darkness above and beyond. The darkness drew them on.

Just at its edge something moved and the two young men were suddenly still. Something laughed, soft and teasing; a shape moved into the twilight.

She was charming: broad cheeks, small round chin, dark eyes bright with mischief, dark hair soft over her forehead. She held out the small fine hands of the People in welcome and even Wirrun, clutching the power and feeling it throb, could see so sign of claws. She looked at him knowingly but it was at Ularra she smiled, turning her firm young body towards him, preening. Ularra's eyes shone and he laughed shortly. She laughed back.

'Come, then, Big One,' she said cheekily.

Ularra stumbled forward, Wirrun grabbed his arm—and they stopped as they were, transfixed, for the darkness came alive and screamed in chorus. The girl cringed, then swung round to face it. There were glimpses of dark women struggling round her, fierce dark women with lashing tails.

'Out!' screamed the voices. 'Catch her!' 'Tear her!' 'Send her out!' 'Have we not trouble enough with things of her kind?' 'Go, you! Take your smiles and your teasing and kissing away!' Their fury was a darkness in itself and Wirrun felt it swirling like a black tide out of the cave. He was shaken.

They reached for the girl with their nails. For a moment she fought back as fiercely, but the tailed women were too many. She sprang away and fled past the two young men and out of the cave. Wirrun would have followed the tailed women into the dark, but Ularra growled and swung after the girl. Wirrun had to run after him and try to hold him. Ularra fought him off.

'Let go, man, I'm not a kid! Up on the cliff—in that hole—Get off! I know what I'm doing.' He was an angry stranger and too strong for Wirrun to hold. Wirrun hung on and shouted for Merv Bula.

Merv came running, looking as he ran from Ularra's straining face to the cave that Ularra stared at on the cliffs. Merv seized Ularra's other arm, and between them he and Wirrun got him away. At the pool Merv tore off his hat, slooshed it full of water and jammed it hard on Ularra's head. Ularra growled and shuddered and at last gave in, and Merv and Wirrun led him quietly down the creek.

'They were after her,' he said once in a dazed way.

'Not our business, mate,' said Wirrun soothingly. 'Let 'em fight their own battles.'

'They had tails . . . She never had a chance . . .'

'They're none of 'em any good to you, mate. Let 'em go.'

Farther down the creek they found another waterhole under river oaks, and Wirrun sat by Ularra while Merv made camp, lit a fire and fried sausages in his pannikin. Ularra was quiet and dogged. 'Fool,' he muttered once avoiding Wirrun's eye.

'You get Merv's sausages into you and forget it, man. I near made the same mistake once, only I had the power and the Mimi.'

'Ah,' said Merv. 'Wouldn't want to make it with that one. That one's no good to a man.'

Wirrun looked at him sharply. 'You know it, then?'

'Knew she was there,' said Merv. 'Should be further north by rights. That's that Abuba.' He seemed unwilling to say more, and Wirrun let the question drop. Tomorrow when Ularra was his cocky self again he would ask more about the Abuba; and about the tailed women from whom trouble seemed to flow in a dark tide. Now he only sat watching Merv at work by the fire: steady and solid, aware of restless spirits and yet not seeming afraid. Wirrun was again glad that the land had sent him such a man.

'Time to roll in,' said Merv when the dark came down; and Wirrun agreed, remembering how they had slept on the stones last night. His body ached from the flight, the rough sleeping, and his climb down from the cliffs. Yet when Merv had rolled himself into a blanket near the fire and Ularra had climbed doggedly into his sleeping-bag Wirrun, lying in his own bag a yard away, was at first too tired to sleep.

He lay watching the channel of stars between the darkness of cliffs and thought of Ularra: Ularra walking steadily with him to meet the Jugi, laughing with delight on the wind, frowning anxiously over Wirrun's own trouble, following him into the cave of the tailed women. He should have watched out for Ularra . . . he'd take more care after this . . . He fell asleep with no haunting of water-music and only the wind singing in the needles of the river-oaks.

He woke startled and confused with his hand on the power: it was still and gave no sign. There was deep dark under the trees and the dimness of starlight beyond. The fire gleamed red under ash, with the rolled-up shape of Merv nearby. The camp was quiet. Too quiet. He put out a hand and felt Ularra's sleeping-bag.

It was empty. Ularra was gone.

Five

Wirrun fought his way out of his sleeping-bag look-ing for the stars and feeling for the time. It was hard to tell under the black shoreline of the cliffs but he knew it was between midnight and morning. He hoped fiercely, he de-manded, that Ularra should be wandering near the camp dazed with sleep. He stumbled into the darkness to look for an angular, loose-limbed blackness moving somewhere. He could not find it.

He crossed the creek below the waterhole and ran along the opposite bank. Still nothing. Ularra must have fallen, sleepy and stupid, and gone back to sleep where he lay. Wirrun began to call.

'Ularra! Wake up, man! Ularra, where are you?'

He waited and listened. No sleepy grunt or stumbling footstep. He called again; and again.

A figure loomed out of the dark and he bounded to-wards it. But it was Merv Bula. Merv grasped him by the shoulder and tried to draw him back towards the creek. Wirrun shook him off.

'It's Ularra—he's gone—we gotta find him. Wandering round half asleep—'

Merv held him firmly by both shoulders. 'No good, Ice-Fighter. Back to the fire till daylight.'

'Not me!' shouted Wirrun. 'Ularra! Where are you, man?'

Merv's grip and his voice were both iron. 'Back to the fire and we'll see.'

Still Wirrun would not hear, for had he not brought Ularra out of his safe job and the milkbar into this danger? Had he not, thinking only of spirits, failed to protect his friend though the power lay in his hand? He struggled again. '*You* go and sit over your fire till morning. I don't need it.'

'Ah,' said Merv, 'but you do. Fire's sense and work and no shivering. You need this one. And you need your head. And you need mine. We got work to do.'

Then Wirrun knew that he was indeed shivering, and that he did need his own head and Merv's. He let Merv lead him back over the creek to the camp.

The fire was already blazing with fresh wood. Merv added more and set a billy in place. 'Tea,' he said.

Wirrun answered sternly. 'All right. No more. Tell me.'

'That Abuba,' said Merv. 'He's gone looking.'

'I know that.'

'Sure you do. That cliff-hole, that cave. He's there.'

'Not yet, maybe. He's gotta find it in the dark.'

'Look up at the cliffs, Ice-Fighter. You'll see her fire. She's lit it for him.'

Wirrun remembered a red point of fire that he had refused to see.

'His bed's cold,' Merv added. 'He's gone long enough.'

'To climb up there in the dark? He can't.'

'Ah,' said Merv. 'That's it. Eh? She'll help him but she won't help you. He can do it. You need daylight.' He made the tea. 'And you need a lot more.'

The cold that lay inside Wirrun was for grasping and using. He was hero and Ice-Fighter: for his People, for his country, and for his friend Ularra. He watched frowning while the tea was poured and took his mug in a firm hand. 'This Abuba. What sort is it?'

'That's right,' said Merv. 'Use the head.' But he seemed to have trouble answering the question and stared at the fire. 'She's a cheeky one,' he said at last. 'She'll coax a man to marry her, see, and then she'll . . . turn him.'

'Turn him how?'

'Change him. Make him something else, not a man. You gotta catch him and turn him back.'

'How?' said Wirrun again sternly.

'Takes time and work—no use rushing off in the dark . . . You gotta make him again. Make him a man like he was.'

Wirrun closed his hand on the power. If he had to do impossible things he must do them. 'How does a man make a man?'

Merv stoked the fire and seemed to think. 'Bit by bit,' he said at last. 'I don't know all I'd like, I just heard the story. It's old stuff, this, and we'll take it bit by bit. Catch him first and then we'll know more. Now we want ironwood.'

'Ironwood?'

'It's got a power we want. We'll need a load or two.'

'Can we find it in the dark?'

'I know where.' Merv banked the fire, drawing ash and charcoal over it to hold it. Then he took a cloth bundle from his pack and unwrapped a small, short-handled axe. He stood up with the axe in his hand and waited for Wirrun.

There was a glow in the darkness of the sky and the stars had paled, but the gully itself was as dark as ever. Yet Wirrun could see well enough, for by now he had lost the night-blindness that is a habit of city eyes. Merv paused now and then to choose his path, but he chose it with certainty and walked like a man without fear. Only a man like this could have brought Wirrun back from the cliffs and forced him to listen by the fire; only from Merv could he have accepted the rule of 'bit by bit'.

They climbed the first slopes of the hill to a darkness of trees. Merv's hands moved over bark, identifying.

'This one and those two, all ironwood. Small, but they'll do.'

He took Wirrun's hand and placed it on smooth, thin bark shedding here and there in twisted flakes, and among blunt-pointed leaves on which he could feel the gloss. Merv's own hands moved among branches, feeling and exploring. At last he took up the axe and used it like an adze, hacking off one branch and drawing it long and slender from the tree. Then he passed the axe to Wirrun.

'Fetch all you can cut—the whole tree if she's not too much for the little axe. You'll find her as tough as her name. Me, I got things to do.' He went away down the slope into darkness trailing his slender branch.

Wirrun set to work, starting on the outer branches that

he could best see. His first fumbling blow only set the branch springing and jarred his hand. He learnt to cut lightly through bark till the pale gleam of wood gave him a target, and then to use the spring of the axe. It was hard work and he did not know why he must do it, but he did it with fierce satisfaction: unleashing all the haste and fear he had kept back, hacking into his dread of the things he must find and do by daylight. He tossed aside branch after branch until he could begin to see a greenness of bark patched with brown and the pale silvery wood that his axe chewed out of it; and then he began on the trunks. When the first small tree creaked and was pushed into breaking he took three branches in one hand, the trunk in the other, and dragged them behind him down the slope to the camp under the oaks.

Merv was working at the fire. A rabbit was cooking in a pannikin to one side of it, but Merv had drawn out red coals from the other side and sat there at work with his knife. He set it down and held his work over the coals, turning it slowly, drawing it back and forth; laid it over his knees again and rubbed at it with a hard rough bark; took up his knife again. As Wirrun watched the coldness came back inside him. Merv was making something like a spear. Slender and about six feet long; hardened in the fire and rubbed smooth, flattened and sharpened at one end; a rough and hurried job that looked primitive and dangerous. Merv said nothing to Wirrun who stood and watched; he only reached into his pack and tossed over a coil of light rope.

Wirrun dropped his load, took up the rope, turned on his heel and went off. He would not speak about the spear. He would do as Merv had said—take the impossible bit by bit and deal with each bit in its own time.

He had chopped down the second ironwood, roped the whole pile together, and dragged it bouncing back to camp when the first sunlight edged the tops of the cliffs. He had to turn and stare in the direction of the Abuba's cave.

'Eat first,' said Merv.

Wirrun swung on him. 'Man—'

'Eat,' said Merv with authority. 'No good on a cliff with an empty belly.' He put chunks of rabbit on a tin plate and

Wirrun tore at them savagely. The spear's slender length rested against an oak, its silvery wood darkened by fire. It was strengthened below the point by a binding of string and had a handgrip of string on the shaft because Merv had not had time or skill to make it well. Wirrun watched it while he ate, but Merv rubbed up his knife and sheathed it, coiled the rope and laid it at hand, set beside it a short staff of ironwood, banked the fire again.

When they were ready he took up the spear, balanced it for a moment and handed it to Wirrun. 'Ever used one?'

Wirrun took the spear. 'Tried it, that's all.'

'Me either,' said Merv. 'I'd have made something shorter only you might need the length. She's not much but she's the right wood. You remember that. What we find in that cave, no matter what, if you want your friend back you take to it with ironwood. Understand?'

Wirrun gazed at him from under lowered brows. Merv gazed steadily back.

'No pity, mind. It won't be true pity. Your mate wants to be a man again. You think of that, Ice-Fighter. Best go.' He took up the rope and the ironwood staff.

They started up the creek. The highest western cliffs were painted with sunlight, but the Abuba's cave was low in the southern wall and always shadowed. They would climb towards it as the Abuba had done, by the eastern wall of the gully above the pool, and where the hillside cut in under the cliffs Wirrun knew Merv would find a way up. He had brought them down that giddy climb from the top without using the rope he carried now. Wirrun carried only the ironwood spear, at first awkwardly and with distrust; but as they went on his hand got to know it and carried it as if it belonged there. Merv's all-seeing eyes saw this too but he said nothing. His face was as dark with strain as Wirrun's own.

They went in silence. Once they stopped to look up at the cliffs, picking out ledge and channel and wind-weathered cave—and the one cave, rounder and deeper and darker, that was the Abuba's. Wirrun felt a tremor like a touch on a tightened string. Once he spoke.

'What kind of thing not a man?'

'Eh?' said Merv. 'Some kind of beast, maybe.'

They went on east, past the dark cave-mouth where pity would not be true pity.

Under overhanging cliffs Merv found a tree, and fallen sandstone blocks, and then a ledge running west, and from that a channel. The rope stayed coiled on his shoulder. It would have taken Wirrun half a day to find the path . . . but Ularra had found it in the dark . . . spirit-helped . . .

Merv had stopped and was waiting ahead. When Wirrun came up he spoke softly.

'The way's easy—she'd have it easy. But the next bit wants to be quick and quiet so take a look. This that we're on opens up in a little cave—see, just up there. That's got a hole that goes straight into hers. Take it quick, in a jump—spear handy, mind, and don't get bit. I'll be back of you.'

He stood aside and Wirrun went on ahead. He laid a hand on the power: it had been quiet all these fearful hours but it was throbbing now. His right hand held the spear as if it belonged there, and he followed the channel up under arching rock that went back into a cave. He saw the hole, an elongated opening fretted by wind and blowing sand through a thinness of rock into a darkness beyond. A sound came through it. Wirrun listened for a grim moment and his blood turned to angry fire. It was a snuffling, whining sound, an animal noise. With his anger throbbing Wirrun gripped the spear, trod softly to the opening and leapt through.

A deeper, darker cave opened round him. He heard laughter in the shadows and his eyes found the Abuba. She stood against the farther wall, charming and cheeky, her dark eyes eagerly alight. She rolled her hips in derision and slipped away into darkness.

Something crouched against the wall where she had stood, something monstrous and shaggy that crouched like a beaten dog. A harsh growl rattled in its throat and it rose and stood on four limbs as man might in stooping, but the limbs too were covered in coarse hair and the hands and feet bore the talons of an eagle. It growled again and faced Wirrun, lips drawn back from long white fangs, he saw its eyes. They were a man's eyes, Ularra's eyes, and dark with misery. They begged for pity. Wirrun's anger sang in his ears and the point of his spear fell.

Coarse hair rose on the beast's neck and back. The growl rose to a savage attacking snarl. Baring its fangs and pleading with its eyes the monstrous thing that was Ularra launched itself at Wirrun.

4

The Remaking
of Ularra

One

. As the great beast flew at him Wirrun acted by instinct. One hand dropped to the power, the other raised the ironwood spear, and he stood poised, ready to leap. Yet the spear-point wavered and dipped for the eyes of the beast still pleaded, and they were the eyes of his friend. And the beast, launched in its spring, seemed to hang there snarling—hair erect, talons striking, fangs bared, yet holding back like a dog that turns in fury on its master and cannot bite.

'Ularra, man!' cried Wirrun in pain and in power.

The beast launched itself again with rattling snarls and met the point of the spear. Wirrun felt its weight as the spear dragged at the hairy hide of its shoulder. It gave a roaring growl, twisted in fury with snapping jaws and striking talons, and its eyes wept.

'Hold steady!'

From behind Wirrun came Merv, grim-faced with his rope and staff, his eyes fixed on the struggling beast. In a moment he leapt forward, thrust the staff of ironwood into the snapping jaws and leapt back. The jaws clamped on the wood and opened roaring. The staff rolled free; there were broken fangs bedded in it and the monster snapped with broken stumps.

Merv threw a loop of rope round the beast as it fought on the end of the spear. He gave one end of the rope to Wirrun, pulled tight and threw again. Leaping in and away he tossed loop after loop and pulled them tight till the beast lay jerking on the rock snapping its broken teeth, baring its rope-tangled claws and weeping with Ularra's eyes. Wirrun tore free the spear with which he had held it and flung it clattering on the rock. He and Merv held the rope between them, each of them one free end; by pulling against each other they held and controlled the beast. They propped themselves against the cave wall to rest, looking only at the monster. It lay on the rock, struggling and bleeding and weeping.

'Shoulda brought poles,' muttered Merv. There were poles for the cutting on the hillside below, but Wirrun knew he meant poles of ironwood. He answered shortly for he was breathless and choked by pity.

'Two men can't do it. There's this hole. Gotta get through.'

He gave his rope-end to Merv to hold, unwound a length of cord from the power and went slowly forward to the beast that struggled and jerked.

'Ularra, man,' said Wirrun, 'we're taking you home.'

He stooped, extending his hands; the beast writhed and snapped its jaws but not at him. He passed the cord round the hairy neck and tied it; the beast snarled and snapped as his hand neared its wounded shoulder. Wirrun forced himself to work at the rope, freeing the hairy limbs for walking. One of them struck at him, he saw the wicked claws curve near his face and draw away. Merv watched with lowered brows.

'Your mate's not rightly turned. Lucky you woke, Ice-Fighter—maybe she never had time.'

Wirrun unwound more cord as he stepped back. Then he and Merv pulled on their ends of rope. The beast snarled and fought, dug at the rock with its claws, came forward a little, pulled back and came on again. At the cave opening it drew strongly back twisting its head away from the light, fighting to keep to the dimness. Merv climbed out of the cave and pulled with all his weight; Wirrun stayed talking and coaxing and even, shuddering, put his hands on the rough hair and pushed. The beast snarled and roared; it struck with its claws and snapped with its broken fangs; but in the end it fought its way into the outer cave. Wirrun climbed after it. He thought an echo of girlish laughter followed him out of the shadows.

That was the worst part of a bad journey. Once in daylight the creature's mood changed. It snarled and fought, struck and snapped, hung back on the rope with the hair stiffened along its spine and the ragged growl rattling in its throat, but it did not fight only in resistance. It fought to gain the shelter of rock, to hide in a hollow, to reach the shadow of trees, and the men could often make use of this. Once when Merv was slow to jump aside its talons gashed his boot and drew blood from his instep. Those talons never reached Wirrun though he came near them again and again; the beast snapped and struck but never quite attacked. Some field of force held it back: the force of the power or of pity or friendship.

It took an immeasurable time to reach the camp. For the men it was time suspended as in dreams. For the beast there was no time, only the eternity of now. But when at last they struggled into camp and tied the ends of the rope to two oaks with the beast crouched sullen and despairing between them, the men were exhausted. Yet even then they could not rest.

'Fires,' panted Merv. 'Here and here. Ironwood.'

Sweating in the heat they dug coals from the banked campfire, laid another two fires and burnt ironwood on all three. However the wind might shift it would carry the smoke of ironwood to the beast. They put water in a pannikin near it with a rabbit from Merv's last catch, but the creature only snarled and drew back. It would not eat or drink.

The men sank down in the shade beyond the fires and drank water. Time was still suspended, but as they rested it began again. They ate a little of the remains of the stew. They even turned and looked at each other. What the look said could not be spoken or written, but they understood.

Wirrun rewound the fur cord of the power. 'Bit by bit,' he said heavily. 'How does a man make a man?' The beast's eyes were on him; the blood welled a little from its wounded shoulder and he was too tired to try to wash it.

Merv shifted and spoke. 'We broke his teeth on ironwood. That's first . . . Burn off his pointy ears with the leaves . . . cut off his claws and make hands and feet . . . skin him . . . give him a new skin and insides.'

Wirrun laughed harshly. 'That all? That's what. I said how.' He had never heard of this impossible magic but he counted on Merv who was of the country. Merv shifted again.

'That's all I know, Ice-Fighter. How is for you.'

In his rage and despair Wirrun stood up and walked out of the camp, leaving Merv alone to watch over the beast.

'Bit by bit,' muttered Merv watching him go. He had done what he knew, but he was no hero or holder of a power. The next bit would come from the Ice-Fighter. Merv stayed in camp and kept up the fires and saw that they made the beast drowsy. He drew water and rummaged in his pack for the makings of a meal. As evening came on the beast grew restless and savage and he tightened the rope that held it. And while he did this Wirrun lay sleeping under trees.

They were ironwood trees; he had walked along the hill until he found them. He lay down under them, battered and weary, gazing upward through leaves at the distant soaring of cliffs; and he thought of Ularra and the making of a man. It would be by no mere cutting with knives. It would be done by Clever Men of the People and by the powers of the country. And though he was hero and Ice-Fighter he did not know the country or its powers. He laid his hand on his own power that was known in all countries as Ko-in had said; and he knew he must journey to the country of his fathers and seek the help of spirits. He did not think how he must make this journey but only that he must make it. And he lay with his hands closed about the power and slept.

And while he slept his spirit slid out of his body as the spirits of his People had done for a thousand ages when they must journey fast and far. He hovered above his weary body and left it sleeping and took only the spirit of the power that lay in its hands. It was like taking the shadow and leaving the stone.

His spirit felt the powers of that country: they brooded in the stern cliffs that loomed against the sky, they watched from the shadows and lay along the winds, and they did not know him but waited to know. He thought of the camp where Merv was alone with the beast amid these powers—and he was there. He laid a power on the beast to quieten it and on Merv for rest and renewal, and he did this by the welling up of power within himself and by willing it. Then he thought of the mountain that was like home to him and lay far down the land to the south; and in a flowing of hills and washing seas, of sunny plain and shadowed forest and a blown-away screeching of Happy Folk, he was there. The quiet of the mountain received him, the township dreamed in the sun on the ridge below.

He stood in his old camp under the wall of rock, and out of the rock flowed the love-singing of his haunting. But his spirit knew that it came through rocks from deep places far off and had laid hold only of the ears and mind that were sleeping in the north.

He laid his fire in the old place, the first place.

'Welcome, Hero,' said Ko-in. His tone was grave, for this was Wirrun's first spirit-journey and the dream-travel of the spirit is a grave matter and dangerous. So Ko-in wasted no time in asking or listening but answered at once the question Wirrun had brought.

'A man does not make a man. That is for greater powers. A man makes the Clever Business that calls up the power. If you cannot know the old business you must call on your strength to make a new one.'

'You gave me a power known in all countries,' Wirrun reminded him. 'Can't you give me a business that's clever in all countries?'

'I know none,' said Ko-in. 'It must be your business and you must make it. Yet I may feed your ears with a thought or two. Before the man can be made the beast must be unmade as you were told: its ears, its skin, its insides. How does a man do this to a beast? How does he unmake the wallaby and turn it into a meal?'

Wirrun let the words of Ko-in feed his ears. 'He cooks the wallaby in the earth.'

'And how do we drive the evil out of a sick and aching man?'

There were many ways; but Wirrun's spirit reached out to Ko-in and took the one he meant. 'We cook the sick and aching man gently in the earth with water and leaves.'

Ko-in bowed his head. 'Is not the cooking-pit a grave to the wallaby and the steaming-pit a grave to the evil? Has the earth no power for its creatures? Tell me, is a grave an end or a beginning?'

This at least Wirrun knew well from the People. 'It's the end of one thing and the beginning of another.' He too bowed his head. 'I thank you, Ko-in.'

Ko-in smiled gravely. 'Only you can make a business from my words, Clever One. When you have used your strength for your friend use it again for your People. Travel well and safely. I may send the night to carry news if you leave an ear awake.'

He sprang up among leaves and was gone. Wirrun heaped earth on his fire and travelled through a flowing of mountains and slow rivers back to the north where his body slept below cliffs. It was safe. He slid into it and felt it pressing the ground again, and the air pumping cool in its lungs, and the power soft and hard in its hands. He slept until evening and woke and went back to the camp.

The beast snarled and grunted struggling on a tightened rope; but it quieted as Wirrun came out of the dusk.

'Been away,' said Merv, heating a can at the fire.

'Far and fast,' said Wirrun. 'I'm hungry.' He laid one hand on the older man's shoulder—very lightly, for his spirit still tingled and he did not know if Merv might feel it prick. 'Time you turned in, mate. I'll watch the night. I got thinking to do.' The beast turned its eyes on him, old with despair. He could not speak to it.

He must sit through the night with the beast and make a business, a magic, his first. It must come not from his mind but from his spirit, and reach out to the powers of this country that he did not know. He must let the beast Ularra fill him with horror and with love.

He did so, keeping up the fires while Merv slept exhausted. When the beast grew wild with night and snarled at the sly-moving dark or the far-off stars he spoke to it quietly and shivered. For the first time since the night Ko-in gave it to him he unwound the cord of the power and held it bare, frost-sparkling in the firelight for the dark to see. The night stilled; he felt its awe. His spirit called to the powers in it that Wirrun, Ice-Fighter and holder of the great quartz crystal, sought to remake his friend Ularra from the beast; that all the land was his country and his business was for all its powers. He claimed their help.

At dawn Merv woke to see Wirrun rifling his pack in search of breakfast.

'Nothing much but sardines and toast,' he called when he saw Merv watching. 'Better come and have it. We gotta dig an oven.'

Merv crawled out of his blanket and went to the creek to splash his face. The next bit was coming sure enough.

Two

It was a hard remaking as it had to be; hard for all of them. The gully, its hours of sunlight shortened by the cliffs, was cooler than the ridges above yet hot enough. The fires of ironwood had to be kept up and the men sweated as they worked. Meals were not easy, for Merv's astonishing pack was at last running low in supplies.

They dug their oven in the sandy soil by the creek.

'No spades,' muttered Merv in displeasure for he did not like to be caught poorly equipped.

'The old People never had 'em,' Wirrun retorted. He was tense with worry about the beast.

It lay in its rope cowed by daylight and the ironwood smoke. It had not eaten or drunk or slept and perhaps had no need. But it watched them with brooding eyes and Wirrun thought the eyes had darkened, and that Ularra no longer looked out of them. They no longer begged for pity. Wirrun toiled at the digging in dread that he might remake the body of his friend and fail to remake his mind.

'He's taming,' said Merv trying to comfort him. 'They gotta tame, even when they're turned back. Can't be quicker.'

They dug with sharp-ended branches of ironwood and lifted out the loosened sand with pannikins. The trench was long and wide enough for Ularra to lie in and nearly three feet deep. The sand they dug was heaped beside it, ready to be filled in again.

'More like a grave than an oven,' said Merv, surprised at the depth of the trench.

'It's that too,' said Wirrun. 'An oven's a grave for a wallaby.'

When the trench was dug they collected fallen sandstone from under the cliffs to lay in it. They paved with flat stones the whole of its floor, and on the stone they laid a fire of ironwood. Wirrun took the small axe up the hillside and brought back more ironwood while Merv, after inspecting his pack, dug yams to roast and filled a billy with yabbies caught in the creek so that they might eat. It gave Wirrun courage that at this time they should eat the old food taken in the old way. The crayfish should have been roasted on stones instead of boiled in a billy, and there should have been no crayfish-flavoured tea to follow, but the meal was the land's gift as it should have been and it gave him strength.

'That's lunch,' said Merv. 'Better think about tonight—a man's no good without his tucker. There'll be duck on the swamp down the creek. If you're all right here I'll see what I can do. Set a trap or two on the way for tomorrer.'

'I'd be in a mess without you,' said Wirrun in thanks. Merv knew it. He went off down the creek with his knife on his belt, a ball of string in his pocket and a few wire snares in his hand.

Wirrun lit the fire in his oven which was also a grave, and sat feeding the fire and wiping the sweat from his face. The beast watched and brooded, and sometimes snarled and fought in sudden anger till the smoking fires quietened it again. The heat of the oven forced Wirrun farther back as the great fire roared and laid down its bed of coals. All the earth about it was warm and the stones beneath cracked with heat. Wirrun fed it and watched the sun pass over and thought with dread of the next bit. When the sun had passed he left the fire to die and went with the axe to bring back leafy outer branches of ironwood. To drive out sickness and aching the leaves would have been eucalypt, but he was treating another evil. As he dumped the last of his load beside the trench Merv came back through the river-oaks. He carried a duck by the legs, its head hanging limply down.

'Just in time,' said Wirrun tightly.

Merv hung the duck from a branch and came silently, watching under his brows. What Wirrun did he did.

They took their digging-sticks and raked over the coals in the trench to hurry their dying. They filled billy and tin cans and pannikins with water and stood them ready. When the coals were black they laid on top armfulls of leafy branches, a deep and springy bed. Then Wirrun took a spray of green leaves to the fire nearest the beast; what he knew of the old business he would carry out. Merv followed.

Wirrun held his small branch in the fire till the leaves smoked and crackled. He strode quickly behind the beast, and it roused as he came and lunged against the rope snarling. Its eyes lit red and Merv stood by the rope. With the power in his hand and dodging as the beast twisted and snarled, Wirrun beat it lightly about the head and ears with his crackling branch. It fought in the rope, snarling viciously, snapping broken fangs, striking with talons, and the smell of singed hair mingled with the smell of burning leaves, but Wirrun knew the beast was not hurt. It fought against healing and against man and perhaps against fear, but not against pain. This light singeing was all that Wirrun's pity could stand of the business of burning off its ears.

Perhaps a power reached it, for it slumped on the rope as Wirrun threw his dead torch into the fire. He and Merv untied the rope and dragged the beast between them to the oven, sweating and grunting. Sometimes it roused and lumbered a few paces and sometimes it pulled back. When it smelt the heat and the leaves it grew wild and snarled and snapped and fought again, and they prodded and levered it over the edge with their digging-sticks till it crashed down on the bed of branches.

'Take the evil out of this man!' shouted Wirrun. He did not know if his lips shouted, but his spirit did. It shouted to cliffs and hills, to watching shadows and the remoteness of trees. 'Give him back his skin and his insides and his brain! Take the beast out of him and make him Ularra again!'

The beast struggled and roared. Wirrun grabbed the billy and poured water into the pit till a cloud of steam rolled out of it. He poured in all the water and passed each container to Merv who filled it again. When the steam thinned and the beast lay still and grunting they pushed earth back into the pit and covered it all but its head. Then they left it.

They had not spoken one word to each other during this business and they did not now. They sat wearily in camp with their backs to the pit and their faces to the fire. Now and then the beast whined as Wirrun had heard it whine inside the cave. Sometimes it grunted as if it struggled in its rope under the sand. Mostly it was silent. Wirrun sat slumped and heavy; his eyes were open but his spirit was not in them.

The sky above the gully was still lit with sun and the tops of the western cliffs glowed. Merv roused himself to fetch the duck and set about preparing a meal. Wirrun stirred, and in a little while rose and left the camp to wander listlessly up the creek.

He went like a feather in a breeze, moving some way and resting, carried on by a thought, stopping again to look at a stone; and as he went his spirit came back to him. He felt like a man who has been through a long illness or a long sorrow: all that could go out of him was gone, all that could be used had been used. What was left must start again. He thought of Ularra and the horror of the beast, and called up strength to wait. He thought of the Abuba and knew she was not wicked but an earth-thing as the land had made her. He remembered the Mimi—she too was an earth-thing as the land had made her. He thought of the tailed women from whom a darkness seemed to flow, and they reminded him of the trouble of his People and the People's trust in him. He even remembered, with a wry smile for so small a thing and a hand ruffling his hair, that his leave was over and his job in the city probably lost with Ularra's.

In this wandering and thinking he came at last through a hush of river-oaks to the wide silent water under the cliffs, and here he stopped in a sort of astonishment. The water pulled at him like a magnet; it drew and charmed him; he longed to strip off his clothes and jump in. He would have done it except for the burnt-out weariness that held him. As it was he stood looking for a long time, telling himself that he would come back in the warmth of the day and never mind the camp's drinking-water . . . And it was here that the Ninya had come; here deep in the gorge and not high on the lookout of the cliffs. That was strange . . . but they might have come through the cave . . . He wandered on into that, but not much farther than the entrance, for he was no more ready for the Abuba or the tailed women than he was for the pool. He went only to the edge of the twilight and leaned against the rock wall to look and remember and think.

He felt the howling through the rock before his mind caught it. He shivered and jerked, thinking at first that it was the beast; but the beast had never howled. This was the wild and heart-stopping howl of a dingo. It came faintly with distance from deep within the cave, and was caught and answered and built into a pack of howling, and died away at last.

Wirrun's face was set, for the blood was cold in his veins. There could be dingoes deep inside the cave but he knew there were not. This was a spirit-howling, and it brought him a deeper chill than the trouble that flowed from the tailed women. Well, he was not ready for it. He went out of the cave and back down the creek to the camp.

The first stars were out when he reached it, and Merv was waiting to serve the roasted duck. They looked at each other and nodded, two tired drained men ready to eat. They would have spoken then, but some struggle broke out in the pit; the beast struggling against its rope, snarling and grunting. It held them silent.

When they had eaten and cleaned the camp and built up the wood-heap and banked the fire, always with their backs to the pit, Wirrun did speak at last. He put his hand again on Merv's shoulder for a moment and said, 'You turn in, mate. I'll be—around.' For he knew that in the night, when the beast was wild and darkness flowed about, he must stay awake with the power, near but not too near. Merv nodded and rolled himself into his blanket near the fire. Wirrun pulled on a sweater and sat leaning against a tree with his legs in his sleeping-bag for warmth. He did not unwind the power again for the business was done. He only sat with the ball of possum-fur cord between his hands feeling it thrum; feeling in its roundness the curve of the sky and the turning of the world; seeing in his mind the crystal coloured like a pink-tinged cloud and magic with the sparkle of rain, the power that was known in all countries of this land.

For a long time he sat awake and listening but the pit

was mostly as silent as the camp and now and then he dozed. But sometimes there were sounds, of struggling and snarling or of whimpering and fear. Then Wirrun sat tense and his spirit sought help for the beast in the pit. In the first hour of morning he leapt out of a doze and sat gripping the power: for the first time there was a howl from the pit and it was the howl of a man. He did not go. He sat rigid and listening for another hour. Then he came out of his sleeping-bag running.

'Oh man—oh man—let me out—' howled Ularra's voice in fear and fury.

Wirrun was by the pit, peering in the starlight, seeing Ularra's face and almost weeping for its wild and angry despair. He was groping through sandy soil feeling for hands and feet free of claws—groping to loosen rope and scoop away sand—bringing water to wash the sandy face and wet the heat-dried lips. 'You're all right, mate, you're all right,' he gabbled as Ularra began to heave out of the earth—and suddenly he laughed a little and dropped down by the pit and slept.

Merv reached the pit only a few minutes later. He found Wirrun sleeping beside the pit and Ularra crouched on it, head down over the billy which was tilted between his jaws while he sucked noisily at the water. Merv frowned and thought. Then he took up one of the ironwood digging-sticks and with careful judgement brought it down on Ularra's head.

Three

In the new daylight Wirrun woke astonished. He was in his sleeping-bag a little way from the pit where Merv had rolled him. Ularra too was in his sleeping-bag; roped in. His head was raised on a pile of branches and Merv was trying to feed him with roasted yam and the remains of the duck. Ularra shouted curses, butted the yam away with his head but snapped viciously at the duck.

'You're driving him mad!' yelled Wirrun struggling out of his bag.

Merv looked up, backing away from the snapping jaws. He answered firmly.

'Gotta tame him first. I told you. He's still a little bit beast.'

Then Wirrun looked and saw that Ularra's eyes, which had once begged for pity from the head of the beast, now held the red light of the beast's anger of yesterday. His joy was dimmed and he came slowly to the pit.

'How long?'

'Ah,' said Merv. 'A day or two, that's all. We'll have him out of the bag with the two of us, and just his hands tied. He'll be thankful when he knows. That was a good quick turning, Ice-Fighter, and none of the old ones to help. I'm proud I saw it.'

'Let me out let me out let me out—' roared Ularra.

'I'm proud you're proud,' said Wirrun to Merv. 'Well, it was my turning sure enough and not the old one, and I don't keep a little bit back for later. This man stood the turning and if it wasn't good enough that's not his fault. I won't have him roped like a dog. He's my friend Ularra. He can suit himself when he remembers it.' He laid the power against Ularra's tossing head and loosened the rope and stood back.

Merv dropped the duck and leapt back too.

Ularra writhed and heaved and sat up. His hands erupted from the bag and seized the fallen duck; he held it hard against his chest with one arm while the other reached for the billy. He tried to put his head into the billy, found that he could not, tipped it up and drank as the water ran down his face. Then he heaved himself free of the bag and stood, half crouching, unbalanced, weak from his turning and from hunger and thirst. Only fear and fury had given him the strength to struggle. Merv saw it and relaxed.

Wirrun spoke to him softly. 'Come on, Ularra man. Back to camp for a proper feed.'

Ularra looked at him with brooding eyes, turned and slouched away stumbling up the hill. Sometimes he went stooped, helping himself with hands as well as feet; sometimes he toppled over and sat and rested; but he did not, as Wirrun dreaded, turn towards the cave of the Abuba. He crawled away out of sight among trees.

'Sorry,' said Wirrun to Merv. 'I had to.'

'Can't be helped then,' said Merv. 'We'll just stick together for a bit.' He took up the billy and one of the sleeping-bags while Wirrun coiled the rope.

They went silently back to camp. The business was over, the turning had worked, but there was no joy in it yet. There was only a new sense of strain. For Merv it lay in the danger of the untamed man wandering free and unseen. For Wirrun it came from the beast-look in Ularra's eyes and in his clumsy shambling movements. Wirrun had slept only a few hours in two nights and days. Merv had been up and busy since he found the hero sleeping by the pit where the beast-man grovelled. Most of his work had been undone when Wirrun untied the rope, but at least there remained a damper cooked in the ashes for breakfast.

They boiled the billy and ate and drank. Wirrun put Ularra's sleeping-bag in its old place and set beside it a pannikin of water, with roasted yam and a part of the damper wrapped in Ularra's spare shirt.

'Man's food,' said Merv, watching. He was alert to every sound and movement, watching for a shadow, listening for a stumbling rush. Wirrun saw it and tried to argue.

'He can't do much, poor bloke.'

Merv was not reassured. 'He'll get his strength back quick when he eats and drinks.' He went on watching and listening for two days more, insisting that he and Wirrun should stick together and that one of them should always be awake.

Wirrun too watched and waited; he watched for his friend and waited to see the turning complete. It was an anxious waiting, but now that his part was done another waiting mingled with the first and troubled him too: he was aware of the cave that waited in the gully. There lay the business that was not yet done, the business of the land and the People; the screeching of the tailed women came often into his ears, or the wild and lonely howling of a dingo. Yet he could not go into the cave leaving Ularra roaming wild and Merv watching shadows; he could not go with a mind half free and unrested. Sometimes his mind caught a falling phrase of music, of dark or bright water and flowing hair; he would have been tense and irritable, an easy prey to the love-singing, if Merv had not kept him busy.

For Merv too had another care: since now they must live off the country he would make the Ice-Fighter free of it as he himself was free of it. He showed Wirrun his own rabbit-traps: snares of wire carefully triggered, set and cocked with a stone or stick or tree-limb on the site. 'Don't take so many but you take 'em like a man should.' He taught Wirrun to set the snares, for rabbit and for other small game. He took Wirrun foraging for berries and roots, and showed him which could be eaten at once and which needed to lie in the creek till the poison was washed out of them. He showed him which creek-holes were rich in yabbies and where to look for fish. He took Wirrun downstream to the swamp and showed him how to snare a duck among the reeds.

When Wirrun first saw the swamp he halted, frowning and wary. Merv waited, following his gaze. 'Grass,' he explained. 'Biggest you ever saw. More like that cane they grow, eh? Or that bamboo. They never grew this, though. Just swamp-grass.'

Wirrun relaxed, remembering that Merv knew nothing of his haunting or the Mimi's advice. Merv had brought him to take a duck, and not because a tall grass grew on the farther margin of the swamp.

Once or twice as they went about the gorge they heard stones rattle under a foot or saw branches wave as something pushed a way through. Once as they walked up a ridge a figure went at a shambling run over its crest and away. Once something splashed in a hole in the creek, and when they reached it the water was heaving and tossing. Wirrun thought painfully of Ularra lying in the water to soak away two days of fires and smoking. He and Merv never spoke of it but only waited till the sounds had gone.

Towards evening of the first day they came back to camp and stood under the oaks looking and frowning. The camp had been visited. The campfire, which had been banked, was black and steaming with the strong smell of wet ash and charcoal; the billy lay beside it. The dead remains of the other two fires were beaten and scattered about the camp. Packs had been torn open and emptied on the ground. Merv strode to Ularra's sleeping-bag and looked up smiling.

'He's took it—man's food! Wouldn't touch it this morning.'

Wirrun grinned back and ran quickly round the camp looking and calling, but there was no one.

'Give him another day,' said Merv.

They put the camp in order again and lit a new fire. That night they slept and watched in turn. During one of Wirrun's watches there was a scuffling in the darkness near at hand. He spoke to it softly.

'Come and have a feed of stew, mate.'

When there was no answer he took a pannikin of stew into the night and left it a little way from the camp. In the morning he found it empty, but there was no sign of what had eaten the stew.

On the second day, still weary after their broken sleep, he and Merv came early back to the camp and rested by turn during the afternoon. Their foraging had by now restocked the camp for several days and taught Wirrun enough of this country. A duck and a rabbit, wrapped in cloth, hung from branches of an oak; a pile of yams lay between stones in the creek. Merv, satisfied, slept in the shade. Wirrun used his turn of watching to build up the woodheap with fresh wood.

He was bringing back his second load when a movement along the hill caught his eye: a loose-limbed figure ambling towards the southern cliffs. It was Ularra, headed towards the Abuba's cave. Wirrun dropped his wood and went quickly into the cover of trees along the creek. He would not interfere unless he must, but he could not let Ularra go back into the cave. He ran up the creek among its trees, pausing now and then to sight the Abuba's cave in the cliff. If Ularra began to climb . . .

Ularra did not climb. He stood under the cliffs and shouted. Wirrun heard his voice ragged with anger and despair, and the cliffs mocking him as they threw it back, and was chilled as he listened.

'Girl, girl!' shouted Ularra. 'Why did you call me, then?' Nothing answered but the cliffs.

'What sort of thing are you, then?' shouted Ularra. 'Did you want a beast to tear you? Call me now, girl! Call me again. I'll tear you.'

Wirrun listening was torn himself and crept away up the creek. This was a painful and private shouting, not meant to be heard even by a friend; but it was the shouting of a man. Ularra must be left alone to work out his pain and protest, and Merv could safely sleep alone in the camp. Wirrun crept on till the gully wall hid him and he found himself beside the pool. He sat beside it to rest in the cool and to wait. He could not by any power take away what Ularra must suffer, but he was full of relief and thanks that it was Ularra himself who suffered.

After a while through his relief he felt the water tugging at him as before. The afternoon was still warm and almost unknowing he tugged off his clothes, folded the power into them, and slid into the pool. At once all his senses were lost in it.

The water wrapped him, icy and silken, and drew him under. The singing drowned him, cool like moonlight and sweet like honey. He gave himself to the water knowing that he would drown. The singing swirled down with him note by note and word by word.

> *I sing in the sunlight*
> *with dark eyes aglimmer:*
> *are you not coming?*
>
> *I sing in the shadows*
> *with dark hair down-flowing:*
> *are you not here?*

His feet sank through a softness of mud among stones and moved a little of themselves, seeking to stand. This instinctive movement was enough to set him rising through the still water. He broke the surface and breathed, and the singing stopped. The bank was at his shoulder; like a sleeper struggling to wake he threw up an arm and drew himself inch by inch out of the pool. Fear did not come till he lay on the bank prickled by oak-needles. Anger and loss came with it, but fear moved his hand to reach for and grasp the power.

After a moment he sat up shaken and rested his head on his knees and let the warm day breathe over him, healing and soothing. He listened: there was only silence under the cliffs. Slowly and tiredly he put on his clothes and went back down the creek. As he went a thought came unquestioning into his mind.

'That was the old water, her own that she keeps for herself.'

He did question it a moment later for he could not recall the flat mineral taste of the old water, and the creek that ran from the pool was as sweet and soft as any creek. Yet he dismissed the question; however the water came filtered and sweet to the sunlight he knew it was the old water. His lips tightened eagerly at the thought that he might go back into the pool and search for the way the water entered, filled with the love-singing. He gave up that idea when the fear stirred again, and he thought of dark water-filled tunnels that might run for miles.

The sun was high on the cliffs when he reached the camp, and evening was beginning. Merv was awake and cutting up a rabbit; he looked under his brows at Wirrun but made no remark about having been left alone. Perhaps the shouting from the cliffs had wakened him. Wirrun brought in the load of wood he had dropped and then, for pure weariness of body and spirit, lay on his sleeping-bag and slept.

He woke in the cool of dusk, with the stars pricking out and the smell of stew in the camp.

'Can't live on rabbit,' said Merv serving it up. 'We'll have fish for a change tomorrer.' He had dished a third portion into a pannikin, and Wirrun carried it to the place he had left it last night.

'Give him another day,' said Merv with certainty.

They ate their own stew in quiet by the fire and Merv spoke again thoughtfully. 'That Abuba. Not its fault. You can't blame a snake when you get bit.'

'I know that,' Wirrun agreed.

'That Abuba's itself: what it is. Your friend made it into something else: what he wanted.'

'That's right,' said Wirrun. He knew now that Merv had heard the painful shouting at the cliff, and that Merv too knew it should not have been heard even by a friend.

'Heard a man once,' said Merv sucking a bone. 'One of them Happy Folk. In a pub, it was. He said a man makes his own god the way he wants. Ah. Might be. Dunno how you'd know. He'd better have said a man makes his own woman the way he wants. And gets mad when she stays what she is, same as him.'

'Um,' said Wirrun. He knew that Ularra had made the Abuba into what he wanted, but he felt that the Abuba had had some hand in this.

'Ah,' said Merv. 'You're young. Tired too, by the look of you—that bit of a nap wasn't much. I'll take first watch. See you when the Cross turns over.'

'You won't see it,' said Wirrun, for the Southern Cross in the sky would have sunk below the cliffs before it turned in the old bushman's sign. He went to sleep knowing that Merv would wake him by some other star-sign.

It was past midnight when he did wake, and Merv had not called him. He was wakened by a grunting and scuffling near at hand. He lay alert and still, searching the camp from under his eyelids. Merv was sitting by the fire and only his stillness showed that he too was alert.

The scuffling came again. It was very near.

'See you, Ularra,' murmured Wirrun drowsily.

'See you, man,' muttered Ularra sliding down into his sleeping-bag.

Four

When Wirrun woke again sunlight streamed into the gorge yet the camp was still. He sat up quietly. Merv grunted in his sleep by the fire: he had given up, then, and abandoned his watch without waking Wirrun. And there lay Ularra in his own place. Even in sleep his face looked worn but he lay free-limbed and himself. Worn! They were all worn, and only sun and a sense of waiting had roused

Wirrun. He got up quietly and went down to the creek to splash his face.

The water felt cold and alive. Strange that it flowed out of the pool in the gully and yet felt so alive. There was no singing in it, or any fear or loss. He stayed looking at it while it ran down his face; and perhaps there was some power in it for he saw clearly the mud-caked spring out west where the heatwaves shimmered with a memory of old seas. He saw the Jugi in its cave, and the tall wispy Mimi sending him forth alone, and the tailed women struggling. He felt again the trouble looming over him while he waited for Ularra. He would wait as long as was needed, but the trouble reached for him. And through it he felt someone else come beside him at the creek. He spoke with his eyes on the water.

'It's the old water, this. Sweetens up somehow.'

He thought he spoke to Merv, but when he looked he found Ularra kneeling beside him. Ularra's face, worn and twisted, was turned up to the cliffs.

'She's old all through,' he said thickly. 'Old and bitter.'

'But she sweetens.' Wirrun let the water dry on his face while he spoke to his friend. 'It was my first time, mate. Sorry I didn't do it better. I was—scared.'

Ularra's gaze came back to him from the cliffs. 'All the time,' he said, 'when I couldn't—when I was—*that,* I counted on you. There was a little bit left somewhere. It counted on you.'

'I know that. It made it worse. I was—scared and bleeding.'

Ularra nodded. 'I saw, man. I saw you bleeding.'

They said no more. They never spoke of the turning again. But Wirrun was thankful, that day and later, for that one moment of direct speaking.

He was glad of it at breakfast, another damper made from the last of Merv's flour. Wirrun saw that Ularra would not eat near the fire in the old way but took his mug of tea and went farther off. He held himself with care like a man who fears he has drunk too much, keeping a distrustful watch on himself and all around him. Merv broke the damper into three equal parts, but Ularra's part he broke again and offered him half.

'The rest soon. You're starved, boy.'

Ularra's eyes flared red and his lips drew back. In a moment he made an effort, relaxed, took the first piece quietly, and waited a while before he ate the second.

Merv did not seem to have noticed. He looked placidly at the two young men and breathed on his tea to cool it. 'Ah. A good day. Feels like a holiday. Only we gotta get some fish before we turn into rabbits.' He drank his tea, put down the empty mug, stood up and stretched. 'Coming fishing?' he invited Ularra.

Ularra looked at him sideways, looked to Wirrun and seemed uncertain. Wirrun crushed a pang of uneasiness.

'You go,' he suggested. 'He'll show you the country. I gotta think what next.'

Like a dog at a word from its master Ularra got up and followed Merv. Wirrun watched frowning. He had never, like Merv, feared danger from Ularra and he would not fear it now. He had done all he could; the rest was for time and for Ularra himself. For Wirrun trouble was waiting and reaching out. He could feel it in the heat and silence and in the shadowed cliffs. They hung against the sky like a great stone beehive angrily humming, and he knew he must soon go into the cave. He knew it with eagerness and dread.

He got up to wander restlessly, and his feet took him again up the creek and into the gully. The pool beckoned, sweet and dangerous, and he passed it with an angry shrug. He would not know what the pool had told him. He went into the cave as far back as the twilight and leaned against the rock with his hands pressed to it. The cliffs stood over him mounting to the sky; the gorge itself lay between the bones of the land. He could feel the twilight leading away deeper and deeper into dark. A First Dark, never broken by sun or moon; an utter dark that would clot here and there into the land's oldest creatures. Could a man, even one with a power, go into such a dark and still be? Would he not cease to exist?

He remembered with panic that he had no torch. It was a senseless thought but he had to fight to crush it. In such a dark as that First Dark a torch was a tiny irrelevance; he would take the power that was all his strength, and maybe a firestick in the old way, and wait for what came. If he must go there must be a way, and it was not by means of a torch. He thought of spirit-travel, sleep-travel—and shuddered. A frail human spirit drifting in that dark among such creatures . . .

He was about to turn away to the light when the rocks vibrated to the sound he had felt before: the weird wild crying of a dingo that was answered and grew. He went away shivering, full of a dread that he would not face though it sank deep into him and stayed. The dingo crying in the dark . . .

When he reached the camp Ularra was there skinning catfish. The billy was boiling on the fire. Wirrun looked sharply round the camp.

'Where's Merv?'

'Gone,' said Ularra. He watched Wirrun sullenly from under his brows. Wirrun's uneasiness tightened into a knot but he forced himself to sit quietly down on oak-needles. Ularra's face twisted into a bitter smile.

'Can't ever be sure, can we?' he said.

'Dunno,' said Wirrun, for he would not at this time pretend to misunderstand anything Ularra said. 'That's your problem; you'll have to sort it out. Where's Merv gone?'

'Home. Left a message.'

'Go on, then. What?'

Ularra's hands were still while he thought. 'Said he was proud to help when needed but he never meant to stay so long and he's got skins to see to. He'll keep an eye, and a fire in a dead tree'll fetch him if he's wanted. He said . . . something like . . . maybe a man can make a god or a woman but a friend's got to come bit by bit.' Ularra frowned, checking his memory. 'That's all, I reckon.'

The knot inside Wirrun loosened for that was certainly a farewell message from Merv. After this he would stick to what he knew and leave doubts of Ularra to Ularra.

'Uh,' said Ularra remembering. 'He said he won't forget.'

'Not easy, he won't,' Wirrun agreed. 'He showed you the country?'

'And fed me all the way. Little bits. Left us some gear too.' He nodded towards their packs and went to the creek to wash the fish. Wirrun strolled over to inspect the gear. He had already noted the billy on the fire and two pannikins near it with their own tin-can mugs. On his pack he found two of Merv's wire snares, a fishing-line wound on a bottle, and a tobacco tin with spare hooks and sinkers.

'He's thorough any rate.'

Ularra coming back with the fish grinned a normal grin. 'He's that. There's even bush lemons for the fish.'

'Yeah? I hope there's salt.'

They laughed like ordinary young men. It was so good that they went on doing it after the small joke was worn out. Wirrun watched with pleasure while Ularra, seeming to have conquered his dislike of the fire, laid the fish on hot stones to grill.

'We won't meet a better man than Merv,' he said firmly.

Ularra's lips tightened for a moment. Then he nodded.

They talked of fishing and hunting and living off the land. Wirrun pointed out that the catfish should have been grilled in their skins; Ularra looked startled and disgusted and they laughed again. They managed to scrape the fish into pannikins and ate them with salt and lemon.

'Man, that's *good*,' said Ularra cleaning every bone. His eyes darted sideways suspiciously as he ate, and Wirrun remembered how the beast and the wild man had starved.

Afterwards they lay on the brown needles of oaks and rested, and after a time Wirrun talked. He spoke of the cave and the anger of the tailed women; of the pool where the water was filled with his haunting and drew him down like a leaf; of the First Dark and the crying of the dingo. As he spoke the trouble reached out to him again so that he forgot Ularra and talked to himself. 'I gotta go in there and talk to those women . . . a torch is no good anyhow, I'd sooner have a firestick , . . and sleep-travel's worse . . .'

'NO!' roared Ularra. He was on his feet and standing over Wirrun. There was red anger in his eyes.

Wirrun sat up startled. 'Eh? What else can I do? I gotta talk to the ones with the tails; that's where the trouble starts. I know that, knew it when I first laid eyes on 'em.'

Words rattled in Ularra's throat but he couldn't speak them. He snarled and grinned, baring his teeth. He made a new effort and roared, 'NO!'

'Look,' Wirrun argued, 'what else am I here for?'

Ularra paced back and forth half-crouching. His mouth worked. Wirrun, fully awake at last, saw that this was unreasonable rage and spoke soothingly.

'Come on, mate, untwist now. I got the power, haven't I? What's going to hurt me while I've got that? Sit down, now. Come on. Sit down and talk it over.'

He talked on until Ularra quietened, looked confused and bewildered, and at last sat down.

'I said I won't sleep-travel,' Wirrun promised. 'I know that's risky. I'll go like I am with the power. You've seen 'em all taking notice of that. Nothing can hurt me.'

'It won't want to,' growled Ularra looking dark and confused. 'I'll tear it.'

Here was a new dilemma, for Wirrun had never for a moment thought of taking Ularra into the cave. That was a dark into which no man should go spirit-troubled—into which no man should go at all unless he must.

He tried a little teasing. 'Now where's your power, then? Been hiding it, have you? How many powers have we got any rate? And who'll be on the outside watching out for us? Who'll put a fire in a tree to fetch Merv if we want him?'

Ularra listened puzzled, but as soon as he understood he broke into a worse rage than before. He leapt up, striding half-crouched in a circle round Wirrun, choked words rattling in his throat. He stooped and picked up a stone, looked at it bewildered, dropped it and struggled for words. There was more than rage in the struggle, there was some deep pain and perhaps despair. He made a great effort like a stammerer and found words: 'That power—the haunting—never stopped! It's near!' He fought with himself. 'That grass—I know—swamp—tall grass—' He took a deep breath and grew suddenly clear. 'You get smoked or you don't go!'

And now Wirrun's face darkened. The haunting was his trouble, his own. He had carried it half across the land and back to its source; he would not be robbed of it now, he would not hear. He growled at Ularra.

'Give up, will you? It's my job and I'll do it. I never asked you to wipe my nose for me.'

'Never asked you!' roared Ularra twisting in pain. He fought for control. 'Not without smoking!' He picked up the stone.

Wirrun sat tight with rejection. His ears might be wearied, his spirit burdened, his body drawn down under water like a leaf, but the haunting was in him. He would not hear. Ularra stood over him, the red light in his eyes, threatening with the stone; and Wirrun, who had not feared the anger of the beast, saw at last that he needed to fear its protection. The shock of it opened his mind to fear itself, the fear of sweet drowning and the dingo in the First Dark.

'All right,' he mumbled. 'I said *all right!*' he yelled. And then, fighting like Ularra to control himself, 'If I get smoked will you stay on the outside and let me get on with it?'

Ularra dropped the stone. He stood confused and lost, holding on to himself. Breathing hard he went down to the creek and splashed his face and stood covering it with his hands. He came slowly back, shoulders hunched, so bitter and defeated that Wirrun felt a stab of hope. But with the defeat still on his face Ularra said, 'Now?'

And there was no other way to keep him out of the cave. Wirrun stood up, sullen and defeated himself. He grunted, 'Mind, you gotta do your bit too.'

Ularra nodded. He looked despairing.

They went down the creek to the swamp, Ularra slouching ahead and Wirrun after him. Wirrun's mind cried out for the sweet burning coolness of the singing, and when another voice rose through it he pushed it down. But the voice rose again: *I think you do need help . . . fight it with the smoke of a tall grass.* In the core of himself he knew that the Mimi's day had come, that Ularra was right, that he would be mad to go into that cave without protection.

They left the creek as the swamp began and worked their way along its margin till the tall grass stood over them. They broke green branches for fire-fighting and chose a stand of grass that stood out into the swamp and beat through it to warn furred and feathered things. Then Ularra put a match to the dead lower leaves of the grass.

They were both smoked. Where the fire met the swamp it hissed and spat and died easily; but flames leapt high in the narrow leaves over their heads and threatened to spring on heated air or gases to other stands. They fought with sweat and tears running down their faces and their lungs aching with smoke, and Wirrun had no time to mourn for lost magic in his fear that Merv might see the smoke and come. When only dainty ruffles of smoke rose from the blackened stalks and they knew the swamp would take care of the rest, the two young men threw down their branches and staggered to the creek to drink.

They went silently back to the camp to prepare the next meal. Wirrun ached inside; yet he saw how Ularra's eyes followed him, brooding and questioning, and that Ularra was still locked in his strange and bitter defeat. He could not leave Ularra there. He roused himself to speak warmly and joke a little and to talk of the next day; and when he spoke of going into the cave he discovered a secret, wicked glee.

That was when he knew, with anger for his own secret triumph, that the smoking had not cured him.

5

The First Dark

One

That evening Ko-in sent the night to Wirrun with news.

He had taken his secret glee and his self-anger away from the camp and Ularra's brooding eyes. Self-anger became self-disgust and laid a slimy slug-track of failure over all he had done or tried to do. The plight of Ularra, torn from the safety of the city; his own enchantment, that he clung to while it crippled him; his shivering dread of the dingo in the dark; all these grew into the certainty of worse failures to come. He needed the strength of the hills leading up to the looming cliffs, and the sharp clean remoteness of early stars pricking a green sky. He went to them, leaving Ularra under the sighing oaks.

He set his sick spirit free and called for power. Power for his friend Ularra who was a man again but whose spirit remembered the beast. Power for himself: if not the power to be free then at least the power to wish to be free. And from somewhere a power came but it was neither of those. It was the power to do what he must in spite of failure: to go limping, if he must limp, with strength and courage. So Wirrun's spirit sought the indifferent stars and came back to him. And the night came, and the darkness thickened round him, and he saw that it waited for him.

'What are you?' he asked the darkness.

It answered him like a woman of the People. 'You know me for you have run from me. I bring one you do not know.'

The night gathered into the shape of a woman with a great sharp horn rising from each shoulder. Wirrun did know it: the horned woman from Ko-in's mountain that had run at him with its horns while he waited for the ice.

125

'Why are you here so far from your place?' he asked it, and it grinned slyly.

'What is one shadow when all the night wanders? Only the hero stays at home in these times. Ko-in stays to watch for strangers. He sends me to bring his wife with news.'

Wirrun was astonished for he had never known of Ko-in's wife. He had heard no tale of a spirit-woman as great and good as the hero, or gentle enough to need the protection of the horned one on a journey in troubled times. He waited to greet her with respect.

It came from behind the other. It was a hag, cruel and cunning. It carried a spear and a large net bag, and Wirrun's angry blood knew what they were for. It was wise of Ko-in to send with it a familiar shadow; without that Wirrun would not have believed that the hero could have taken a monster for a wife.

The shadows watched and grinned. The horned one spoke. 'Truly a wife for a hero, Bimpo-in who feeds on the People. She brings news.'

Wirrun held in his anger. It was not for these two old shadows bred by the land, and he had no right to be angry with Ko-in whom he loved. He only said, 'What news?'

Bimpo-in answered. Her voice was as cunning and cruel as her shape. 'Ko-in greets you. The trouble you seek is in his country too, but Ko-in is strong. From those that come and go he has found out the beginnings of the trouble.'

Wirrun could believe it. He remembered Ko-in's questioning of the Mimi when she wandered a stranger in his country. He nodded. 'Go on.'

'Small beginnings,' said Bimpo-in, and the two shadows nodded and grinned. 'There is one stranger lost in the deep places and that one angers the wives of Kooleen. For Kooleen and all his wives and children are tailed; they mock at the People and all who wear no tails. Now Kooleen would make this stranger one of his wives, a slimy thing without a tail!" The two hags hugged themselves and cackled. 'The wives are shamed and angry. They keep the stranger fast in a cavern and will not let Kooleen come.'

The shadows stood grinning. Wirrun knew well the darkness of trouble that flowed from the tailed women, yet he did not fully understand. He questioned the one with the spear. 'Are others angry too, then? Why does the trouble spread? Why do they leave their places and send others out of theirs?'

Bimpo-in shook her bag. 'Have you not ears? Are not the wives and children of Kooleen many, and their place far to the south? The angry wives divide, they and their children. Some hold their own place and some the caverns of the north, and so they drive others from their places and leave them nowhere to go. Are you a fool and earless?'

Wirrun frowned but stood thinking. 'Why does the old water flow in new ways? Is that from Kooleen and his wives? Or from the Ninya, maybe?'

Bimpo-in sneered. 'You have sent the Ninya home, Hero. Leave the land to care for its water.'

'That's my business,' said Wirrun sternly, 'and while I hold this stone you'll give me an answer.'

The bag shook impatiently. 'What answer? The Ninya's ice cracked some rock. The stranger is a water-spirit. One or the other may have opened new ways for the water. It is nothing to me. I have told what I know.'

The water-spirit trapped in the rocks where the dingo cried . . . the pool that sang and drew him under like a leaf. He would not know—but he was shaken. It was all he could do to send the shadows off with thanks to Ko-in. They flowed back into the night.

Wirrun wandered for a long time under the stars. He thought of two troubles, his own and the land's, and of the deep places where the stars were shut out. And Ularra lay under the oaks awake and despairing.

In the morning they went together to the cave. Wirrun carried a firestick with a smouldering point and Ularra looked at it with flashes of anger. He himself carried some remains of cold duck tied up in a spare shirt, and Wirrun frowned at that. He had said over and over that this first trip was no more than an exploration, that he would be out again soon; holding down his own foreboding and fear he had done and said all he could to lighten Ularra's. But Ularra came prepared to wait and kept his dark watch on himself, and his eyes still held defeat and sometimes fear.

It was the first time Ularra had entered the cave since he had seen the Abuba driven out of it. He gave it one flaring look, stood rigid, and fixed his eyes on Wirrun.

'You'll be cooler waiting under the trees,' said Wirrun

tightly. 'I won't be that long.' Ularra nodded. Wirrun wanted to tear himself roughly away for he could not much longer hold down his secret knowledge that the smoking had failed or hide eagerness and dread. He nerved himself to make one more effort, to leave Ularra in the old light-hearted way. 'Untwist, mate. Nothing to worry about. *You're* all right.' He patted the net bag at his belt. '*I'm* all right. See you.' He turned and strode into the twilight.

He looked back once. Ularra's tall and gangling shape was sharp against the light; he stood there as though he would not turn away until Wirrun came back from the cave. It was hard to leave him there so lost, but Wirrun waved the firestick and strode on. The night led away in front. He went into it.

As he went he wondered if perhaps after all it was only a small night, a single cave leading nowhere; if the tailed women had come into it through some spirit-path he could not follow. If that were so he could only wait in the cave itself and hope they would come again, and the dread could die away and the quivering hunger go unsatisfied; he could release this tightness. For a moment, reaching a hollowed wall of rock, he thought it must be so. He stood in the cave-night looking for darker shapes and saw at last a blackness to the right. He felt his way to it: it was a slit opening into deeper night. He stepped through.

Now the firestick became a red eye with a few inches of sight. He held it close to walls and floor peering with his one red eye. If he went with great care the dim red glow might just save him from potholes and ledges; it was not enough by which to find a way. He groped forward round a boulder and over a hollow but he could not tell where.

He turned back. The dark slit through which he had come was now a grey slit into the outer cave. He would have to work along walls to keep some idea of where he was. He found the wall and groped along it with his firestick. Something stirred behind him: a breath of air from outside, or a bat's wing or a fall of dust. His hand was on the power, questioning, but it did not throb. He went on.

Staring eyes—he stood rigid—the power was still—he raised the firestick. They were painted on the wall: eyes of charcoal and pipeclay, round and solemn and sad. As he moved the firestick over the wall the painted figure raised arms and spread its fingers in the red glow; it adjured him. He had not yet reached the First Dark. The fires of his People had lit this cave and their voices had sung here. If he lit a fire now he would see their hands spread like those of the figure, outlined in ochre, reaching out to him from the past and from forgetting. He felt those hands above him as he groped on along the wall.

His stick's glow vanished into a darkness it could not light, an opening deeper into the land. Wirrun hesitated, tightening his grip on that dread that would send him back and the hunger that would draw him on into any danger. In this second cave he could find himself even when his firestick burnt out: he need only crawl along walls and feel his way till he found the grey opening to the outer cave. But from here? Should he go on? Or should he wait under the painted hands of his People until something came to him? The power gave him no sign. He thought that if he could he must go deeper into the land before he waited.

He groped about for a loose stone, freed the end of the power's fur cord and drew it from the bag, unwound a length and tied it to the stone. That he wedged into the worn base of a boulder. Then, unwinding the cord, he entered the blackness. He could go at least some distance before the cord ran out.

He stood still and extended his arms: each found a wall. He was in a rock passage. He went on slowly, an elbow against one wall, the dark pressing close to his firestick and his uneasiness growing. There should be old things in this thick dark, yet as he fed out its cord the power lay inert, a stone without life. Then why did the air stir? He stopped to listen. Did something breathe? Had a stone moved under the rustle of a blind cave-snake? Was that the slither of dust or the scuttle of a spider? And why did the cord vibrate in his hand? Caught on a roughness of rock, maybe, and the air and the dust stirred by his passing. Yet there should be old things.

He went on.

Space widened and gaped, but only his skin felt it. He had reached the First Dark. He felt it like a massive monster, ancient and aware, waiting without warmth or cold or movement for his next most dangerous step. He did not take the step.

He set down the firestick with care: it was useless now but at least it remembered the light. He unwound more cord in the hope that he might crawl a little—and the dark thinned and light was glowing in his hand. The power under its wrapping shone in the First Dark. He pulled off the last of the cord and had light, dim and magical like starlight. He saw that from the broad ledge where he stood the dark vaulted up and down. With the light in his hand he dared to shout 'Hoo!' and heard the cry ring wide and come ringing back many times over. But for all his daring he knew he could not find a way down into the vault by the starlight of the stone. And while he thought this the power gave one throb in his hand and was still again.

He shouted, 'Come back here! What are you?' but the thing had gone. It had come and gone in a flash, spirit-fast, and he frowned and was uneasy again. There should be old things here in such a dark. Could they have felt his coming, felt the power, and fled to avoid it? He had not allowed for that, but the Mimi had once warned him that the need to obey was not always the wish. Well, he could not move without their help. He must keep still, play their game, and try to catch the next that came to peep. He sat down.

It was as well, for the moment he had dreaded and wished for was on him and his limbs and brain were weak and if he had been standing he might have run. The rock vibrated and hummed like a great bell humming into silence and the singing was under and over and all around. *Are you not coming . . . coming . . . coming . . . sings the bright water . . . sings . . . sings . . .* He shook and sweated as he gripped the rock and fought it. When it hummed into silence he wiped his face with his sleeve and sat fighting for resistance and strength.

So he was not ready when the power throbbed once more and was still, and that angered him and gave him back his wits.

'Come, whatever you are!' he roared, and the vault gave back the roar over and over but the power was still. There was only a clink of stone that his shouting might have disturbed, and a scuttle of tiny legs over his hand.

Wirrun swore. His frustrated mind remembered another spirit-telling: *There is no spirit in this land that would not help Wirrun the Fighter of Ice.* That had been the Yabon after the battle on the shelf, and he thought morosely that the Yabon had been wrong. To prove it he shouted again into the First Dark:

'Come on, then, all you that'll help the Ice-Fighter! I'm waiting, me that sent the ice back. I need help. What's coming?'

Silence. The stone was still. He swore again.

The power began to throb and its light to pulse.

He waited, rigid.

They came: darkness billowing like smoke. They had no shape firm enough for speech or seeing. Ancient and formless things of the First Dark, they only rolled about him like smoke and thinned away from the light in his hand. Wirrun was awed. They might be the land's First Thoughts, stored and remembered with the waters of its youth. He bent his head and covered the power and let them come.

He felt the dark thicken till he struggled to breathe. It supported him and bore him along the ledge and down, far down, by some long and twisting slope. The fur cord hanging loose from its net trailed behind him and reached its full length and was gone. Stones never disturbed slid behind him, ancient dust slithered. He stood on level rock; his foot touched water and the shadows drew him back. Without them he was nothing, he had ceased to be; no more than a passing thought in the unimagined dark.

But the First Dark had its own lights. He saw them, small cold lights that thinned the dark as they came and glimmered high and low. Others were coming. The shapeless shadows drew away from them into hiding and Wirrun uncovered the power. It flared and sank and flared, pulsing as the power throbbed. It and the tiny points of light were reflected in a dark pool at his feet, he could not tell for how far, which lights were reflected and which moved over rock.

When the little moving lights were near he saw that they were eyes and he knew them: the old bright eyes of the Nyols, the little grey people. He was glad to see them.

'You call,' they said in the soft rumbling voices he re-membered. 'We come.'

They were clustered at his feet and on rocks over his head watching him with their old bright eyes. Behind them he could see other shapes, most of them strange and some of them fearful, a crowd of shapes gathering in answer to his call. There were small hairy man-shapes, and bouncing shapes, and groping shapes like women without heads. He wished the Yabon might be among them but its place was on the surface of the land. These were all dwellers in the dark. He searched among them for the angry tailed women but none of those had come.

He spoke to the Nyols. 'Where are these tailed women, Kooleen's wives? I want to talk to them.'

They rumbled softly together exchanging glances like glow-worms and flickering the black pool with lights. They answered him in several voices. 'They not come.' 'They run, they hide.' 'They angry. They not come near.'

'They won't, won't they? Well, I'll have to go to them. Can you take me?'

Little grey heads were bent. 'We take you. Other one too?'

Wirrun was puzzled. 'Other one? What other?'

'Other man behind. One that follows.'

Wirrun's brows drew down. He swung round to the dark where the dust slithered, where a snake had rustled and a stone had fallen; behind him where, since he left the first cave, something had moved and breathed.

'Ularra!' he roared. 'Come out of that!'

Nothing stirred but the air. He turned back to the Nyols, those strong little wrestlers who watched bright-eyed. 'You fetch this other and we'll see,' he said.

They flowed past him in a tide of little grey bodies and scrambling limbs. They came back bearing Ularra strug-gling in their midst, and set him before Wirrun with his parcel of cold duck in his hand.

Two

Wirrun and Ularra faced each other in the First Dark in the dim light of the Nyols' eyes and the pulsing power. The tightness vibrating between them sent the old things wavering back. Wirrun glowered from under jutting brows. Ularra's face was set and determined, holding back fear. Wirrun drew breath to speak but Ularra got in first.

'It's no good, man. I got no choice. That smoking never took—it's like you never had it.'

So he had seen. Wirrun flinched and dropped his eyes. He growled, 'How did you get here any rate?'

'Same way you did.' Ularra opened his large hand and up sprang a released bundle of fur. The cord of the power had brought him silently following Wirrun. 'I was right behind.' His eyes widened and narrowed. 'Them old ones took me down after you.'

Wirrun swore. He waved the cord away. 'Shove it in your pocket, it might do you some good. Old ones! Look at 'em, then. Go on, look around. The ones without the heads, see? And the bouncing ones. A man's not meant to be here, mate.'

Ularra gave a small tight smile. 'A man's not, maybe. I'll do all right. If you can do it I can.'

'Do what?' roared Wirrun. 'What do you think you can do?' Ularra muttered something. 'Anxious! A pity, that is! Anxious! What about me, then?'

'I never said anxious,' Ularra flared. 'I said anchor.' But Wirrun, being launched, never noticed.

'Haven't I got enough on my hands and now you down here before you're ready? And getting you into the trouble—what about that?—standing there with the power and doing nothing? Anxious! What about dragging you out of your job in the first place? What about that?'

133

Ularra's eyes were sombre. His head was bent as if he listened to something other than Wirrun's raging. 'What about living, man?' he said gently. 'What about the wind?'

Wirrun turned abruptly away. The old things murmured in the silence. Now that the men had stopped quarrelling they drifted near again.

'Well—' said Wirrun at last. He looked for the Nyols. They clustered round him, waiting. 'Can you find these women of Kooleen's? Give 'em a message and bring me the answer?'

They nodded.

'All right. Tell 'em I know they're holding a stranger here and I know why. It's doing no good to anyone, just making trouble all round. Say—say I've come to take this stranger—back to its own place. Then they can stop worrying and go home. Tell 'em to bring the stranger to me here.'

'They not come,' said the Nyols, but some of them scurried off into the dark and some of them stayed.

'Well—' grunted Wirrun again. Ularra watched him with grim satisfaction; he knew that this change of plan was made on his account but he approved of it all the same. Wirrun ruffled a hand through his hair. 'Well . . . might as well have some lunch while we're waiting.'

Ularra nodded and began to untie his bundle.

They sat on the rock by the dark water, the rivers and rains of her youth hoarded and remembered. They ate cold duck while the First Dark flowed with ancient shapes watching curiously. They were two men in the eye of a cyclone, not speaking but clinging to peace.

And the love-singing struck again: a tingle in rock that Ularra could barely feel but that Wirrun heard like a bell humming into silence. The shadows stilled and listened. Wirrun sat tight and racked. Ularra watched him with brooding eyes that held fear. It died at last.

The Nyols nodded wisely at Wirrun, seeing that he heard what they did. 'That one sings,' they said, telling him aloud what till then he would not hear. 'That one Kooleen wants.'

He tried to reject it—but he had known since the pool drew him under and since Ko-in sent the night with news.

That his trouble and the land's were one; that to heal the land's trouble he must meet and resolve his own; that here in the immense and waiting dark Kooleen's women would bring him his own haunting. While he still trembled the rocks hummed again, chilling him with the lone, wild howling of the dingo.

'And that,' he whispered. 'What's that?'

They nodded again. 'That one cries. That water-spirit.'

And that too he had known: that the singing and the howling, the hunger and the dread, were the same. Wirrun stared into one dark and Ularra into another; they would not look at each other for there was fear in the eyes of both.

The shadows were listening again, this time to something Wirrun could not hear. The Nyols grew restless and rumbled together, all their heads turned to the curtain of blackness beyond the pool. Soon Wirrun saw a star-flicker in it: the search party was coming back. The waiting Nyols scurried to meet it rumbling excitedly.

The tide of bodies flowed back carrying with it a taller and angrier shape with a lashing tail. The Nyols had caught one of Kooleen's women. They brought her to Wirrun as a flood might bring a struggling wallaby. He and Ularra stood up.

'No use fighting now,' Wirrun told her holding the power. 'You're here.'

She faced him sullenly. 'I got no business with you, Man.'

'I say you have.' Wirrun spoke harshly because of the care he must take now that his haunting was named. 'This water-spirit. You don't want it. You only want it away. Bring it here and I'll take it away, back to its own place. And you can go back to yours and stop making trouble.'

She sneered. 'What am I, Man? I am one. The wives of Kooleen are many and fierce with anger. All these little no-tails could not hold them. Can this one take the stranger from them and bring it to you? Earless words.'

Ularra growled. He was shaking, for the tailed woman brought his own haunting near. Wirrun put a hand on his arm but it had been a man's growl.

'Those were your words,' Wirrun told the woman. 'These

are mine.' He held up the power pulsing with light. 'Tell Kooleen's women what I say. Bring 'em here with the water-spirit. And make it fast.'

The woman flounced off and went tail-swinging back into darkness between banks of Nyols that parted to let her go. Ularra shook himself fiercely.

'Untwist,' Wirrun told him. He was angry with Ularra: angry that, still troubled, he had forced his way into the spirit-troubled dark; angry that he would not wait in safety but must tangle Wirrun's feet with his fierce protection. But Ularra was his friend; he was angry because of his care. He said firmly, 'They're only earth-things. You're a man.'

Ularra sat down and laid his head on his knees.

Wirrun sat with him. They waited again . . . *The dark-flowing water . . . like dark-floating hair* . . . the rock hummed sweetly. Wirrun sat tormented and at last laid his own head wearily on his knees. He must not part with his senses now—he had almost leapt up and rushed into the dark leaving Ularra alone.

'Is it bad?' whispered Ularra.

Wirrun's mouth twisted. 'I wish you'd stayed where you were told,' he muttered harshly.

The old things wavered and murmured and drew into shelter. Something had disturbed them. Nyols scrambled higher and hung watching. The black curtain of the dark was disturbed and wavered too: shadows were moving in it. They slipped along walls, slid behind boulders: the tailed women, creeping and hiding. When Wirrun was sure of it he stood up quickly with the stone.

'Come on, you women! Come out and talk.'

They had to obey. Out of the dark, out of niches and hollows and round the shoulders of rock, they gathered into a crowd and came forward with sly grins to see how the others hung back. The smiles became titters and grew into shrill laughter. They pointed at Wirrun and Ularra, rolled their eyes, nodded to each other and laughed. The vault gathered their laughter and threw it back and forth. The First Dark shrieked with mirth.

'No-tails!' the women screamed, holding each other as they laughed. 'Unfinished! See how they cover their

ends—even they are ashamed! No tails, no tails!' They cackled and shrilled and held their shadowy sides.

Wirrun waited with a hard smile and a hand on Ularra's
shoulder. He could feel its stiffness. He feared that the
beast would rise again and leap among the women red-eyed
and raving.

'No more!' he roared. 'That's enough!'

They tittered and sniggered into silence; the laughter
died among the rocks.

'We got no time for games,' said Wirrun. 'You know me
or you wouldn't have hid. And you've had my message or
you wouldn't have come. Where's this water-spirit?' But he
knew they had not brought it.

They looked at each other with secret smiles. 'If the
power says bring the water-spirit we must bring it. But it
will never reach you, Man.' They nodded and grinned and
twirled their tails.

Wirrun frowned and said nothing, only waiting. They
nodded and grinned a little more and then had to explain.

'Slimy as weed, slippery as a fish, that water-spirit,' they
told him. 'If we take it from its place, in a flash it slips into
the water and away to Kooleen. It will never reach you.'
They smiled in triumph.

'There's enough of you and I've seen you fighting. You
can keep it from the water.'

They shook their heads and tittered. 'Who are we, Ice-
Fighter? Only poor wives of Kooleen. We cannot live in
water or grip slime.' They nodded to each other sideways.
'We have no great power like yours to make the stranger
obey.' They glanced secretly at each other. 'Lend us your
stone, Great One, and we will bring the no-tail fish.' They
hid smiles behind their hands.

Wirrun gave only one bark of laughter and shook his
head as mockingly as the tailed women themselves. Their
eyes flashed and their tails began to twitch. 'Wait,' he ordered them, and turned to Ularra.

'You'll have to tie me up,' said Ularra at once; and even
if he had Merv's rope again that was more than Wirrun
could have done. There was no help for it. He glowered at
Ularra and turned back to the women.

'You'll take me and my friend to this spirit and *I'll* fetch it out.' Their eyes were sullen and their tails lashed. 'There's more,' said Wirrun. 'I'm doing you a favour and I'm not doing it for nothing. When I've got this stranger out of the way you'll go back to your own place and stay there. Right?' They muttered and twitched, for they had enjoyed the excitement of battles with Kooleen and their power over the water-spirit. 'I lay it on you,' said Wirrun with the stone pulsing in his hand. 'First you take us there and back and give us what help we need. After you go to your own place.'

They flounced and sulked but they were ordered. 'If the slimy one goes we go. What should we stay for?'

'Good. And one more thing. The old water's finding new ways. Springs are drying and deserts are green. What made the new ways?'

They shrugged. 'Who are we to know the ways of the water? Ask the old ones that hide.' They remembered something, giving each other glances and a grin or two. 'The slippery one has long nails. It scraped and scratched to open a way but it could not slip through. We heard it howling.'

Wirrun thought for a moment. The Ninya or the water-spirit: what difference? The old and formless ones would know, for the land's dark heart was their own being. He would not bring them out of shelter into the faint light. He called to them where they hid.

'Eldest Ones, I lay it on you. When the stranger's gone you'll find the new ways of the water and close them up.' He was not sure of his power to command these ancient things that might be her own First Thoughts; but they had come first to his call and he was sure of their help.

He turned back to the tailed women. Now the ordering was done and the doing had to be faced, the dread and the hunger resolved. He, knowing, must go where Ularra had gone unknowing and fight for the power to command himself; for if he were lost there was no hero at hand, no Clever Man with a power, to bring him back. He could not keep the hoarseness out of his voice.

'All right. Take us to this place.'

The long months of waiting and seeking were like a river that carried him on into the monstrous waiting dark, aware, without cold or warmth. He was burning to go and cold with fear: fear of the cold fish-spirit, the slimy thing that sang like wild honey and howled like a dingo. He would not look at Ularra. But Ularra looked darkly and forebodingly at him.

Three

The old south land lay under the sun like an open hand, but its secrets were hidden in its heart. There in that unknowable dark it held them all alike: its old remembered waters and the bones of forgotten creatures; its secret dreams of fretted, fragile beauty and the drifting shapes of old lost fears. And now it held with those, as deeply hidden and unknown, a lost love-singing and the torment of Wirrun and the pain of Ularra. It hid them, and knew, and was silent.

They fumbled their way deeper in as the old things flowed with them and led them on. The faint little lights of the Nyols' eyes flickered and the power pulsed on Wirrun's belt. So they travelled in a small moving starlight, and in this immensity of dark it was no more than a half-thought never uttered. Sometimes it lit a hidden spark, sometimes only the looming rock and flowing shadows. Kooleen's women shrilled and tittered ahead or watched at hand with slitted eyes and their tails curved like cats. The others that came with them Wirrun did not see. He was poised always on the twin points of hunger and dread, of longing for the singing and fear of the singer and himself. He fought for power.

They waded deep through water and crawled through sand and dust. They climbed up and again climbed down. They walked upright through echoing vaults, edged along narrow twisting places, squeezed themselves through slits. Once the inert dark warmed and breathed; there was a gushing of hot water and the curl of steam. Once Wirrun rested on a thing that crumbled: a skull, long and narrow and strange.

The first time the singing struck at him Wirrun was picking his way down a rough passage. He stood frozen, fighting it with teeth and hands clenched, while Ularra watched frowning and the spirits looked on curiously and listened to the song. The second time he and Ularra were jammed together in a slit, scraping a way through. Wirrun drew a sharp breath that jammed him tighter and gripped the rock and closed his eyes—but he heard Ularra's indrawn breath and opened them again. They were close together with the light of the power pulsing on their faces. He saw the shock on Ularra's face and knew that he heard with his ears what had haunted Wirrun's own mind all this time. Jealousy flared through him like a fire in grass.

> *Are you not coming?*
> *sings the bright water,*
> *are you not coming?*

The phrases dropped like falling leaves, the voice was as clear as a bird's and as sweet and sharp as wild honey. Ularra was dazed and his hands too gripped the rock.

'Man!' he whispered, and Wirrun snarled.

> *The glimmer-bright water*
> *alight with the glances*
> *of glimmer-bright eyes.*

Ularra shivered. 'It's a fish, man,' he whispered hoarsely. 'It's a bit of slime.' But Wirrun saw that the brooding had gone from his eyes; they were hard and afraid like Wirrun's own. He bared his teeth at Ularra like a dog.

'My business, mate. You keep out.'

The rocks sang into silence. The eyes, angry and afraid, fell away from each other. The Nyols waited indifferent but respectful. The two men stirred and went on. But Wirrun was always aware now of Ularra near and watching, grimly watching.

They skirted a pool, crawled through a low passage, and

stood upright again in a vaulting dark where the eyes of
the Nyols twinkled from near to far and the darker shadows flowed between. The singing struck them again. Here
it rang soft and free and an echo picked it up.

> *Are you not coming?*
> *sings the dark water,*
> *are you not coming?*

Ularra groaned. 'A man can't—a man can't—' He stood
rigid as Wirrun did, fighting with himself.
'Mine,' panted Wirrun. 'Mine.'

> *The dark-flowing water*
> *like washes and ripples*
> *of dark-floating hair.*

It was cool as moonlight. Wirrun broke into a stumbling
run. In one leap Ularra was on him, gripping him in a vice.
'That's cold stuff,' he said harshly, 'that dark water. Old
and bitter all through.'
Wirrun fought him. 'Keep out—keep off! I been all this
time—Mine. Mine. You just got here.'
Ularra fought to hold him. 'I'm here. I'm staying.'
'And who brought you?'
'You did, man, you did.'
The spirits watched and listened, drawing a little farther
off. The singing died. The knowing dark waited immense
and unmoving. Ularra's grip loosened, Wirrun threw it off
and the two stood panting.
'A man can't—' muttered Ularra again, and Wirrun
laughed hard and bitter; but Ularra looked dark with despair.
'You not come?' said the Nyols.
Another passage. A cleft through which Wirrun fought
his way possessed. The singing again: sweet and cool, echoing into a chorus.

> *I sing in the sunlight*
> *with dark eyes aglimmer:*
> *are you not coming?*

'No good to a man,' said Ularra and his voice cracked. Wirrun, rounding on him, saw that he had picked up a stone. Wirrun ranted.

'Haven't you had enough, eh? Haven't you had enough? Come here on my power—my power—dogging me like a beast—like a beast—'

> *I sing in the shadows*
> *with dark hair downflowing:*
> *are you not here?*

Ularra stood shaking and shaking. He threw the stone into a clattering dark. 'Can't ever be sure . . . can't ever be sure . . . But I'll tell you something, man . . . there's all kinds of beast.' He pulled the possum-fur cord from his pocket and thrust it at Wirrun; it fell between them and merged into the dark. 'You keep it,' gasped Ularra, his eyes flaring with fear. 'You need it.'

And through the pain of the haunting another pain struck Wirrun. He hardly knew what he had said or done but it should not have been said or done. He could only look pleading at Ularra as the beast had looked pleading at him. And Ularra's eyes were still hard and afraid.

There was shouting ahead, and the tailed women running in a crowd. The haunting gripped Wirrun and dragged him after them.

'Wa!' they were shouting. 'Slimy weed! Slippery fish! Fireless fool with no place! Take yourself out of our place, no-tail! Go back where you came from, slime-weed!' Tails lashing they worked at the stone of a rock-face. In a moment they had pulled away three large stones and were screaming insults through a cleft where the old water trickled. Wirrun rushed in among them and forced himself into the cleft. He was cold with horror and burning with need.

The water slipped over a ledge and clinked into a pool. The singing echoed and rang and he shuddered with longing. The power flared into brightness and he crawled along the ledge above the magical, cooling, enchanted water that his burning body craved. Something moved in it, flowing and lovely, and came out of the water on the farther side.

He saw her at last and knew her from her singing, and the knowing held him while he looked.

She was silver like moonlight and lovely and dew-wet like a flower. Her dark hair flowed over slender shoulders to the rock where she sat, and she combed it back with delicate fingers. Her dark eyes were truly lit with moonlight, soft and shining, and she smiled with the sweetness of honey. She was dark and silver like moonlit water, lovely and remote like a dream. She longed for him, the singer in the dark, and his longing flowed back and he began to slide over the ledge.

But something scraped in the entrance. Something breathed hard. Ularra shot from the cleft and halfway across the pool in a dive, and cut the water so that it rang and echoed like the singing.

Wirrun shouted and dived too, fumbling with the power, but Ularra was already near. The water-spirit watched and quivered. As he came close she leaned towards him and held out two slender fingers.

Four

When the Mimi had vanished into rock and those who came to honour her had gone, when the Yunggamurra had howled in despair and the howling had died in the dark, she had done all that was left to her. She had crawled on through the First Dark not knowing where but aimlessly seeking.

Her brown had paled to gold under its silver slime and her moonlit eyes had widened. She could see those fretted shapes of stone that glittered like ice: she was used to the dark. She had lost sunrise and sunset, north and south and the wheeling of the stars: she abandoned them and thought only of up and down and the secret flowing of water. She grew used to the weight of the land lying on its rocks. Only the pain of loneliness never softened or passed; that and her fear of the others in the dark, in whose place she was a stranger.

There came a time when she slipped on a trickle of water into a cavern with a different feel. A pool was cupped in it, wide and deep with ledges of rock above; a good pool, but she had found many of those. She lay quiet to sense the difference of this pool and found it with relief that was almost joy. Nothing old had lived here or came here. The rock and water were old as the land but the cleft that led in was new. She might rest here safely.

She did not choose to stay. She only stayed.

Rest and safety were healing. Her delicate slime was renewed, her dark hair grew sleek again. Sometimes she even played alone like a dolphin. She made one expedition to stock the water with blind fish and the cavern with pale spiders. It became her place.

But there was still the pain of loneliness. When she sang it was not to draw Wirrun of the People or Kooleen the tailed one but for memory. She sang for her river where the waterfall roared and faded and roared again. She sang for her sisters: for the glowing eyes and wild-honey smiles and slender shapes that showed her to herself; for the laughter and clinging hands, the water-tangling of dark hair and limbs, the sweet bad mischief of the games. When she sang the cavern caught and answered her singing till her voice was one of a chorus. Her sisters were there when she sang—but they never spoke or played or showed themselves. Sometimes she howled for this. The rock caught both the howling and the singing and carried them far.

And others heard. They lay quiet and listened. In a hundred years or so they might have come to whisper in the dark, perhaps to play a little. Only Kooleen the bold one with the tail came at once from the south to see.

When he saw he laughed, as he always laughed at those who were shaped like the people and wore no tails. The Yunggamurra laughed back. She was filled with wild excitement by his visit. She slid into her pool and played like a dolphin to amuse him more. Kooleen narrowed his eyes.

'You will be one of my wives,' he said.

'Yes,' said the Yunggamurra for the sake of the company of spirits. Her sisters would have howled in fury.

The rock carried the words as it had carried the singing. The wives of Kooleen heard them and came eagerly to see. Her cavern filled with dark tailed women, new sisters. The Yunggamurra climbed from her pool to greet them with joy.

The joy was lost in a shrieking fury of women lashing their tails. Before she understood it Kooleen was gone, the cavern closed with stones, and she a scratched and beaten prisoner.

First she struggled to remove the stones. Then she pleaded. Later she searched for another way out, working at a fault in the rock below the water. It was useless; only the water, which before had trickled in to fill the pool, now began to flow a little. The Yunggamurra was defeated.

Sometimes Kooleen came to tease his wives, and laughed to her through the stones and called her his little fish. There would be another shrieking battle, and after it the Yunggamurra howling alone. Sometimes the wives would shriek taunts and insults through the stones. That was all she ever heard, but it was better than before.

When she sang it was not to draw Kooleen for he was her own kind and not to be charmed. She did not hear what others whispered, that the Ice-Fighter was at hand. She still did not know it when she felt the old sweet wickedness working in her and the game beginning. She only guessed that somehow, here in the deeps of the land, men of the People were near.

And the game was beginning! Her singing vibrated with magic and echoed into her sisters' chorus. Her moonlit eyes glimmered, her dark flowing hair shone. Her lovely silvered body quivered with the old fierce waiting, sharpened by long loneliness in the dark. She sang with the echoes and measured the pauses to build up doubt and wonder. She spread her fingers delicately like a dancer and smiled at them and listened and waited.

She heard as the others did the Ice-Fighter calling for help. She would not have gone if she could; to her he was a man of the People whose name she had heard in the dark. The game should bring him to her. She did remember that they had called him hero, and that lit her to fiercer excitement.

An uneasy stirring beyond her cavern, a pressure of Kooleen's wives who whispered and muttered: they lay close and hid, and she smiled her wild-honey smile. Did they think a crowd of tailed shadows could spoil her game? What did they know of the hunger of a love-sung man? She sang again, sending into the rock and the dark her sweetness, her remoteness, her waiting.

The pressure of uneasy wives had thinned: most were gone and only a few waited. Now, if a water-spirit had power with rocks, she might move the stones and slip away to freedom. But she would not if she could—not now—not when by some wonder a man was close—after so long— She sang of tenderness and loveliness and longing.

When she felt the nearness of many spirits she hugged herself and laughed. They should know her now. They should see what they kept closed up among them lonely in rocks and dark. They should see the game played, the man not stolen in sleep but coming free and eager. Let them see.

When next she paused in her singing and heard the voices of men she trembled. Two! There were two of them! And one a hero, and only one Yunggamurra. No sisters to help if help were needed—her fierce waiting was pricked with fear. She had forgotten the fear for every game holds a point of fear and in the old days it had been small. But now! She nerved herself. This game, played alone in the deepest dark, should ring for ages to come in the laughter of her sisters—if only she could play it—and they could know—

She heard the men near and slipped into the pool to wait for the moment of love: that strange sad moment that belonged in some way to the fear and sweetened every game . . . The stones were moved amid shrieking . . . it was coming . . . Now! They had found her! Soften the smile, light the eyes to a dewy shine, and watch, watch, watch . . .

There he was, the man, creeping above on the ledge, as burning and eager as herself. And after him in the entrance the second. She placed herself quickly on rock and leaned forward with longing and sang. Her shining eyes watched and waited spirit-old; and what they saw sharpened the needle of fear. For these were charmed men as they should be, and filled with torment as they should be; but each of them knew his torment as he should not. And where she had looked for only one hero there were two, each holding tight to his purpose. For both the purpose was strong and desperate, but for one the purpose was not hers—

That one leapt from the entrance into the water as the Yunggamurra summoned all her power. She saw him coming and was pierced with fear because she could not read his purpose. The man on the ledge shouted, at first with jealous rage as was right and then desperately as he plunged into the pool. The other was close, and yet she did not know—But she put out two fingers in the old way, like a crab's claw, and easily held him under the water.

Now the second was near. He had a strong power—he ordered and she had to obey—sullen with fear and defeat she drew back her crab-claw. The man under water bobbed to the surface and was still. The other stayed by him; he did not come on though his power had defeated her. Fear ebbed; now she was curious and a little sad. She watched with moonlit eyes.

It was sad that he lay so still so soon, the man who had come to her singing and played her lovely game—the man she had loved for a moment and failed to read. He had not struggled at all.

Five

When Wirrun saw the water-spirit shining in the starlit dark he knew her for his own: his strength and purpose and power, his dream and his haunting, all that he needed. This was what had called to him from the mountain, whispered in the desert, carried him on the wind. It was for this that the land was troubled and the spirits restless: that Wirrun of the People might find and claim his own. The certainty held him and Ularra shot past into the pool.

He shouted with rage—but the power burnt his hand and the water-spirit moved and he saw Ularra's face as it went under water. Dread seized him, he shouted again in desperate warning and fumbled for the power as he leapt.

The delicate silvery shape drew back, watching with old and fearful eyes. Ularra bobbed up and Wirrun grabbed him. The old water lapped his face: a man's face, stern and calm. Wirrun had seen the sternness already as Ularra sank; but the other thing, the weary dread, was changed now into this deep, accepting calm.

'No,' grunted Wirrun panting and fighting to drag Ularra from the water. 'No . . . a man can't drown so quick.'

It was true; but even as he rolled Ularra over, the ancient air of the cavern stirred and sweetened. Something passed through it, something warm and strong and gentle that stayed by him for a moment and was gone. And he knew it: it was Ularra's spirit.

His own spirit called after it, a cry for forgiveness and restoration while he worked to revive Ularra's body. Useless work, only that he could not believe it. A man can't drown so soon . . .

He worked on, pumping steadily at Ularra's lungs. Nyols and small hairy things crept into the cavern and looked. They looked longest at the water-spirit for they had seen dead men before. 'Drowned like a lizard,' they told each other nodding wisely.

At last Wirrun's aching body gave in; his mind was locked away somewhere behind glass. Gently he turned Ularra over again. The face was so deeply, so strongly, at peace. 'Mate,' whispered Wirrun, pleading, but Ularra's peace was not to be broken by a word.

He stood up stiff and aching and his eyes fell on the water-spirit. It watched as old as moonlight, knowing and yearning and uncaring all at once. *Old all through, man. Old and bitter . . .* His eyes narrowed and hardened. The thing had done its work. Now it should show like a hag and not as remotely lovely as before.

He said, 'What are you?'

She had drowned one man too easily and the other would not drown. She answered sullenly. 'Yunggamurra.'

He repeated it. 'Yunggamurra.' *A fish, man. A bit of slime.* 'You'll stay here, Yunggamurra, and wait.'

She glanced indifferently at the open cleft. The tailed women were there smirking and staring but it had not mattered for some time now. She was already ordered.

He saw that the cavern was full of old things that drifted and stared. He spoke to them harshly. 'This was a hero.'

They looked at the face so sternly and strongly at peace, and shifted and murmured.

'Take him to a hero's place,' ordered Wirrun.

They only looked again, and those that had faces turned them away. They did not know a hero's place. But the formless ones, the land's First Thoughts, flowed even into the light and thickened around Ularra and bore him out of the cavern. Wirrun found that this, the thickness of dark bearing Ularra away, was more than his mind could now accept. He retreated behind his wall of glass, bewildered. The Nyols closed about him and he went with them like a child, following the shadows. Kooleen's women closed up the cavern behind them and stayed by it. Other shapes went with the Nyols deeper into the land.

Behind rose a crying wild and chill and lonely that rang away down corridors of rock and was caught and answered and came back from all sides till the dark was shaken. Wirrun shuddered and waited thinking that this crying came from him; but the Nyols looked behind and hurried on, and he knew that it was the Yunggamurra's howling. The rock pulsed with it, crying for Wirrun who must not yet feel pain or cry.

He could not see what went ahead through the dark where a man may cease to be. He saw only the little eyes of the Nyols and the shapes that flittered near. Peering close in the dim light he gave careful attention to broken rock, to dust and sand and water, for these things he could comprehend; and he went obediently where the Nyols led. When they held him back he waited obedient.

Those ahead were busy, darting like glow worms about some wide dark place. Light blossomed, the red and gold light of fire, and he frowned over that: what fuel had they found? The flames rose; he saw the cavern, and the journey through dark had meaning again.

The fire lit the cavern to frost-sparkle and rainbow-shine. Its flames leaping and playing flung back curtains of dark and let them fall again. Now here, now there in the moving light stone glistened and flowered and soared. Glistening folds of stone swept down from an upper darkness, glittering columns and spires rose into it. In its old dark heart the land had dreamed of beauty and its oldest shadows had found the dream.

To the right a pool caught and doubled the frost-sparkled fretted shapes. Above it jutted a shelf of rock over which flowstone had laid a drapery that hung fringed to the water. On this drapery of gleaming stone the shadows had laid Ularra with spires glistening round him. Wirrun could not come near, but he climbed a boulder on that side and looked down.

'Pretty,' crooned the Nyols clustering near. They stole glances at Wirrun, and he saw and answered them.

'It's a place for a hero.'

'It grows,' they told him, and he nodded and looked quickly away. He understood what they said but he could not yet think of Ularra wrapped close in the gleaming stone.

Ularra's loose-jointed legs lay neatly, his long arms rested at his sides. The dark swept its curtains over his face and away as the firelight played; sometimes it showed sternly and calmly at peace and at others it moved and darkened. Clearly Wirrun heard Ularra's voice in its pain: *Can't ever be sure, can we?*

He rubbed a hand over his face. Yes, Mate. We're sure. I'll never need to be so sure.

It did not seem possible to climb down, to go away from the cavern and leave him. But it was made possible. When the busy Nyols could find no more fuel the fire died. The dark drew its curtains close again, and only the power and the glow-worm lights of the Nyols drew a secret glint from stone. Not Wirrun but Ularra had gone.

Wirrun came down from the boulder and carefully thanked the shadows. They took him back through the weary dark to the cavern where the Yunggamurra now lay silent and the tailed women waited. The women confronted him.

'The slime-weed. The no-tail fish. You take it now?'

His face twisted and he tried to pass but they flounced ahead of him.

'A bargain! It was a bargain!' They hugged themselves in anger and jerked their tails.

Wirrun drove his fist into his palm. 'No more!' he shouted, and they were silent and sullen. He knew it had been a bargain, but he wanted with a sudden fierce disgust never again to see that silver shape or hear the falling phrases of the song. 'Maybe I'll be back,' he said more quietly. 'Now I have to think of my friend.'

'Friend,' rumbled the Nyols. They had known the word for a long time but still did not understand it as men did.

They took Wirrun on. The tailed women stayed by the cavern and stared after him insolently until the next passage hid him from them.

In the passage some of the Nyols stooped, rumbling to each other and gathering something between them. Wirrun found it pressed into his hands, a soft and growing bundle: the cord from the power. Loosely bundled it was too big for its bag; he struggled to force it in. It had gone more easily into Ularra's large pocket—and if it had stayed there Ularra might be here now—something large and dull inside him sharpened and tore and he groaned.

They took him on through the huge aware dark: through slits and caverns and passages, through water and dust and sand. Sometimes he forgot what he should do and they herded him gently like a mob of small grey sheep herding the dog. They took him past a pool that reflected their glow-worm eyes in a vaulting dark, and there he saw Ularra's spare shirt and stood gazing at it uncertainly for a time and turned and left it. They led him up a mounting slope to a higher level and through a passage to a lesser dark.

'You call,' they said. 'We come.'

And they left him. The power had ceased to glow.

He stood alone and bewildered turning here and there to look at the dark, not knowing what to do. He could not escape from behind his wall of glass. After a time he found a greyness away in the dark and looked at that; and while he looked his mind suddenly saw, as clearly as if his eyes had seen, the hands of his ancestors outlined in ochre on the walls above. The hands of his ancestors reaching from the past, spread over him in pity; the eyes of charcoal and pipe-clay knowing and sadly forgiving.

They knew he had faced his haunting and found no power over himself; that to save him had cost the making and losing of a hero. He felt a choking hardness that would not break into sobs; and he dropped to his knees beneath those pitying hands and crawled to the grey light.

So Wirrun came alone out of the First Dark to mourn for his friend Ularra. Behind him, though he did not hear, the rock vibrated again to the howling of the dingo. The Yunggamurra mourned too. She howled for dark and loneliness, and for men who would not play her game but lived or died too easily.

6

❖❖❖❖❖❖❖❖❖❖❖❖❖❖❖❖❖❖❖❖❖❖❖❖❖❖❖❖❖❖❖❖❖❖❖

Singer in Sunlight

One

The mourning of Wirrun for Ularra was such as could be borne by only one man: the man who climbs the rugged track to hero. It was mourning embittered by every step that led to it. Not softened by friendship for friendship sharpened Wirrun's failure into a spear. Not relieved by hatred of the killer, for hatred and enchantment were still horribly one and he could not untangle them. Not sweetened by discovery of Ularra the Hero for a friend's greatness should be seen while he lives. Not warmed by gratitude, for when a hero dies for a friend who has failed gratitude is a mean and cowardly thing. There was no help for Wirrun.

For three days and nights he roamed the gorge not knowing where he was. Flashes of vision came and went—

He was sitting in the creek with a cut on his leg. It bled and he watched—

He was rewinding the cord on the power. He threw it down and wearily took it up again—

Are you not coming?—he writhed, hating himself for hearing and for the stab of hunger—

He sat eating fish that someone gave him in pieces. He looked and saw it was Merv Bula and said, 'Get out.'

Merv knew the curtness was inability to speak. He put the fish at hand and went. Not smoke but the lack of it had brought him: there was no campfire. He had found Wirrun wandering alone, his spirit gone, and had made his own camp under the cliffs and watched and followed. Twice more he put into Wirrun's hands food that the hero ate blindly.

Wirrun's spirit had gone out of him to plead with the powers of that country. 'Bring him back. Bring him out of there. I'll live haunted and never listen.' The powers with-

154

drew into cliffs and shadows and far blue hazes; they could undo a magic and reshape a form but they could not remake life. That river flowed from another source.

Wirrun thought they refused him because he could not, even while he promised and pleaded, live haunted and never listen. *Sings the dark water* . . . he cursed and beat at rock.

Pleading broke into anger. He raged at the unmoved powers. He raged at the singer, the slimy evil howler. He raged at himself for a weak fool and a coward; and at last he raged at the land itself, the cruellest monster of all.

'Old hag—old beast—you called didn't you? We came— you took us—dropped us both into hell. What for? What for?'

I did not call, said the land. *You were mine and I aided you. No more.*

He had not heard that voice when he listened for it but it reached him now in his crazy anger: remote and near, stern and gentle. It was the beginning of sanity. Anger broke into purest pain and he threw himself down on that arrested strength. He lay at the still centre of pain till the land drew its darkness over him and itself sent him help.

The air stirred and sweetened. Leaves moved and whispered.

What about living, man? What about the wind?

'Oh mate!' cried Wirrun's agonised spirit. 'Ularra, where are you?'

A man's place . . . a man's place . . .

'Nothing surer. Never was. Wish I was with you.'

Hush, man. Listen, man. Listen . . .

He lay at the still centre of pain while Ularra's spirit drifted near, in the wind, in the grass, in the slipping of the creek. He let Ularra speak to him, in words he had heard or spoken and in new words.

A man can't drown so quick . . . unless he wants to . . . a beast's too much for a man . . .

The air stirred and the trees murmured.

Had to take it from you . . . my own way . . .

The night trilled with insects and softened into young moonlight.

Dreaming only I never did it so good . . . the wind and a man's place . . . thanks, man . . .

And as the sweetness passed and the grass whispered into silence:

Can't drown so quick . . . unless he wants to . . .

Pain broke at last into weeping, and Wirrun could lie weeping on the earth until he slept. At dawn he woke and went down to the creek and washed. Merv Bula saw it from under the cliffs and came down to light a fire and bake a damper.

Wirrun accepted him with a look and ate and drank in silence. Merv asked nothing. Over a second mug of tea Wirrun found his voice, rough with disuse and hunger and thirst.

'He's in there . . . deep down . . . under the cave . . .'

'A man?' said Merv quietly.

Wirrun raised bloodshot eyes with a spark in them. 'None better. Died saving me.'

'Ah. He had no choice, then.'

. . . unless he wants to . . . Wirrun said roughly, 'There's always a choice.'

Merv nodded. 'A man's choice,' he amended. 'He'll be glad of that.' He took a rabbit from his pack and began to cut it up for a stew. Since he asked nothing but was only there Wirrun was able to tell more.

'The beast. It was too much for him. He couldn't trust—'

'That'd be bad, then,' said Merv with deep sadness. 'He'd need to find out. Poor boys. Poor boys.'

Pain rushed over Wirrun again and he laid his head on his knees. And still he had not told the worst.

Merv could not know how much was untold. He only watched and stayed: stocking the new camp he had made, bringing Wirrun's pack from the old one, quietly taking Ularra's things away to the cliffs. He was not waiting to hear more but for the right time to go. He did not like to see the Ice-Fighter listen wincing to something unheard, or the darkness that came over him then.

Wirrun was finding how to use his pain to defeat the singing. It struck at him often, and the hunger it roused filled him with shame and horror for Ularra's sake. He could harden it now into hatred but he could not yet speak of it to Merv. Yet he wanted to speak for he wished the People might understand his failure—and while he wished it he found himself rejecting failure, rejecting it for Ularra as well as for himself. Shielded by hatred from the silvery singer with the moonlit eyes he thought again of his bargain with the tailed women. Yet nothing shielded him from the chill of the First Dark.

To go back to the darkness where Ularra was, where forever stifled today; to be led again by shadows where he and Ularra had fought; to see that shirt again; he could not. He fought his dread all day and at night while Merv slept. Near morning he knew that for him as for Ularra there was no other way.

Only he and the power could bring out the Yunggamurra. If he did not go hate-shielded into the First Dark and bring it out then the trouble of spirits and People would go unhealed. That would make Ularra's death a mockery indeed, a useless failure, a slaughtering by Wirrun of his friend. He had to go.

Merv woke early to find him filling a billy with yabbies for breakfast. It should have been a healthy sight but the darkness was still on the Ice-Fighter. They ate in silence; and afterwards when Wirrun spoke Merv's face darkened too.

'I never said what he saved me from. I'm sung.'

Merv's glance went quickly over him: not bone-pointed or sung with the stones or string. In his body at least the hero was not sickening but recovering. Merv waited.

'A long time now,' muttered Wirrun. 'Turns out it's all of a piece with this other trouble. It's a—love-singing—an old thing down there—got *him* a bit, too. That's why—' He stopped, out of words.

Merv's voice shook a little. 'You went knowing? Both?'

Wirrun nodded. 'We fought,' he whispered. 'I called him—I don't know what—'

'Poor boys. Poor boys.'

At least it was told now. Wirrun coughed to get his voice back. 'Trouble is, I gotta go down again. No good without. Gotta bring this—thing—out, send it home.'

Merv's eyes shifted. 'You want help.'

'No!' shouted Wirrun spilling his tea. He got hold of himself. 'Not another one. No fear. You keep well out where you can't hear no singing. Stay up on the cliffs.' He ran a hand through his hair. 'I just want you to know, that's all. Know and keep off.'

There was silence for a moment. Almost in despair Merv asked, 'What *can* I do?'

'If I don't come out don't try. Just leave it. Only tell Tom Hunter, that's all. They got a right to know. And he—Ularra—he came from that country. He's got a right. Tell Tom.'

'And what about your country, Ice-Fighter?'

Wirrun smiled tightly. 'From sea to sea it's all my country.'

'That's all, then? That's everything to do?'

'Look,' said Wirrun, 'you don't want to get in a twist. It's safe—beaten—that's what he did for me. Long as I can handle myself I can handle the rest. If I can't—well, just tell old Tom. And don't let no one in there after us. Right?'

'Right.' Merv stood up and turned his back to look at the cliffs. 'Two of you . . . young blokes. You cut a man down to size, Ice-Fighter.'

'Not you. No one cuts you down.' Wirrun hesitated, not wanting to say the next part badly. 'Only I want you safe out of this. Thanks, mate, but I'm right now. You get going. I can't fetch this—water-thing out till you do.'

'Today?'

'I'd feel safer.'

Merv began to roll his pack.

'And don't hang around on top,' said Wirrun urgently. 'Don't watch for fire. It travels, this singing.'

Merv finished rolling his pack and shouldered it. Wirrun walked beside him up the hill. A little way up Merv stopped.

'No more. You gotta get your strength back.'

Wirrun struggled for words to say good-bye. 'There's this old spirit-bloke,' he said. 'Ko-in, sort of a grandfather. There's my friend Ularra, he's gone now. After them there's you.' He held out a hand.

Merv said nothing. In a gesture that was strange yet old, dignified and right, he folded Wirrun's hand between his older hands and pressed it to his chest. Then he turned away and went on up the hill.

Wirrun watched for a moment and went back down the hill to the new camp. He poured more tea and thought of going into the cave. But not today. Not yet.

It was hate that sent him. He was wakened next dawn

by the singing and the eager leaping of his blood, and his spirit rebelled. It was not enough to reject the cool sweet magic; it still struck. There was still that piercing moment and afterwards the shame and horror. The singer must go to its own place and he must put distance between or he would go mad. He must go now, before pain softened and his shield of hatred softened with it.

He ate a little cold baked yam and made tea. He took no firestick but unrolled the cord from the power and left it safe in his sleeping-bag. The crystal lay in his palm: grey-white stranded with pink, the colour of the dawn sky. He held it for a while for strength before he laid it carefully in its netted bag. Then he went up the creek again to the cave.

He did not notice that he trembled and his knees were weak. He had enough to do to keep his mind narrowed to its purpose, to walk tight-lipped and frowning through the twilight of the cave and on into its night; to find again the darker slit and climb into the second cave; to feel his way along the painted walls. Without a firestick he found the entrance to the passage only by groping. He went a foot or so in and shouted.

'Hoo, there! Come on, you Nyols! It's the Ice-Fighter needs you.'

Then he leaned against the rock and waited.

It was bad waiting. The First Dark probed along the passage knowing he was there. Ularra would have stood here fingering the fur cord, waiting to follow . . . He narrowed his mind to its purpose again and watched for the first points of light, wondered only if they would come, thought nothing of the last journey or the end of this one.

Pinpoints of light flickered and came, soft voices rumbled. The Nyols peered with their bright lizard-eyes in the faces of small grey children. 'We come,' they pointed out.

'Take me back to Kooleen's women,' he asked and let himself be led as he had before. The power began to glow and pulse, strengthening as they went.

The way seemed long. Wirrun looked only at the nearest rocks and the pinpoints of light. It was not as hard as he had feared for now he knew where the journey led and there were no stranger shadows drifting with them; this journey alone with the Nyols was a different one and less fearful. But sometimes the other stabbed at him out of the dark: in a shoulder of rock remembered, the crumbling of a skull, a slit through which he knew the way. He trod on Ularra's shirt and could not leave it again but had to push it away inside his own. He stood trembling where he had ranted at Ularra and was helped by Merv Bula's thickened voice saying, 'Poor boys. Poor boys.' After that he could hear the shrill squabbling of Kooleen's women; it was easier to hold to his purpose but harder not to think ahead.

Kooleen's women felt his coming and began to shriek in welcome. 'He is here, the one with the power!' 'The Ice-Fighter keeps his bargain!' 'He comes for the slippery thing! Out! Send it out!' A little farther and he saw them: shadows clustered in the starlight, flashing grins and jerking tails. Already they were working at the stones that blocked the cavern.

'Here, then, Ice-Fighter! The singer is waiting and wishing for you!' They stood grinning round the open slit. His mind leapt ahead in panic and found a solution: he would order the Nyols to take the Yunggamurra home. Five minutes to find out its place—then be rid of it—try not to see—Shaking he crawled through the entrance. The power flared.

It was there, a silver glimmer in the dark watching with old moonlit eyes. He longed and sickened and called up hatred: Ularra's face stern and calm in the water. He spoke hoarsely.

'Yunggamurra. Where's your right place? Where did you come from?'

It said, 'Up.'

He frowned. 'I'm taking you out of this, sending you home. But I gotta know where.' He held up the stone and the spirit watched it like a child watching a candle. 'Tell me where.'

She did not believe what he told her for that was not how the game was played; but she was ordered and had already answered. She tried harder. The moonlit eyes dreamed.

'My sisters are there. The sun shines and the river flows. The water leaps far over rocks.'

He had heard the leaping water . . . He saw that anger

was useless for the creature had tried to obey. But his mind, held tight to its purpose, met this new problem slowly and struggled to think. He asked, 'How did you come here?'

The shining dark eyes widened and aged. 'Through rocks. In the dark. Many ways.' She thought again. 'With the water and against it. This way and that.'

He watched intent, grappling with the problem. 'A long time?'

'Alone in the dark, a long time.' The bird-sweet voice was cool and indifferent but he had seen the spirit quiver. He felt a quick unexpected pang. Lovely and loathsome, delicate and enduring, gallant and terrible. He frowned again and thought.

'Does the river come out of the rocks? How did you get in?'

'There was a storm. The water spread wide. I was carried into the sea. In the sea I found the old water trickling.'

The sea. 'What sea?'

It frowned, was puzzled, folded itself in indifference again. 'There is only one sea. That sea.'

'What if I took you back to the sea? Could you find your way home?'

It shook its head quickly and was wrapped in its own flowing hair. 'The sea is a cold wet fire. It burns. I cannot live in it.'

Wirrun brooded in silence. The Nyols listened and peeped like inquisitive children. The tailed women whispered and sniggered. The Yunggamurra saw and heard and gave no sign.

In this place where Ularra had died Wirrun faced his own shame and dread: there was no easy way out. The water-spirit, a creature of sunlight and rivers, had been in the dark a long and twisting time; it was lost. If he sent it away with the Nyols they might wander and search for years and the trouble go with them. He himself would never know when he might meet it again, when its singing might pierce him from some creek or pool. He must take it with him into daylight, give it time to recover and find itself, treat it like any earth-creature.

He said, 'You'll come with me. No slipping off in the

water to Kooleen, mind. No singing. No howling. Just come.'

He did not see the fear in its eyes. Like a diver filling his lungs with air it slipped into the pool to wet itself and came.

Two

'Wa!' cried the tailed women waggling their fingers and jerking their tails. 'It is going, the slippery thing, the no-tail!' They leaned towards the Yunggamurra grinning and shaking their heads. 'Ko-ki! The slime-weed is going! You will never see Kooleen, fish-thing! Go, now, go!'

Gleaming wet and silver the Yunggamurra passed through them following Wirrun. These were the sisters she would have welcomed in spite of their tails; even now, jeering and mocking, they were company of her own kind. But she gave no sign that she saw or heard, yearned or resented. Slender as a strand of weed in the water and cool and remote as moonlight she walked between them after the man with the power. She had played and lost. That was a rare and terrible thing; what came next she partly knew and did not understand. But she was a Yunggamurra.

'Go, no-tail! Go, slime-weed!'

'That's enough!' roared Wirrun in disgust. 'You go too; trouble-makers. Back to your own place and leave others to theirs. That was the bargain.'

They laughed and swung their hips and curled their tails. The power would not hold them forever but he knew the bargain would.

The Nyols gathered round and the journey began. The water-spirit came behind all the way and never spoke. It slipped easily through narrow slits that he climbed through with care, but once or twice it was scraped by rock and he heard its quivering indrawn breath. Once it paused, holding up dainty fingers and wiggling them like a child. He paused too thinking it was hurt, but he saw that its eyes smiled a little. He frowned, wondering, and felt again that strange unexpected pang. It was looking at the glow of light on its silver fingers; after so long in the dark this twilight was bright to it.

When they reached the long pool it slipped in and he jerked with quick suspicion. But he saw that it followed still, a ripple in a cloud of hair. At the beginning of the long climb up he called it from the water. It came dripping and delicate out on the rock, its old bright eyes showing nothing; not eager, not reluctant, only ordered. Wirrun grunted a little and muttered a word to Ularra, yet he did not know why. The water-spirit made no claim, its wild-honey voice was silent, his shield of pain and disgust was not lowered. There was only that small odd pang that passed before he felt it.

He did not see how the Yunggamurra mounted the slope for the Nyols were all about him. Climbing or carried it came with them and was there, a remote glimmer, on the ledge. It followed down the passage and into the cave where the power ceased to glow, where the Nyols rumbled a soft farewell and went away. He feared that in the dark the spirit might slip away with them, but when he turned suspiciously he found he could still see its glimmer. The gorge must be in full sunlight; there was more light in here than before. He could easily see the slit to the outer cave. The spirit's eyes were fixed on it too but they showed no feeling.

He must still grope his way to the slit with care. The spirit watched curiously and followed at a pace slowed to his. At the slit it hung back.

'Go through,' ordered Wirrun sternly. It laid its silver fingers on the rock and groped through. He followed.

The Yunggamurra was cringing against the wall of the cave, eyes closed, an arm shielding its face. He frowned in surprise and looked for the cause. There was only the long twilit tunnel of the cave and a dazzle of sunlight at its mouth. He thought of the Nyols that came and went underground and above, of the Mimi coming from the blackness of rock into light. He had not thought that a daylight spirit long underground might be hurt by the sun.

'We'll wait,' he said gruffly and sat down.

In a short time the Yunggamurra lowered its arm; a minute later it stood upright and faced the cave. Still looking only at the floor it waited, ready. He felt that peculiar pang again.

'We'll go nearer and wait again.'

It followed him down the cave from twilight to morning and when he stopped, watching under his brows, it turned its shoulder to the cave-mouth and hid against the wall. The day's heat came in like the breath of a monster. Even for him, coming from so short a time in the huge First Dark, the heat and light were sharp.

'You gotta get used to it if you want to go home,' he muttered.

It was the first time he had seen the spirit in daylight. He looked warily. Its silvery colour came from a covering of silver-grey slime. Where the slime had been scraped by rocks it showed a golden colour underneath; he wondered if that was the dark and if sunlight would brown it. Over its shoulders the dark hair tumbled and shone, moving lightly with the air because it was now dry. The creature was smaller than he had thought and its face was hidden in its long-nailed hands, but nothing could hide its slender curving beauty. In shape as in movement it flowed.

It raised its head and looked at him with those lovely dew-shining eyes that held only waiting and age. He turned roughly away and led it farther, to the edge of the sun. Here again it cringed and hid and quivered, and in a moment cried out its first words since the journey began.

'There must be water!' it cried in agony.

'There's a pool,' he said quickly. 'Down the hill a bit.'

'But I cannot see to go!'

He did not mean to torture it, only to be rid of it. He said, 'Shut your eyes and give me your hand.' It did as it was ordered and he took the small silvery hand and led it to the pool.

There was no magic in its touch. He felt a quick disgust that had nothing to do with Ularra. The hand was inert with none of the response or telling of a human hand. It was cool and moist like a frog without firmness or the frog's tense life. It felt like twigs in mud and slime. The spirit sensed the pool when they neared. Its hand slipped free. It sprang with no splash into the water and sank out of sight.

Wirrun gathered oak-needles and wiped the slime from his hand scrubbing it clean. The creek was shallow where it ran from the pool; the spirit could not slip away without his seeing it. He sat on the bank to wait.

The Yunggamurra went deep, down into the soft mud below. The water pressed her down as if it would hold her till the man with the power had gone. She curled and straightened, feeling its softness and sweetness—the sweetest she had felt since the storm. It soothed the bare burnt places where the slime was scraped off and softened the slime that was left. She looked up at the surface through water-light to the shadows of trees; and she did what she had not known a Yunggamurra could do. She wept.

She had not thought for a long time of daylight filtered through soft brown water and patterned with the shadows of trees. To see it again was sweet; and perhaps soon she could look at the trees, and beyond them to those widths of world she had forgotten. She could look but she could not stay. The man had her.

She wept only a little while. When her eyes found the light soft and dim she floated up into stronger light and looked again. She thought wistfully that she might sink to the bottom and stay a little while till the earth whirled once or twice around the sun; and the man would be gone. The pool could be hers, for nothing lived here. But that was not the way the game was played. She was a Yunggamurra; the man had come called by her singing and defeated her. When her eyes were stronger she floated higher.

Now she could see through the water to a blueness of sky and the wavering shapes of trees. For a year she had been in blackness, but to a spirit that in itself was a little time. In the sudden joy of trees she forgot it and looked for her sisters: where were the silver limbs and the dark clouds of hair? She shot up through the lid of the water to look and in the strangeness of looking remembered. She put back her head and gave a soft wild howl.

'Stop that!' shouted Wirrun, at once rigid.

She looked at him remembering that too, and cut off the howl.

Wirrun had waited by the pool for a long time suspecting some trick. There was nothing he could do about it for the thing had needed water, but he watched darkly. When he saw the silvery shape through the brown water he breathed hard in relief. To lose it, let it loose among men who knew nothing of it, would be the worst failure of all. He grew patient in his relief and watched it float higher, understanding that it treated its own light-blindness in the best way. Emerging it took him by surprise and he shouted his order—he could not become chilled or enchanted, he must stay in charge. But when the old yearning moonlit eyes looked at him half seeing and the howl broke off, that unrecognised pang needled him again. Why should it howl? All he wanted was to send it home.

'What did you howl for?' he asked it gruffly.

'For my sisters,' it said with the same indifference as before, and waited to be ordered further. When no order came it floated in its own spreading hair and looked and looked: not at Wirrun but above and far off, at trees and sky and cliffs and perhaps birds.

When sunlight had left the gorge and Wirrun was hungry he called. 'Can you come out now? There's another pool lower down.'

It came out of the pool into the creek. He walked down the bank to his new camp and it followed, sliding or swimming or sometimes walking in the creek. When they reached the small pool at his camp he spoke very sternly.

'I could tie you into a bag like a fish. I won't if you behave. You're ordered not to leave this pool till I say and to come when I call.'

It nodded and sank in a swirl of dark hair.

Wirrun lit his fire and cooked a meal and ate. Then he lay in the grass and watched the fire die while evening turned to night. He was deeply tired, deeply sad; he understood that. But he was also guilty and ashamed, and that he did not understand. He had made the hard journey into the dark and kept off horror with the business in hand. He had sent the tailed women home so that quiet would spread through the land; he had ordered that the old water should return to its old ways. He had taken charge of the water-spirit and kept off dread and enchantment. The thing was beside him now in the pool, Ularra's killer; but it was there because it must be and he could do nothing else. Why shame and guilt? How had he failed this time?

There was a bulk that he had grown used to and now felt: Ularra's shirt inside his own. He took it out and lay with it in his hands and was shaken again by pain and hate. Hate: that was it. He had forgotten for many hours to hate.

Was it then only the singing he hated? Only the howling he dreaded? Only his own danger and not Ularra's fate? What sort of thing was Wirrun of the People? He had betrayed his friend again.

The air sweetened and stirred, the grass whispered, but he did not hear it for a long time. He was weary to death and sick. The grass whispered on.

There's all kinds of beast, man . . . all kinds of beast . . . there's gotta be pity . . . pity . . .

He heard it at last and knew what that odd recurring pang had been. Pity . . . for Ularra's killer . . . how strange men were.

Three

That night Wirrun slept where he lay and did not feel the deep cold before dawn or the chill of dew or the eyes of the Yunggamurra watching from the pool. He woke aching. He ached all through with the weariness of this bitter time in the gorge. His muscles ached with cold, his belly with hunger, and his mind with the sadness of a hate collapsed under the weight of pity.

He lit his fire quickly and while it warmed him made a damper with flour from a bag that Merv had left hanging on a branch. Merv would see his smoke and know he had come back safe; he hoped the old man would stick to instructions and keep away. He had forbidden the singing, but while the singer lay in the gorge no man should be put at risk . . . And even while he thought this he heard the singing, clear and sweet and cool as before: *are you not coming?*

The longing struck—he sprang up in fury but could not find the spirit. While he glared at the pool the silvery face rose from the water amid its hair, looked with wide fixed eyes at his fire, and quickly sank.

It had not sung. The singing was in his mind. The spirit itself might be to him no more than a handful of slime, but the singing was barbed deep into his mind.

He ate, tidied the camp, banked down the fire, folded Ularra's shirt away in his own pack, prepared his gear for fishing. Then he went to search under fallen branches for bait. He would be eating fish again today: doing his hunting in the creek. When he had a few crickets and worms he came back to the pool and called to the water-spirit while he baited his hook.

'Yunggamurra! Up you come.'

It rose without a ripple on the far side of the pool, its back pressed into the opposite bank like an animal at bay, only its head above water. It stared past him at the camp and then at him with something like dread. Wirrun cast his line on his own side of the pool.

'It's all right,' he told it but he was puzzled. The spirit was held by the power, yet the power had done it no harm. It had suffered at first in heat and sunlight but he had allowed it time to recover. He had forbidden only its singing, its howling, and its freedom in a country that was not its own. What should it dread?

'Do you want to go back to the dark?' he asked.

It shook its head, tangling and untangling its hair.

'Just as well. You can't do that. Do you want to go home to your sisters?'

It nodded.

'Well then,' he retorted in exasperation, 'you better try and help me. Instead of staring as if I was going to eat you. What are you scared of any rate?'

It looked at him with darkened eyes and beyond him at the camp. He glanced over his shoulder: his pack; a branch from which two hessian bags swung keeping Merv's provisions from the ants; a small heap of yams; a curl of smoke from the banked fire. He considered.

'Are you scared of fire?' It quivered. 'That one's only smoke.' Its eyes darkened. 'I won't let it hurt you any rate. I'll look after it.'

The spirit said nothing but eyed him with reserve. He frowned and gave some attention to his line. It was natural that a water-spirit should dread fire but this one would have to trust him if he was to get it home. How it watched: as if it knew something dreadful that he did not. He could not meet its darkened shining eyes. He spoke to his line.

'You've had a bit of time out here now. Could you find your own place yet?'

The spirit shook its head.

'Tell me about it, then. Go on. Talk about your country. I might know it.'

It answered in its cool sweet voice almost exactly as it had before. 'The river flows and leaps over rock, a long leap. The sun shines. My sisters are there.'

'Yeah. Well that could be a lot of places. You'll have to do better than that. What else is in your country?' It only looked at him. 'Come on—you lived there a long time. You must know your own country.'

Its eyes yearned. 'I know it well. The river is my country.'

'But didn't you ever leave the river and go about the land? You've got legs.' The loveliest legs, slender and silver with curving thighs. 'What are your legs for?'

It gazed dreaming. 'We walked in the shallows. And there were rocks; we often came on to the rocks to play. The fish hid in the shadows . . .'

Wirrun waited hoping, but though the Yunggamurra dreamed on it said nothing more. He was distracted by a bite at his hook and in a moment pulled in a catfish. He unhooked it taking care of the spines and laid it in safety on the bank. The water-spirit had stopped dreaming. It watched with the sharp interest of a hunter of fish. He rebaited and cast out again.

'Which way did your river flow?' he called.

'Many ways, a gathering of many rivers. We travelled wide. East and west, north and south,' it said proudly having remembered them, 'and never left the river.'

One of the big systems, then. He thought of the nearest

and most likely. 'Was there always water? Were the rivers dry, some of 'em? Only run when it rained?'

'There were such rivers,' said the spirit indifferently, and he saw that indifference hid a passionate pride. 'We did not trouble with them. Our rivers had much water, a great water.'

The pride belonged to the yearning perhaps, but probably the river was permanent. There were few of those to the west entering the Gulf—and surely none with falls? East of the Cape, then? One of the big Queensland systems?

The Yunggamurra sank without permission. No matter; he needed time to think. He was getting nowhere on this line. How could he have guessed that the creature would know its own river and nothing beyond? He'd have to find some other approach, look at some of his maps maybe . . .

The Yunggamurra rose suddenly on his side of the pool and fixed him with a new look—was it mischief? It leapt upward and swung its arm: a catfish came swim-jerking through the air and thudded on the bank. The spirit sank with a gurgle that must be laughter.

Wirren sat frowning at the fish until its jerking took it almost over the bank. Then he put it safely with the other, wound in his line and gathered his gear. No point fishing any more; two big catfish were enough. But why had it thrown him a fish?

He gutted and washed both fish and wondered uneasily if it were safe to eat them from a Yunggamurra's pool. That was the danger of things out of their place: only the People of their own country knew the rules of safety. He decided that a whole river-system infected with love-sung fish would have earned a reputation wide enough for him to have heard, wrapped his catch in a wet cloth and took it back to camp. There he went through the pockets of his pack to find the maps he kept there but had not needed.

The water-spirit disturbed his thinking. He needed to be free of it without losing sight of its pool. He took his maps a little way up the hill and sat behind a rock from which he could watch concealed. He would study the river-systems in search of new questions, staying in charge without letting the creature confuse him.

The Yunggamurra too was confused. She lay watching

shafts of sunlight filter thrown brown water while she puzzled about the man. He had a power . . . had used it twice . . . and now he left her alone again and free. He questioned and questioned about her river . . . as though he would truly send her home. It was strange. In the stillness of light and the fluttering current came the thought that perhaps the man did not know.

She rose to look at him again. He was not even in sight! It was too much to believe, that he did not know—yet if he did it was almost as strange. To be alone and out of the dark; a night of stars, a day of sun and sweet water, of fish that were truly alive, of weed and moving shadows and a bank fringed with grass. It hardly mattered that she could not leave this one small pool . . . unless the man did not know?

She sank again. Free in this small water-world she needed only her sisters and their play. It was a pity that the man would not play—not the old game again but waterplay. She knew he would not; he was too stern. He frowned even when she threw him a fish. Yet he left her alone in the sweet sunny water . . . she forgot him and played.

She chased fish and played with shadows, danced with weeds and rode tumbling in the current. She played dolphin-games, rippling silver in the shadow of her hair. Where the creek flowed in over waterworn rock she curled herself and dammed it till it trickled past her shoulders— then, laughing like bubbles or the trill of a bird, she let herself be washed like foam over the rock's edge and down into the pool.

And Wirrun watched. Hearing the laughter and looking from behind his rock he watched the water-spirit play: sharply sweet as wild honey, magic as sunlight on water, lovely and merry as a girl. He watched with his maps neglected on his knee, half a smile grooving his face and his eyes shadowed in sadness. And he saw the spirit, as the stream tumbled it over the rocks for the third time, suddenly stop its laughing and turn a face full of loneliness and longing to the sky. He had forbidden it to howl but he knew it howled in its heart. It howled for its sisters.

He bundled his maps together and stood up and strode down to the pool. 'The flood washed you into the sea!' he shouted to the spirit. 'Which way? East?'

It looked at him with old eyes that had forgotten him for a while and now remembered. 'The river flows south and west. It turns north to the sea.'

He scrabbled with his maps on the bank. That could be anywhere . . . anywhere . . . on the southern shore of an eastern inlet, even a small stream on a southern promontory . . . memory and longing would make a big system of a creek. He swore and began to smooth and fold the maps. He had to do better than this; there had to be a way. He went heavily back to his camp and built up the fire to grill one of his fish. At once the Yunggamurra went under the water and stayed there.

In the afternoon he went over his maps again looking at rivers and creeks one by one, trying to probe the uncertainties of scale. How many that seemed from the map to enter the sea flowing east might in fact turn north for half a mile or so? How many looping between coastal hills might be said to flow south and west? A new question occurred to him and he turned his eyes, absent and thoughtful, to the pool. The sun had gone out of the gorge and the Yunggamurra had come out of the water to the rocks above the pool. It sat watching him, its eyes as absent and thoughtful as his own.

He was wrung with sudden pain—how pity could hurt! If only it felt warm and alive, and not a thing of mud and slime . . . He put the idea angrily away and went to ask his question.

'You went north to the sea but how did you get back into the rocks? From the east?'

It gazed at him absently and answered with its thoughts still on other things. 'From the sea. The sea is not east.'

Under his brows his eyes narrowed. 'Show me the east,' he ordered.

It waved one arm in a careless graceful gesture. 'Into the sun's path. That is not to the sea.'

'How, then? Which way? Where was the sea?'

'It was north. I was blown in the storm. I came south to where the old water trickled off a northern coast.'

The Gulf? Had it after all come in from the Gulf? Then where was the waterfall? He needed more maps—there must be a river with falls—he was about to turn back to camp when the spirit spoke again.

'Your friend is between us,' it said like a seeker who has found a truth.

Wirrun was suddenly rigid, a staring stone. He could not speak. The old moonlit eyes watched him, knowing more than he did.

'It was the game and he sought it but he did not play. He sought peace and found that. Should his peace lie between us?'

Wirrun's voice shook with anger that the creature should dare to speak to him of Ularra. 'My friend was a hero. He died for me.'

'And for peace. For love and peace. Which lies between us?'

'He's not between us,' snapped Wirrun, for Ularra had made it true. '*You're* between us.'

'Is that why you seek my country and leave me free?'

He laughed harshly and touched the stone on his belt. 'I don't leave you free.'

At that the Yunggamurra laughed too, a magpie's note, and slipped down into the water. In a moment it rose again and threw him another fish. Wirrun left the fish flapping and jerking on the bank and strode back to the camp to build up his fire. Angrily he threw on more wood than he needed and built it high. Tomorrow he would take the slimy little brute back to the Nyols for a bit and put a fire in a dead tree for Merv. He would send Merv for some good maps of the Gulf and find that river with the falls.

In the night by moonlight the Yunggamurra sang, but not the love-singing. It sang softly of falling water and swirling bubbles, a song that held no magic but its own. All the same Wirrun raged at its cheek and longed to stride down and forbid it. He did not dare because the Yunggamurra sang so teasingly; he could only sit stiffly in the dark and listen, and watch the spirit play with reflected stars, and later try to sleep knowing that it still played there.

'Oh mate!' he groaned to Ularra's spirit, but this time no help came. The leaves whispered only with a sound like gentle laughter and in time Wirrun slept.

Peeping from her pool the Yunggamurra saw: the hero was sleeping beyond the range of speech with his power beside him. Did he truly think that power would hold her all this time and even while he slept? Because its magic guarded him even in sleep did he think his stone had memory and will? That it would obey him when he did not speak? He trusted to that; he did not know, he did not know!

But if he did not know what use in staying? She might stay for an age and the game never end. Or she might slip away, as she might have in all the times he left her free, and find some pool where no old thing lived and the fish were sweet. What would he do then? Would he think his power outworn and throw it away? Her laughter bubbled softly; but she did not go.

She chased and caught a water-spider. 'He will send me to my sisters,' she told it before she ate it. She smiled with joy and then was still with sadness; for he could not live among her sisters and he was not like other men. She slipped under water to catch a fish and came up again to sing to the moon: softly, not to wake the hero. She sang to him while he slept and when the song was finished broke into laughter. She had thought of a new game, a game to play with the hero.

She would not go; she would only lie on the water like foam and let it carry her. She thought how angry he would be and laughed like bubbles and birdsong while the current carried her out of the pool. As she slipped along under shadowed banks to find a new hiding-place she wondered if he would throw away his stone.

Four

Wirrun woke early and remembered the song of the waterfall. He was surprised and a little disturbed to find that while he slept he had forgiven the Yunggamurra for speaking of Ularra. Forgiven or not, he would take it in hand again and return it for a while to the dark as he had planned. That would teach it to laugh at him—or rather, it would give him time to fetch Merv and send or go with him for maps of the Gulf.

He lit a small careful fire and cooked breakfast, keeping away from the pool so as not to alarm the spirit before he was ready. It was very quiet this morning; though he often glanced secretly from under his brows not once did he see it peep or play. He thought how he would take it back to the cave ordering it to stay with the Nyols till he returned. It would be distressed, of course—indifferently obedient as it had been at first; but he would remember that there must be pity. He would explain how soon he would be back, and that he needed maps to find its country, and that he would bring it back to its pool in the sun as soon as he could. And when he did come back it would be glad and laugh teasingly and sing about the waterfall . . . and be like mud and slime to touch . . .

And while he thought of this and frowned over his tea he heard the singing.

It was a song of the flowing of weeds and the swimming of fish: silver-sweet, cool, unmistakeable. And it came from somewhere down the creek towards the first camp.

He could not believe it at first. He thought the spirit was singing under water and that this confused the sound. But the sound was clear and sweet and true. He went to listen by the pool.

He ordered the spirit to come up from under the water. It did not come. That as much as his ears told him it was not there. It had left the pool. He stood rooted on the bank shaking with rage and dismay. He had gone into the dark to rescue this thing—treated it with care—sought to find its home! He raged at its ingratitude and broke off to curse, and raged again at himself.

How could he have been so blind, so stupid? To trust that the power would hold it for any time and even while he slept! He had never thought or questioned; he had trusted rather to the creature itself and its longing for its country. To forget it was an earth-thing, wild and lovely and free of evil! To bring such a thing into the light where unwarned men might hear it—and then to lose it! In fright he raged at the spirit again and then again at himself.

And while he raged a cool sweet song came floating up

the creek, a song of the freedom of all Yunggamurra and the winding of rivers.

He could not stand there helpless with fright and dismay. He must recapture the creature. If he could find it and creep near—while it was still proudly taunting him with its freedom and before it found its way out of the gorge—if he could take it by surprise while it must obey the power, and order it back to its pool, then he would have time. Then he could return it to the dark till he found its country and never mind how it felt. Let it think it was sent away forever—let it play gallant and indifferent—let it crawl on its lovely silver knees and beg for pity. He knew it better now.

The Yunggamurra sang of sunlight and the slipping of currents.

He listened and tried to judge the distance and examined the cover along the creek. He chose the eastern bank where the hillside rose steep and rocky and the trees came nearer the bank. Then he began his stalking.

He went like a shadow and kept to the shade: creeping between rocks, sliding behind a tree, crawling through bushes. It was slow and he had to stop often to watch and listen. Above the old camp and its pool he chose a rock behind which to crouch, expecting a wait of some time. The creature was sly: it would be hiding as closely as he was.

There was no waiting. The Yunggamurra sat boldly on the bank on his side of the pool, its back confidently turned, combing its long dark hair with its fingers. Wirrun's anger softened: it was like a child, pleased with its own cleverness and sure it had won. Or like a bird that knew nothing of the hunter. He stood up very quietly to examine the hillside and ran stooping through shadows to a treestump below. From there he crept into a gully and went very softly down in the shelter of its bank.

From the mouth of the gully he sighted the spirit again. Still sitting openly in sunlight, back turned, combing its hair. While he watched it began to sing, a song of moonlit nights and the deep sleep of heroes.

Like a shadow Wirrun slid from the gully to the first of the river-oaks. Still singing the Yunggamurra slipped into the water. A moment later the song came from far upstream.

Upstream?

Patiently and slowly Wirrun repeated his stalking in reverse. His heart lifted to see the spirit in its old place where the water ran into its pool. Of course it had never meant to leave him until he had found its country; it had been thoughtless like a child but not sly or cunning. It waited for him now. He came out from the bushes.

The spirit laughed, waved, and was gone. He caught a silvery glint from under a bank lower down.

It was hard to admit that the thing might be playing with him. He frowned heavily, decided that his cover had been poor and took a more careful route back to the old camp. From there he heard singing lower down the creek. He knew that lower pool: its banks were high and well covered, easy to approach. With great care he worked his way down to the river-oaks by the creek; he could move more quickly and freely there and follow the creek itself down. He ran lightly past the pool at the camp.

A light splash behind him—a catfish landed jumping at his feet—a bubble of laughter and a ripple travelling the wrong way, upstream again.

He had to accept it: she was teasing him. Did she think she'd get away with that? Wirrun rubbed his hair into curls: at this rate she would. He was about to push the catfish back into water with his foot when he realised that it was now lunch time any rate, that he might as well catch up on food while he thought, and that while he had no knife there were matches in his pocket. He lit a fire and grilled the fish whole in the old way, and sat on a log to eat it in his fingers and think.

He thought of the creek as far as he knew it, of all its deep holes and shallow places. He thought of the Yunggamurra and how to make a Yunggamurra trap. After that he waited till he heard the singing again far upstream, trying to call him back. Then he ran as quickly and quietly as he could down the creek to the swamp.

He stepped lightly on firm ground around its margin to those stands of bamboo, the tall grass, and felt only one spasm of pain at the sight of the small burnt patch. The next moment he was calculating whether that patch could be seen from the creek. It could not; both before and behind it there were stands that reached farther into the swamp and hid the burnt one. He examined those two stands, listening for the singing as he looked. Soft boggy going—he and Ularra had avoided them for that reason though they reached so much farther into the swamp—but if he placed a dead branch or two between them he thought he might leap fast enough from one to the other.

Quickly, for he knew the speed of spirits and she would be wondering where he was, he found two dead branches and pushed and tugged them into the mud and tested them with his weight. With a smaller branch he made himself a hide in the stand of bamboo farther from the creek. Hidden between tall stems and shaded by drooping leaves he sat watching the place where the creek ran in and listening for a song.

She could not escape from the gorge without passing through the swamp, or pass through that without his seeing her; and if he were her game she would come because he was there. He thought with a pang of guilt that she was only playing, that she would not come this way to escape but only because he had drawn her. It could not be helped. She did not mean to be evil or dangerous but he must not leave her free till he had found her right place. He watched relentlessly.

A long time went by. He played the game of patience as his ancestors would have done: he never moved or forgot to watch but sometimes flexed his muscles silently to keep them ready. A frog leapt on his foot and away again; mosquitoes buzzed and stung; a small lizard stayed for a while on his hand. Over his head the leaves whispered of smoke and Ularra, and his spirit whispered silently back that it did not matter; the cure had failed but now as then he did not want to be cured.

He waited. In an hour he heard the singing close in the creek, a song of hiding and finding. He smiled. After half an hour he glimpsed her at the mouth of the creek, and after another half-hour glimpsed her again. In a while she stood straight, looking at the swamp with something like fear, her eyes old. She drew back and sang a little and was silent. He had to wait again, flexing his muscles.

Then she came. With bravado she walked light-footed over the surface of the swamp: a lovely sight but he only grew tense and ready. She turned his way, bright-eyed and honey-smiling. He waited while she passed the first stand of bamboo and neared the second; then he struck a match and put it to the dead lower leaves.

This was the one second that counted. At the first crackle he exploded across his bridge of branches and struck another match. From there he plunged muddy and leaping through the swamp itself and held her penned against two fires of tall grass.

They were leaping fires now and the smoke rolled from them. He thought she would come springing back in terror and he would catch her—he had even planned to hold the slippery creature by the hair. But she stood frozen, eyes huge, as if she were already caught and could do nothing. Smoke rolled over her and she writhed in it—she dreaded fire—he need not be crueller than he must. He came plunging to catch her in her panic, and wound the dark hair round his left arm and tried to draw her away. She only stood, her feet sinking now in the mud, her lovely silver turning to lead, coughing and writhing, gazing strangely at him and the fires.

'You did know,' she whispered and slumped against his arm.

What had he done? Blood pounding he grasped her, expecting a light floating weight and the slither of mud. But the grey slime had dried and hung in strips and the weight was human and alive. His blood stopped pounding and began to sing fiercely: the Mimi! She never could believe how little man knew! *Fight it with the smoke of a tall grass*—how could he have known from that? With lungs aching and eyes streaming he carried the Yunggamurra deeper into the smoke. She lay with eyes closed, seeming dead but feeling alive.

He held her over the small licking flames and saw strips of dried slime fall away and burn. He watched with hard disgust something more horrible: a million tiny leeches crawl from the pores of her skin to fall into the flames. Her eyes were fixed on him again, dark with old knowledge and streaming with the tears of smoke. He gazed back stern and pitying, and they wept and coughed together while the smoke rolled, the leeches burnt, the flames sizzled in the swamp and died. She never fought. When there were only dead fires and lazy smoke he lifted her and kissed her and her lips were smoke-dried but soft and cool and clean. He was suddenly ashamed and bewildered.

Squelching in muddy boots he carried her to the creek and up to the first pool. Clothed and booted he walked deep into the pool and held her in water to heal her of the fires. The love-singing was loud in his mind: *are you not here?*

She and not he had come. He had always known, in spite of all pain and enchantment and evil, what he must do with the Silver Yunggamurra. But the love-singing was drowned in a clamour of warning bells while he stood holding the living golden girl.

7

The Water-Girl

One

So he had known after all. She was clothed in flesh; the game was played. What was she now? What should she do?

Her body felt tight and hard, stinging from the terrible smoke. He held her in the water and she felt the current flutter as soft as ever on her skin. But she could not ride the current; she was as heavy as stone. The water flowed past and did not move her at all.

She shifted her legs and arms feeling their new weight and the man let her go. At once she plunged down under water to restore her burnt face and frizzled hair. That was bad, it was frightening. The man had to lift her again because she could not raise herself, and under water she could not breathe and could scarcely see. Had her water-country gone with her silver foamy self? Where were the fish? And the light precise weeds pointing the way of the current?

She had no country left; she must live in the world of dry sunny air. It was too much. She closed her eyes and mind and let her heavy feet move as they would while the man half-carried her a long way to his sleeping-place. There he wrapped her in something soft and laid her in the shade. It was easier to be heavy lying down. She opened her eyes again to watch him.

He was sitting on his pack watching her. He too was scorched by fire.

Neither had spoken at all. They were filled with the silence of time and old magic, of red plains and tall rocks and dark places. It was in their eyes too, and smoked the sunlight.

He broke the silence at last with a few mumbled words: 'I'll call you Murra . . . I'm Wirrun.'

That was a saying fit to break old magic. She lay and listened to it: that he was Wirrun and she Murra. Not a Murra or the Murra but Murra. She had never been so single before. She lay listening to the word while he fell asleep exhausted and until she slept too.

She slept through the rest of the sunlight and through evening into night. When she woke in the last of the moonlight he still slept; the man: Wirrun. He lay in the same place, tumbled on the earth like a child's stick-doll and sleeping like death. He had left the night to her.

There were shadows that sat in the moonlight and watched curiously. She saw and ignored them; she was very young and very old and enduring, and the night was hers. She threw off the soft wrapping with those new heavy legs and arms and lay working them: finding the strength of bone, the pull of muscle, the soft response of skin. She sat up, stood, walked in the moonlight. There were strength and balance to match the weight, and as she used them the weight seemed to drain away. She walked on sticks without breaking them—on grass without bending it. That was not like walking over water or lying on a current; but in the dry sunny world it would do.

Finding the rhythm of her body she swayed and danced—see! she was still slender and light and lovely! Her new darker colour belonged to the shadows of day and night as her old one had belonged to the water. She laughed a little and chased a bandicot. See! She still played! She was herself.

Herself. Murra.

The moon had gone and she was hungry. But she did not know the food of the dry world. She would wake the hero Wirrun and tell him she wanted food. She ran back, not bending the grass, to push him awake with her foot— and had to learn first to stand on one foot only, and then anticipate the double warmth she would feel when her warm toe met his warm leg. And while she paused over these things she looked down and drew back her foot. She would not wake him. He slept like death and was tumbled like a stick-doll. She stole away.

She went back to the only source of food she knew: to her old pool. There were fish and beetles and spiders waiting, she knew where. But she was frightened by the water, twice frightened. Once was because of the way her body had trapped her when she went under water after the smoke. Twice was because now water was wrong for her and her sisters were fierce. He, Wirrun, did not know it; he had taken her into the water for healing. But she knew.

She sat on the edge of the pool and wished for water and fish but was afraid. The reflected stars made her smile: how they would jump if she tried to catch them! She reached down for one and fell heavily into the pool. And after all she felt lighter in the water than out, and could stand up and breathe.

It had happened, then: and her sisters were far away she did not know where. She found that now she could ride the water a little—go deep if she took the dry air down with her—see when she learnt to understand what she saw. She played water-games that were near enough to the old ones. She felt the slither of a fish and caught it by habit and feel.

She came out to sit on the rocks and eat the fish and went in again to catch more. When Wirrun woke at dawn she was sitting in her old place above the pool and there were three fresh catfish at his fireplace.

Two

When Wirrun woke and saw the lovely flowing shape on the rocks he would have believed the smoking was a dream if it had not been for her colour darkening to his own—and for the three catfish. He was astonished. That limp, stricken doll of yesterday—already she had learnt to move and swim and catch fish?

He was moved by the fish. Hadn't he dragged her, lost and a stranger, out of her world and being into his? She should have hated him and instead she had brought him

fish. He lay a while longer pretending to be asleep so that
he could watch.

Still playing: combing the waterweeds with her toes. The
eyes dew-lit, the smile still sharply sweet, movement as
flowing, shape as slender as before. His heart turned over.
Maybe she was a girl now, Murra, but still she was not like
any human girl he'd ever seen. Lovely, gallant, enduring,
and playful as a child. He could not bear the moment of
knowing and loving, and got up to light the fire.

Murra at once began to sing about the heaviness of heroes clumsily tumbled in sleep. Her voice was as sweet as
yesterday; and as teasing. It was enough to make any man
grab her and drag her off into the bushes—except that he
was almost sure she did not know it. His ears rang again
with a warning like bells and he pushed a hand through his
hair.

He had seen his friend changed and knew what it was to
bear. He had been warned that there were all kinds of
beasts and that there must be pity. It was he who had lit
those fires and smoked the water out of the water-spirit;
and now she was a stranger in his hands as Ularra had
been. He must take care.

He had not meant to take revenge for Ularra; but it lay
in his mind like a stone that the revenge was terrible already.

He cut into the song about the heroes with a carefully
cheerful shout: 'What's got into these crazy fish, jumping
out of the creek like that? Reckon they're safe to eat?'

She considered the question in some surprise and saw
that the hero was teasing. She smiled with delight and
splashed down into the pool. He smiled too at the splash: a
person and not a spirit was swimming.

While the fire burnt down to coals he went down to the
creek below the pool to wash himself and clean the fish.
There were two immediate problems that he could already
see: to clothe Murra, and to feed her with a breakfast
cooked at a fire. For weightier problems he needed time;
he would concentrate on these two first.

Murra swam down to the outlet of the pool and gave
him a third. With her face floating in a cloud of hair she
said soberly, 'I should be kept from water. It is the rule.'

'That so?' said Wirrun cleaning fish. 'Who says?'

Again she considered the question. It was a foolish one but she answered. 'It is I who tell you. Murra says.'

He smiled at her. 'If you shouldn't be in the water you'd better come out.'

She sighed, frowned, nodded. 'It is right.' She swam back to the rocks and drew herself out. He hoped his other two problems could be solved as easily.

When he called her to breakfast she came warily, watching the fire, keeping at a distance, yet not as nervously as he had feared. She watched with reserve while he ate but at first refused her own share.

'I have eaten already. While you slept and the fish jumped out of the creek.'

'Never mind. You can eat a bit more. Have a little bit.'

He offered the pannikin. She sat unmoved. He held it a little closer. She gave in, took a piece of fish in her fingers and put it whole into her mouth. She chewed with a thoughtful frown.

'Soft. Dry. The bones wander about.' She added sadly, 'But I must not eat it raw. It is the rule.'

'Why did you, then?'

'I was hungry and you slept. I do not know dry food. And my sisters are not here.'

'Tonight you can try rabbit stew.'

'It will be hard.' She sighed and repeated her experiment with the fish. Full of admiration at her good sense and tolerance Wirrun approached his second problem confidently.

'Better put that on,' he said tossing her a knitted cotton shirt from his pack.

She gazed at it without comprehension.

'Like this,' he pointed out, showing her that he wore one too.

She seemed bewildered. 'Do you not like me, then? Am I not beautiful?' Since he only looked away with tightened jaw she argued warmly to convince him. 'I am beautiful, that is sure, for all the Yunggamurra are beautiful. There was never a Yunggamurra that was not beautiful.'

He broke in roughly. 'You're as lovely as the day and I like you very much. Put it on.'

She gazed at him with old eyes and made no move to

touch the shirt. It seemed that there could be nothing about clothing in the rules. Wirrun tried an appeal.

'I like you so much I don't want other men looking at you. I'm jealous.'

She frowned severely. 'You give me no reason. There are no other men here.'

'But we won't be here forever—there will be men! There's one up there on the cliffs could be watching us now! You need to get used to things like that shirt while we're here.'

To leave the creek between the cliffs for a wider world was a new idea that clouded her courage, but she was not convinced about the shirt. She grew sterner.

'Jealousy can only insult me. Which do you deny in me?—honour or understanding or will?' And, as he looked puzzled, 'Tell me. Am I stupid, weak, or a cheat?'

She was none of those and he had no answer. He saw that he must give her a real reason but it was hard to find. 'It'll keep off the sun and the wind and the flies.'

She disposed of that easily. 'It will save my middle from these dangers. Must my arms and legs and face be chilled and bitten?'

Wirrun scowled. 'I'll get stockings for your legs if you like, and gloves for your arms and a hat for your face. Only I haven't got 'em here.'

She blenched but was not defeated. 'Because you do not need them. Then why this?' She touched the shirt scornfully with one toe.

Wirrun struggled. 'Look. Would you wear that in the river with your sisters? I mean, just say you wanted to: would you?'

She gave a short bubbling laugh. 'I would not.'

'Why not?'

'They would laugh and jeer and drive me away. Or tear it off.'

'Right. Well that's why you do have to wear it here.' He saw that she was turning that over in her mind and tried to complete the reasons. 'And because I do; and the only other way is for me to take mine off and I'm not going to. You changed to me and not the other way round.' Because he had still not made it clear he grew heated. 'Look, can't you see? If you're my kind I gotta think about you and take care. If it's the other way round it's easier to forget—think you can look after yourself. Can't you *see* that? Maybe it's stupid but it's true. Did I look after you like a person yesterday? Not me. I made a trap and caught you to keep other people safe.'

Murra gave a small defeated sigh and picked up the shirt. He moved to help her but she frowned and drew away. She examined the shirt for a moment looking sharply from it to Wirrun's own, and struggled into it with a wild waving of arms. She laughed like a magpie at this performance, wriggling inside the shirt to feel it as it fell loosely around her and laughing again when it tickled. Her long hair was still caught inside the knitted neckband. Wirrun, smiling, leaned forward and gently freed it.

That made her look sharply again. She fought her way out of the shirt and back into it, freeing her own hair this time. She took it off and put it on again, and went running down to the pool to lean over the bank and look at her reflection and laugh and laugh. The drooping shoulders of the shirt brought its sleeves below her elbows and its hem hung below her knees. She tugged at it and let go, watching it stretch and pull back. She smiled at its faded blue and poked at its softness with her fingers.

Wirrun watched, sad and smiling. What a shame; but he needed to have her in that shirt. She knew so little of the dry world—but he had made her a person. Very well; she must be treated like a person.

Murra pulled off the shirt and came back carrying it. While Wirrun banked the fire and cleaned up the breakfast things she watched closely and now and then put the shirt on or took it off. It was hard to work while she crouched there watching.

'What's it like being a Yunggamurra?' he asked to turn her attention away.

Her face stilled. She sat fingering the blue knitted cotton. 'It is to flow with the water and ride it; to be one strand among weeds, one voice in the singing. To rise to the sun or sink from the wind as the others do. To be no one but to be many, and to play.' She hesitated. 'That much I can tell. You must be Yunggamurra to know the fierceness of wanting.'

He did not think so.

'What is it like to be hero?' she asked.

He was surprised into an answer and more surprised at the answer. 'It's finding out if you are or not and never mind what they tell you.'

'And are you?'

He had thought so a dozen times and afterwards found he was wrong, but now he could say yes without pride or pleasure or doubt. What had it taken, since the day Tom Hunter came, to turn the name of hero into truth? Work, mainly. And the call of the wind. Ularra's need and sacrifice, Merv Bula's support. Ko-in's teaching and the Mimi's help. Hunger and dread fought off. Pity learnt. A long rugged road with a lot of helpers and more failures. There was no pride yet in being a hero.

Murra came with him to set traps for rabbits, watching sharp-eyed like a hunter and walking soft near the warrens, and he saw that the grass did not bend under her feet. She was not all girl, then; not yet any rate. The traps puzzled her, but when he explained she nodded quickly and seemed to find this way of hunting a game of suspense.

Between warrens she invented other games. Chasing birds was a failure; she frowned in discontent and Wirrun dreamed of taking her with him on the wind. Swinging from a low branch was good; he made her laugh harder by giving her a push. She would climb a tall rock and jump off, gasping with delight and terror. Wirrun jumped with her once. She laughed excitedly when he scrambled up beside her and laughed more at his heavy landing. Most of the time she wore the shirt but he was never sure when he might see her in her own shape, the shirt swinging from her hand or draped over her head and her eyes teasing. Once he had to pick the thing out of a sapling while she watched wickedly and pretended to have forgotten it.

She sat down often, missing the support of water; and Wirrun stood waiting while she rested, or perhaps showed her another of the dry world's foods. His restraint and shyness puzzled her. He smiled, but sometimes with pain—as if she had won the Yunggamurra's game and he had lost? She began to watch him secretly and kept the blue shirt on as often as she remembered.

When they had set traps and dug yams they returned to the camp to eat cold cooked fish. After that, while gold sunlight poured into the gorge and the cliffs hung blue-hazed from the sky, they lay or sat in the shade looking at each other and looking away.

Murra took the shirt off and quickly put it on again.

Wirrun picked a grass-stem and bent it into knots. In a careful voice he asked a question.

'What do you want to do now?—where do you want to go? Back to your own country?' He heard her quivering breath and found her looking at him almost in fear. He frowned. 'Well?'

'We cannot go to my country,' she whispered. 'You do not know the way.'

'If you want to go back I'll find it. Somewhere up where the sea's north.'

'West,' she whispered.

She had said north but he let that pass. 'Don't you want to go back and see your sisters?' She shook her head, staring as if he were some kind of monster. 'Why not, then?'

'Your friend is between us!' she cried. It was almost as though she howled again.

'Murra! No! You forget that, girl. It was an accident. Like a rock falling.'

'He is between us.'

'No, I tell you. He was at first—but not now. I swear.'

'You say it but you cannot show it.'

He smiled a little, brooding, and she watched him with old eyes. 'Ularra wouldn't come between me and a girl.' He looked at her straight and gave her the simple proof. 'You're wearing his shirt.' And, when she seemed not to understand, 'Would I give you that?'

She jumped up, tore off the shirt, ran to the creek and dived in. Going back to the water.

He could only sit and watch with the worry inside him like a stone. If Ularra stayed between them it was she who would keep him there; but what had he said to make her think it? And what could he do? He counted over the possibilities as he had done all morning while he watched her play.

He could drag her off into the bushes like the hungry beast he was—Murra, under whose feet the grass did not bend, whose joy was so sweet to him. The stranger, old and enduring and young as a child, lost in his dry country. And afterwards, what?

Take her back to the city or to some country town? Leave her alone all day in a one-room flat or the yard behind a pub? Take away her play and the freedom of waters and give her instead the dirty streets, a cotton frock and an old stove? No, of course he couldn't. It wasn't possible.

Take her back to her country, then? Saying, 'Thanks for a great time, kid, and don't you want to get a job somewhere near your sisters?'

Or just leave her, perhaps; here in the gorge, safe from the bewilderment of men. Men would be safe from Murra now. She could feed herself all right, and play with the water and the trees until she grew old and wrinkled. And perhaps in time she would find her way out of the gorge: Ularra's way.

There was no solution at all that he could see . . .

Three

For an hour Murra played fiercely in the water while Wirrun watched and brooded. For ten minutes more she played consciously, catching his hungry gaze and rejecting it. After that she climbed on to the rocks and sat cold and dignified and lovely; she was now almost as brown as he was. She began to stare at him defiantly, and at last she left the rocks and came striding back flattening the grass with angry feet.

She seized Ularra's shirt and pulled it on. 'I should be kept from the water,' she accused Wirrun. 'I have told you. It is the rule.'

His blood was pounding again but he was long used to that and could answer coolly. 'Stay out, then. It's up to you.'

'No it is not. It is you who should keep me from the water.'

'I don't keep people from what they want, water-girl. That rule seems like a pretty tough one to me. You've got a right to suit yourself.'

She gazed at him severely and sat on a branch. 'You know nothing about Yunggamurra.'

He was unashamed, being used to this sort of scolding from the Mimi. 'True enough. Never heard of 'em before. But you're not a Yunggamurra. If the rule says you shouldn't go in water, why do you?'

She pushed at a twig with her toes. 'The rule is hard,' she confessed, and added defiantly, 'But I cannot find my sisters, they are not here, they have lost me and cannot come! So . . . I am not afraid . . .'

'Scared of your sisters? But you want your sisters! You wanted 'em bad enough yesterday any rate. What's up now?'

'Now,' she cried, 'I want to be! As everything that is wants to be! Each thing wants to be what it is and I am Murra. I want to be Murra.'

He was watching her from under heavy brows. 'And so you are. What else can you be?'

'Yunggamurra,' she whispered. 'That is what you should know.'

'Go on, then. You tell me.'

She hunched up a shoulder and spoke from behind it. 'It is a hard game, the Yunggamurras' game. The man cannot win. You think you have won because you have caught and tamed me—'

'Not me, water-girl. I don't hold with taming.' She peeped at him over her shoulder and fingered the blue shirt and he smiled. 'Some day I'll get something fit for you to wear. A rainbow, maybe?'

She brushed aside the teasing and faced him again crying, 'Some day! Some day I shall not be here to put on your rainbow! That is the game. My sisters will find me. They will call and call and I will hear and hear; and one day they will find me in water. They will catch Murra more surely than ever you caught Yunggamurra. They will take me back to the rivers and the games and I will be

Yunggamurra again. You should keep me always from the water.'

There was silence for a moment. Wirrun broke it harshly. 'That's it, then. We better find your country and take you back.'

She threw back her head as if he had tried to hit her. 'But I want to be Murra! You have caught me and changed me—I have put on the shirt! Do you not want me? Do you not care?'

He almost did hit her. Eyes blazing he seized a dead branch and hurled it down to the pool. 'Of course I want you!' he roared. 'Bloody little fool! Of course I care! Haven't I followed your bloody singing half across the country and into the Dark? Haven't I watched you playing and left you alone while I tried to work out what was best?' He saw that she was bewildered, trying to follow what he said, and he sat down and fought with himself and whispered curses until he could speak calmly.

'Look. Water-girl. I do want you—it's eating me. But what am I going to do with you? How can I keep you playing games?' And carefully, slowly, as he found the words, he told her about the world of men. About money. The Happy Folk. Jobs. Flats. About cities and towns and soft-drink cartons dancing in the wind on a pavement. About the People and how they lived, in settlements and on the fringes of towns. About the dry sunny world into which he had dragged her and how she might live better in it alone in the gorge than with him. And as he talked more passionately the ages of knowledge came back into her eyes and they were not dewy but moonlit.

She went to the heart of the matter. 'Do you like to live this way?'

'Like! No. It's the way men live.'

'But you are a hero with power. Where is this money? I have not seen it. Here you set traps and dig yams and catch fish.'

'You can't catch everything you need in a trap.'

'No? Yet you have said that I might. What do you need more than I need, that you cannot catch in a trap?'

'Shirts. Traps. Other men. To walk over my country.'

'Is it wide, your country? Has it many fish and rabbits? Is it yours?'

From sea to sea . . . spread with broken fences and rusting wire for traps . . . rich in rabbits to be eaten and the skins sold . . . dotted with Inlanders needing wood for their stoves or a day's work now and then . . . A rich country if your needs were small and you loved it. And his own.

'You have not told me. What more do you need that your country cannot give?'

He rolled over on his stomach and smiled at her tenderly. 'You.'

The moonlit eyes clouded. 'So you must go back to the money. For you have caught me in a trap and I will not stay.'

'If I knew you'd be happy I'd take a chance on that. If you were happy you'd stay, never mind how they called.'

'You followed my singing so far only because you would? It is easy to be called and not to hear?'

'Easy, no. It depends what you want and I wanted Murra. If there was even a chance you'd be happy I'd take it—that's just the ordinary chance of being alive.'

Now it was she who sat listening to something unheard. There was nothing to hear but insects, for the air was heavy with heat though only the cliffs were still gold in the sun. Perhaps she listened to those: to the strong silent singing of stone and the murmur of distance. Or perhaps she listened to a far-away waterfall.

'But there's not a chance,' said Wirrun, 'and it's no good me telling you. You don't know. You don't know being hungry or cold—or work—or getting old—'

'That is not the ordinary chance of being alive?'

'For me it is. It's my world and I can handle it. For you there's the river and your sisters and your games. That's too much of a difference; for me any rate. I can't drag you out of your own world into mine.'

Her eyes were as old as lizards and as soft as moonlight when she stood up. 'If you cannot that is all.' She pulled off the blue shirt and tossed it away and shook the dark hair till it flowed around her like water. 'While I am Murra,' she reminded him firmly, 'you cannot order me with your stone.'

His voice was rough. 'I don't want to. I just said.'

'And I cannot draw you with my singing.'

She turned and ran away over the grass, not bending it, and he heard her splash into the pool. He buried his head in his arms.

> *Are you not coming?*
> *sings the bright water:*
> *are you not coming?*

It was barbed deep into him; he would never be rid of it.

> *The glimmer-bright water*
> *alight with the glancing*
> *of glimmer-bright eyes.*

Knowing her and loving her had changed even his memories. There was no longer any dread or magic in the haunting; it was gay and teasing and alive, Murra and not Yunggamurra.

> *Are you not coming?*
> *sings the dark water:*
> *are you not coming?*

An echo carried down from the cliffs. Wirrun rolled over suddenly: an echo? And in his mind the singing had never run so continuously.

> *The dark-flowing water*
> *like washes and ripples*
> *of dark-floating hair.*

He sat up. She was in her old place on the rocks, dripping wet, leaning forward and singing, smiling her wild-honey smile and teasing with her eyes; calling him out of his world of money and jobs and flats, into her world of freedom and the old ways of his People. When she saw his face she laughed like bubbles and birdsong and slipped down into the water.

Not draw him with her singing—what did she think he was? Tugging off his own shirt he remembered that she knew what he was as he knew what she was. She would never be like any other girl; she was Murra, water-girl, half spirit and half person. And some day she would hear her sisters calling.

Glossary

Abuba—dangerous spirit, resembling a young woman, who lures men and changes them to beasts.

bandicoot—small, insectivorous marsupial.

billy—a pot or container in which water is boiled.

boot (of car)—trunk.

bore—deep well, usually artesian.

Bunyip—dreaded monster spirit of great power; dwells in shallow water to trap men for food.

corroboree—a large, noisy gathering or festival of the People.

Cross, the—the Southern Cross, a constellation.

damper—unleavened bread of flour and water baked in hot ashes.

dingo—wild dog of Australia.

doss—sleep, lie down to sleep.

Dry, the—rainless season of the year in a monsoonal climate.

firestick—a torch of wood.

gibber-plains—plains strewn with rocks or boulders.

gum (tree)—eucalyptus tree.

hakea—tall shrub.

Happy Folk—the whites of Australia who continue a life like that of Europeans; especially, the city dwellers.

Inlanders—whites who have lived close to the land long enough to have developed some feeling for it.

Jugi—huge, red-eyed, inimical spirit-dogs.

Ko-in—Hero of the People, now a spirit.

Kooleen's women—spirits who resemble women, but with tails.

Little People—very strong spirits, like children of the People.

Mimi—rock-spirits; tall, thin, frail, and shy.

mulga—a slow-growing type of tree.

Munga-munga—spirits who resemble girls, but with claws.

Nargun—creatures of living rock; considered Great Powers.

Ninya—ice-spirits living in underground ice caverns.

Nyols—little spirit-People who live within rocks; very strong.

Pangalunga—spirits who resemble men, tall as hills; anthropophagous.

pannikin—small pan.

People, the—the black Aborigines of Australia.

power, the—a crystal of quartz wrapped in opossum fur; magic talisman.

swag—a traveler's bundle of belongings, food, etc.

tucker—food.

Tu-ru-dun—same as **Bunyip.**

Wet, the—the rainy season.

yabby—crayfish

Yabon—shape-changing, friendly spirit.

Yunggamurra—river-spirits, sirens who lure men by singing.

NOTE: The spirits of the Australian People bear little resemblance to the pale, ghostly things of European mythology. The spirits of the People's legends are normally invisible but otherwise have many of the characteristics of life. They work or seek prey to eat, they suffer pain and emotional reactions, and they have a real existence and physical ability. They frequently are limited in territory. They do not spring from the People, but from the land, and many are older than mankind in the land.

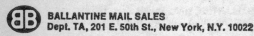